Soul of the King

Rasool Darweesh

Soul of the King

Olympia Publishers
London

www.olympiapublishers.com
OLYMPIA PAPERBACK EDITION

Copyright © Rasool Darweesh 2024

The right of Rasool Darweesh to be identified as author of
this work has been asserted in accordance with sections 77 and 78 of
the Copyright, Designs and Patents Act 1988.

All Rights Reserved

No reproduction, copy or transmission of this publication
may be made without written permission.
No paragraph of this publication may be reproduced,
copied or transmitted save with the written permission of the publisher,
or in accordance with the provisions
of the Copyright Act 1956 (as amended).

Any person who commits any unauthorized act in relation to
this publication may be liable to criminal
prosecution and civil claims for damage.

A CIP catalogue record for this title is
available from the British Library.

ISBN: 978-1-80439-205-8

This is a work of fiction.
Names, characters, places and incidents originate from the writer's
imagination. Any resemblance to actual persons, living or dead, is
purely coincidental.

First Published in 2024

Olympia Publishers
Tallis House
2 Tallis Street
London
EC4Y 0AB

Printed in Great Britain

Acknowledgements

To… Every flagrant critic.

"We have given him the way either to be thankfully or faithlessly."

The Holy Quran

The novel does not examine reality, but existence. Existence is not what has happened, it is the field of human potential, it is all that man can do and become, and all of which he is capable.

French writer,
Milan Kundera

Apology

Some scenes of this novel are true, and they are neither inspired nor imagined by the author, so this must be apologized for in advance, because these scenes may cause harm and psychological effects to the reader, which may last with him for a long time.

Introduction

After the funeral of my father, my mother came knocking on the door of my room, I let her in and kissed her forehead; she was full of speech, but she didn't know exactly where to start her dialogue. Her eyes were staring all over the place and then fell straight toward me, and her hands were confused moving them at one time, allowing the fingers of her right to hug her counterpart on the left. She moved for moments and remained for others. She knelt looking like an exhausted woman who would ask for kindness from life.

And so, she repeated the same situation while I was gazing at her silently. I stood bewildered and then walked away from the office chair. I came to her in concern saying, "Mom, what's the matter? Is it my father's departure and what he had left in your head and heart?"

She was stunned and did not pay attention. I said, "Mom. You are a believer, and this is God's justice and destiny. I mean, we don't always expect our relatives to stay alive forever, we expect leaving us at any moment as they expect us to. Therefore, we don't have to moan too much when someone dies, it is expected since the beginning, even if the deceased is my father, may God rest his soul."

My mother did not care about what I said, she went on saying, "My son. At this moment, I would like to tell you a secret, no one from our family nor relatives knows about it but only me, do you understand that?"

I got closer to her. I hugged her, embracing the world, kissed her forehead, and smelled the paradise. She patted me on the shoulder and took me by her side to the old green couch in the middle of our lounge. She put her hand on my right thigh next to her, looked on the balcony of the lounge. Then she said, "My love, my only son, where is your father's body now?"

"In his grave, he rests between the graves of his parents, God willing. God bless them all, they are the formers and we are the latecomers."

"Are you sure?"

"Mom, what's the matter? Why this question? It is only one week since he died, may God rest his soul, and make his resting place paradise, our grief will not change anything."

She put her hands on my face, pampering me as a child, looking carefully into my eyes for a long time. Then, I stared in her eyes deeply for a long time, and I saw what was behind her eyes. She was reading me as a white book, while I was lost in her black oval eyes, showing oval lines of years around them. I went to the far horizon in her eyes until I lost sight of them. She patted me on the cheek like she wanted to wake me up from what I became, pulled me to her kissing my forehead.

"Dear, listen to me carefully, and remember, my son, what I will tell you."

"I hear you ma, say, say, I'm with you."

"The one buried among the graves of your grandparents… is not your father's body."

I got out of my place right away, stood up, kissed her again on her head, put my palm on her forehead, and I felt her temperature. It could be the fever of loss taking and dragging her into delirium and beyond.

Then, she said in a voice closer to a whisper:

"Rasool, your mother is not sick, she is in her full mind, she does not ramble nor abandon, just concentrate with me a little please. My son, I am fine and thanks to God."

She moderated in her session, and she became more likely to speak and reveal; her words became clearer and soft while speaking, and she started talking and even revealing:
"I'll tell you about the circumstances of your father's death, washing and burying him, yes. I'll tell you about all that. You will tell me about the circumstances of his burial among the graves of your grandparents as you claim and say, you know, women in our country can only reach the graves after burying the dead people, this is a religious and social legacy, my son. Call it whatever you want, but with time it has become a law."

I've moved away from her again, maybe the space between us is enough to understand what she's saying, and she's going to know what I'm going to talk about later. But she added confidently, in a low, thin voice that I could hardly hear:
"Your father's body was brought by the dead transport vehicle, and you know that of course, and while you were busy with all the mourners, I asked the driver of that vehicle, that young man named Falah, I asked him to stay adjacent his car to the back door of the dead bathtub, where the dead bodies entered, and then, as you know, this door is locked from inside. That is exactly what happened until opening the opposite door after the process of washing and shrouding completed, so the depositors, the men of relatives and acquaintances, whoever wants to say goodbye. Then, they raise the dead to the casket, and here the hands crowd to carry it, while the women keep watching the event from a faraway distance. Later, the deceased is taken to the cemetery mosque to pray on him, and then, the dead is buried in his grave after being indoctrinated and said goodbye. Isn't it?"

I answered her with approval, "This is certainly what happens with all the dead here, and it is exactly the same as what happened with my father. I said:"Nothing new, Mother."

"My son, Rasool, what happened with your father is half of the story, only half of the story! Do you understand?"

I wondered what my mother was saying.

"How?" I asked her.

"After taking your father's body into the washtub, the washer began to work, removing the white cloth from the body, that cloth officially marked with the seal of the Ministry of Health. Then, began pouring water from the bucket. This process is generally known as 'dead washing.' There are those who helped him, handed him a bucket of water and other necessities. After completion, the dead-washer performed the mummification process, putting cotton, sander, and eucalyptus. And before he put your fathers' body in the coffin that time, he asked his assistant to call me through the door from which the body was inserted, he asked his assistant to stay in the back, so that no one else could come in. This unexpected precautionary action provoked some attendees. But the effect of the calamity did not allow them to comment or talk out of respect for the deceased and his family."

"Mother, women can come in to say goodbye to the deceased. This is a normal matter which is not a problem."

"My son, this time, the dead washer called to show me something special about your father, something in your father's body. The dead washer opened the shroud from the abdomen and chest. Then, he placed his index finger circularly on a soft surgical (hernia) and only suing a longitudinal leather stitching appeared, which seemed clearly defined, stretching from the left, where the top of the heart area, to the top of the navel; I asked my God to give me patience and fortitude. There were seven stitches in a semi-slanted image. I held myself as much as God gave me patience and endurance. As I was seeing the beginning of the dangers, I wiped my tears; I chose to wait and to remind calm to be reasonable. I asked the man, with the help of the driver, to return the body to the car of the dead after we opened its door to the back door of the bathtub. After that, I asked him to put some palms and cotton in another shroud and tie it tightly to the shape of a human body. The two men understood that there was an emergency and an abnormal thing. The dead washer tightly tied (the fake body) and then took him out to pray on him with the mourners. So, the dead washer himself buried the body without opening the shroud on the face side. Moreover, he spread the news that this situation was 'in accordance with the will of the deceased and the wishes of his wife and son."

"Mom, do you mean …? Should I return my father's body from the morgue? I'm not going to do that Mom. Who can get him in there? Well. You also mean we only prayed for cotton and fronds while my father's body was …"

"My son. We took the body to the morgue with the help of the driver and the dead washer, and we have never told anyone. Now, you must visit your father's body there, and you must examine and confirm that wound in the body. Once you are sure about what they did to your father before or after his death, then we will accept what Allah almighty appreciated and wished."

"How can I know if the criminal won't be there?"

"My son. Make sure that there is a trace, an effect that will remain, and the offender always falls into the trap if he tries to escape from his crime, because he usually commits into another crime."

My beloved mother has undoubtedly put me in front of a

painful responsibility. I run behind fictitious answers to multiple questions, and I may find answers to some, but other questions may hide and close their eyes in front of me.

Those questions may open some doors but some of which may be tightly locked. It is the heavy responsibility that has been thrown at my head. Since that time, whenever I have hidden myself, or held the pen to write, I have written about what had happened, but my mother's voice had been stimulating:

"My son, you must write the novel *Soul of the King* after you heard the story of your father's death." Then, she put a white letter back in my hand which I opened to read the first line:

* Characters: Al-Mualemi, Mikael, Hamidel, Ezrael, The King, Pure Mind, Hamid, Falah, Maya, Kamel, Arak Leader, Ministers, Al Wajih, Alawi, Al-Qurain, Shawzan.

And then, I read the second line:

* Places: Arak Republic, Burqan State, Cedar Republic, Kingdom of Tablistan, Persia.

I lifted my head, and I found her to have her eyes on my chest, staring at me as she was reading me without blinking her eyes. Then, she said:

"I will visit you again, my son, you must write the novel, (*Soul of the King*) for yourself, write it for yourself and it will succeed, let the show, the writer who demands fame is rarely successful. And when you have done writing *Soul of the King*, I'll visit you. I promise!" Then, she left… My mother left me while I have been waiting for her to come back[1]

---

[1] I had this dream (just as it is) on Wednesday, 29/11/2017 at around 2.45 p.m.

Chapter 1
Eternal Theatre

(1)

"Peace be upon you. Go to the Death Registration Department, receive a statement, and bring it here, so you can receive the body of your deceased."
This is how the morgue employee greeted Hamid as he was sitting at his desk behind the glass, addressing him through small holes as he looked at his wide white dress, after which Hamid stood with his head, silent and hesitant, not knowing how to talk with the employee and what to answer.

"Do you understand me?" He asked him urgently again.

While Hamid was waiting for the employee to be alone to tell him what's on his mind, he put his right-hand fingers all over his scalp, scrubbed with his thumb on the sides of his head, as if he did not know what to say, his silence was prolonged, and he remained confused and stammered in his place.

"Yes, my brother, I have a lot of work, all right, is there anything?"

The employee asked him, but with greater severity, as if urging him to remember what he wanted, or he had to leave.

"In fact, I want to talk to someone working with you, someone named Falah, he asked him hesitatingly."

"Yeh, say like this, you want Falah, he has a break now, dear, but if you want to receive the body of your deceased, bring a statement from the Death Registration Department. This is a normal routine that everyone knows here, and if you want to wait for Falah as you say, you are welcome dear. Sit down there, over there, please. Until he gets back."

Hamid sat in the second row, on a long metal bench in the waiting room, reading the faces of those waiting without resting his back and relaxing behind. He was watching some of the audience console each other, and seeing others console their colleague. Some of whom raise their voice and call from time to time:

"May God rest his soul.

"Survival to God, we are to God and we shall return to Him." His friend answers.

"Eh, everyone on it will die but God remain with majesty and honor."

After a few minutes of anticipation and waiting, a young man in dark complexion and in his mid-thirties, entered. His head hair extended to his beard where they met. His thick black beard became extended without breaks. A black spot emerged in the center of his forehead, which is known as the sign of prostration. It is a black circle intermittent, descending and hanging over his nose, like summer clouds tired of waiting and wanting to fall.

Four of the attendees directly went to him, shook his hand as he was still praying to his God and repeating:

"We are to God and to Him we shall return, thank God anyway."

This comer seems to have lost a loved one, too. Hamid persuaded himself to show his sorrow to that man, to act like others, he went and said:

"God bless your condolences, brother. Stay for God Almighty."

The man with the black label did not answer him in any word, he nodded his head only as an expression of a repeated answer. They stepped aside from him, then he left also.

The man crossed the hall and went to the office door where the receptionist was sitting. He sat next to him without permission. Hamid wondered and asked himself about this man:

"Does he work here and has a death case too? If so, thank God, it is normal and there is nothing wrong with it. But what if he doesn't have a death case?"

Suddenly, Hamid's phone rang, he took it out of his pocket, and growled:

"It's my wife Maya, chasing me from one place to another, wherever I go.

He answered her while hiding his boredom, he acted a fake welcome:

"Welcome, dear Maya.

"Where are you? We're waiting for you."

"In the hospital, honey, I finish the official paperwork of the father, God bless him."

"I am hungry, but I will wait for you until you return, I will feed your son and let him sleep."

"No problem, honey, goodbye now."

The call even though expected it increased the amount of embarrassment he already had. He stuttered and was confused until he felt that everyone in the waiting room was looking and monitoring him. Hamid relaxed his body on the long metal chair waiting for Falah with others.

Suddenly, the employee, sitting behind the glass, raised his hand to his side:

"Brother, Brother."

"Me?"

"Yes, you, come here please, how can I help you?"

"I was asking about a man named Falah."

The thirty year old man with the intermittent black mark

intervened, saying: "I'm Falah. Yes, how can I help you?"

Hamid put his fingers on his black hair dispersal, dispersing and rubbing it as usual, and then whispered to himself:

This is the discreet confident man my mother told me about, how he came to the cemetery, and I didn't notice him? I don't even remember seeing him before! I must now be incredibly careful when talking to him, there is something wrong. He came nearer to him asking:

"Are you also a receptionist?"

"No, my colleague is the receptionist, I work as a morgue ambulance driver, the driver of the dead. My name is Falah, how can I help you?"

As soon as he uttered the word 'driver of the dead,' Hamid's eyes widened again.

He told himself calmly as his hand was moving between his head and his waist: He is that witness to everything, only these three know the truth in all its subtlety: my mother, the driver Falah, and the dead washer, while the dead washer assistant, I don't think he knows but to carry out the orders. And right now, I'm fourth. it's the list of the secret operations I want to reveal all its secrets.

Hamid approached near to Falah's ear whispering and asking him:

"Can I talk to you in private, please?"

Falah came out of the office and asked his colleague a permission from behind the glass. He took Hamid to the end of the equilateral corridor; whose walls and roof are all dyed white. Hamid began to talk hesitantly:

"I'm, I'm, I'm…"

Falah put his right hand on his visitor's shoulder, approaching his ear and telling him:

"I remember you, I've been waiting for you three whole days, and we only have a few days left, maybe only four. You are too late, but the good is always what happened."

"My mother did not tell me the truth of the tragic news except yesterday, after only three days of consolation."

"I was afraid that it would be left with no attention nor an end. The administrator might come to check the morgue and the coffins as usual, check the official statements and compare them together. Later, we might fall into a taboo or, we fall into a calamity that we do not know its end."

"I first want to see the body of my father, please, as my mother recommended to me."

"It can't be done in the morning, Mr.... You told me, what's your name?"

"I am Hamid, Hamid Kamel."

"We will not be able to carry out the order in the morning, you see the number of people and their clamor, as well as the large number of fellow staff, the issue here is very complicated."

"Oh, okay. Then, what's the solution?"

Falah turned to his back, looked at everyone in the waiting room and gave his back to Hamid, no one could hear him but Hamid, he said with a mouth that was almost closed:

"Bodies are never handed over here until the morning when there are many people, and the movement returns to normal. But in your case, you must come in the evening, when the number of employees and parents is much lower than you see now, come tonight, and I will let you in without the knowledge of the guard, we will ignore him, yes, we will ignore him. Come at 10pm exactly, don't come before ten."

Hamid greeted him with his permission: 'May God bless your parents, goodbye.'

"Goodbye," he answered.

The evening came after a long wait, in which Hamid's eyes had not closed since he left the reception area in the morgue, and during that time he could not eat anything, only the water was enough to fill his needs of hunger and thirst.

He returned home watching his mother's movements from far away, and he was keeping away from facing his wife Maya, and even talking to her, something in his chest started to stop him and keep him away from her since his mother told him the truth, pretending to do anything to get away from her. He knows that a husband never leaves his wife but feels guilty.

Few hours later, the deadline approached, and as Falah recommended and agreed on the most delicate details; Hamid set off to the Capital Hospital, parked his car away from the morgue, parked it with the cars of the patients and their families, far enough behind the green garden, in the open public parking. He disembarked, looking left and right, he went to the morgue indirectly. On the way, his mobile suddenly rang. He said sadly:

"It's Maya again."

He took his mobile out of his pocket slowly, and when he saw the caller's name, he rose from the horror of what would ensue:

"Falah." He answered quickly and said:

"Hello, yes..."

"It's exactly ten pm, but wait, don't approach the gate unless you don't see the guard there."

"Just standing? "

"And don't come unless you see me at the outside gate, and then I will give you a ringtone on your phone, okay?"

Hamid stood on the sidewalk from the other side, waiting and raising his phone in front of his eyes watching it. While the air breeze moved his wide dress, he was avoiding the eyes of others and their curiosity, hoping not to meet any of his many acquaintances.

A few minutes later, Falah appeared and came to the guard in his uniform. They had a little talk, Falah's hand moved a lot as if he represented or created a dramatic situation, realizing that a distant eye or relative was looking at him.

A brief time later, the guard went inside the building next door, and Falah soon pointed to Hamid with his right from afar. Hamid came looking in all directions. Then, Falah pointed his right hand at a metal electric door as if it were an emergency door. Then, said:

"Enter through this door, and wait behind it from the inside, never move, I will be back to you after the guard returns from the bathroom."

Hamid did what he was asked for but kept wondering: so, this is how it works easily here, those who are inside are dead, who wants to see or meet them? Bodies like soft trees lying and wrapped in white cloths, peaceful inside their coffins, while calamities and disasters come only from those living, from the people of this world.

Falah came to him about five minutes later, closed the electric door behind him with the key, then moved the handle to make sure it was locked and tightened.

"Come in, come this way, quickly."

Suddenly, Hamid's phone shook in his hand with a new message, which he opened: Oh my God! Maya repeatedly, do you know where I am, even if I'm on Mars?

He silenced his device and then turned it off. Hamid followed Falah as a shadow who said without looking behind him:

"Look, Hamid, these are the morgue refrigerators of the dead that you were hearing about in the Capital Hospital, your father's body there, in refrigerator number five, exactly, that row on your right."

He walked in front of him, as he guided him and explained to him the instructions and recommendations:

"Open the refrigerator by pressing the handle inside like this way, then turn it down and drag it out. Just like that… And the door will open smoothly."

He turned after him and did not find Hamid near him. The newcomer retreated to where he entered waiting and panicked behind the metal door. He could not step forward, so he stayed there and went back as if he had a bit of nausea and dizziness. Falah came back to him blaming and saying:

"Hurry, Hamid, we don't have enough time, move faster." He returned to his side and pulled him out of his hand, and then pointed out by his finger:

"This is your father's body wrapped in white cloth, in mortuary refrigerator number five, stay here, next to him; check it out as carefully as your mother asked you, wait here until I come back, I'll be out with the guard."

Falah left Hamid quickly as a deaf machine, without waiting for a response nor answer from him. Hamid put his confused hands on the handle sensed its coldness and began to take a slow look from the ground to the handle, recognizing the distance between his feet on the ground and the refrigerator. He quickly recalled some of the events installed in his mind on the tape of his father's life. His legs rose and feared their betrayal, he clung to the handle, and put his head on the square metal door, and without looking beyond, he whispered so his father may listen:

"I came to you, Dad. Do you hear me?"

No answer.

He hit his fist at the mortuary refrigerator door:

"Hear me?"

It is nothing.

"Dad, don't you hear me?"

He felt the low temperature of the place and the coldness of the mortuary refrigerator door that began to run in his body. He was scared and very tired, stuck his forehead to the metal door as he wished for its mercy, then he pulled himself to the ground slowly and lay down on it, closed his eyes. He was relieved of the fatigue and lack of sleep as he had not been sleeping for almost four days. Since then, only, I took the opportunity to talk with him, and I immediately replied:

"Yes, I hear you."

Hamid opened his eyes hastily, rose from his place, as if someone was shaking him so hard to wake him up, he started looking in horror in all directions, and suddenly opening the shroud from his father's face without fear or disturbance, looking and searching for the source of the sound he had just heard clearly, he moved his father's face who did not respond:

"Dad, are you alive? Do you hear me and talk to me?"

He waited for the answer as he was flipping in the cold face. But nothing ever happened. He soon shouted in the cold and still space of the room: "Hey, anyone here? Is there anybody?"

Then, he whispered to himself: as if I heard a clear voice, but it's not as human voices! I think it's like whistling or buzzing! Oh, my God, maybe these are the illusions, the ones we're hearing about. I seek refuge in God from the devils.

At this moment, I listened very strongly to him, did Hamid call me the devil and take refuge in God from me? God forgive you, Hamid, God forgive you! He certainly means me, but the problem of man is that he does not see what is hidden from him, that he must feel, to reach the stage of realization, then he will see what can and can't be seen. Hamid was aware with my voice more than focusing on his father's bluish face. He was waiting for another word or one breath but that was impossible. However, he did not respond, and his father failed to pronounce even a single letter. The body's mouth and nose were filled with cotton and tied to a white cloth from the chin to the back. Hamid, as a loser, gradually withdrew to the ground, until he returned to his position and lay down again. He sought refuge within God from the accused Satan. Then, he closed his eyes and reviewed his memory of the last time he saw his father, and then gradually returned to this moment, where he is now, which human beings call current or present. I can see him now very clearly, while he cannot see me. Hamid was still confused about the sound he had just heard, so his memories were mingled with that moment he was in it, and before he was invaded by the flames of dreams, I said:

"No problem, Hamid, you will know me eventually."

I gave him another chance, but of a sudden, I found his mind asking himself: who is he, the one with that voice and the buzz? Or are they only the hallucinations, those that come from the majesty flames of death, and abound as we get closer to the bodies of the dead and the smell of nothingness? Does nothingness sound as well as existence? Hamid lost hope while complaining; he cushioned his right arm and closed his eyes. Thus, the opportunity was once again ripe; I landed next to him and approached him gradually, then I settled over his forehead and between his eyebrows exactly. I condensed in him like ether and concentrated in his forelock, and I began chatting him at lightning speed:

"I know, Hamid that you will come here, to see your father's body, and then you will wonder about what happened to him in His life. I also know that this body of your father will not talk to you and will never say to you a single word. What is left of him is an inhabitant body which is immobile and has no soul. This body that you see now is nothing but a dress he took off, and now it is lying dead without any movement. There is no harm to this (dress) if it stays here in the mortuary refrigerator behind you, or is buried in or on the ground, near billions of people who preceded it. The result is one clear and unambiguous, namely, the nothingness of a clay body and the launch of a spirit into the space of heaven. Its birth in the other life, and its stability in the World of Eternity, where we humanize it, as his lovers have humanized (him)."

Hamid's body moved in response to this act of dialogue. He put his hand over his head in response to the disorder of his mind and the signals sent to him. I stopped talking with him for moments, and when he stopped again, he was stable. I said to him:

"I should not have kept you tired and bewildered, reeling between right and wrong, and lost, looking between truth and falsehood. In between all of these, you were cursing and insulting the king of Tablistan. You think he is a major reason for the sufferings of your father Pilgrim Kamel, which led to his death and his departure from the world. You have never thought that your insults will never harm him, but it is a clear situation that explains those conflicts and worries stuck in your chest. Hamid, you should know that your God will achieve what you want in case you provide your pure and absolute faith only for Him. But if your prayer is not answered, then you must know that your faith has not reached the needed amount. I am innocent of what you describe and blame, and far from the accusation you are sticking to me. Hamid, you should also know, that it is not the task of your God to do what you want and need. God has given you the ability to choose and has given you the right circumstances to achieve your goals, but he has never cared about what you do or want. You are simply like the rest of humans; they do not return to him unless the world narrows or spit them. As far as we are concerned, all good will be forgotten by you, human beings, and unjustly thrown behind your ungrateful backs. While all evil you attach to your *Imams*, your elders, and your sultans, and even on the hanger of those who rule you, king, prince, or sultan. In your own situation, while your chest is full of rancor and hate, you are the slave of lust. You see that your curse and insults are a means of expressing the things in your chest, but you know nothing but that expresses what is inside you. Oh, Hamid, I am Kingel. I am the Soul of the King, who has now been accused by all the evil that has afflicted the people of the Kingdom of Tablistan, and no one will remember any worldly good thing that has hit you and brought to you. You have undoubtedly been afflicted by great evil and great good, but you have never been grateful."

I gave his mind space and some time to reassure him that his body would not move or wake up, I talked with the soul between his two sides and I said:

"Hamidel, Oh soul, here is your human being accepting the body of his mortal father, and this is what will tire him and burden him increasingly, if he tolerated the case, he would survive. But, if his strength is weakened or lost, he will be mad and domed. He must realize that his father's body will never return to his first image, he is an undoubted mortal and dead, how am I satisfied with that, and he sees me as a major reason for that? The ruler does not lose the right to his people after the annihilation of his body and its demise, because he is responsible until the Dome day. A great responsibility that does not end if those injustices and needs are inherited. As the relatives believe in prayer and charity on behalf of their dead's, the true Soul of the King does not stand idly by, unless it is unable to save itself in the other life, and its fate is to Hell. I am now in the highest heaven; I need a life in which I rise and increase. Its ascension does not end. Therefore, I chose absolute love, because after I got rid of the king's body, I had nothing left of fear and panic. The souls love the oppressor and the oppressed at the same time. They love the master and the slave, the light, and the darkness. Because they realize that every creature only performs its assigned role and is always in dire need of help, to sow love in it, and what creation needs to its counterpart and its opposite to manifest itself."

Come with me, Oh Soul, come with me, Hamidel. there, to the farthest horizon, the higher horizon, to where the world of secrets, the world that will tell you how Hamid's father reached the end of his life in the world, to where he demolished his worldly age by his own hands. From there, the tale will begin, and the dust will dissipate. You must leave your body beside the body of Pilgrim Kamel. You also must keep something of yourself and your light in your body so that it does not perish and die as Hamid's father died. Keeping a part of you will survive Hamid's body and let it in a small death, in deep sleep, and will inevitably wake up after you return to him and spread in his body.

Hamid leaned to his right shoulder and cushioned it, and he fell into a deep slumber. I took the opportunity and went on to talk to Hamidel, who was awake in his forelock:

"The events of the world, Hamidel, do not perish and never disappear, and their time or place never ends as the people of the world usually think, but the human body loses the ability to follow them; Oh, Soul. The human body has the ability only to preview its immediate time, which rotates in front of its eyes in motion, which the people of the world call the moment or now. Because of the nature of his materialism, man sees only this moment, but the souls remain free and able to see all the moments. O, soul. It's the chapters of the eternal play that Soul lives but not bodies. It is that play written from time immemorial on the *Lined Panels*. What you must do, Hamidel, is only to leave your current heaven, the *Lowest Sky* that you are in now, and leave with me to the *Second Heaven*. From there, we will remove the veil from the *Preserved Board,* and any chapter of the *Eternal Play*, and then watch it together, yes, we will watch it together, you and me."

We will see and observe all its events, which human beings mistakenly think have been eroded and vanished forever, but they remain etched there on the *Eternal Board*. You will see from there what man was destined to do first, and what he chose and on purpose second.

"Will I go to escort you to second heaven as you say? Hamidel asked me as she is troubled."

"Yes, but, as I told you, you must keep something from you in your mud body lying next to that dead body in the morgue, to keep something of your trace. We will leave for the second heaven, but you will not be able to travel with me to the rest of the highest heavens except as a soul which is completely separated from her body. Then, that body which you are wearing now, will die."

Hamid and his mother wanted to know the causes of *Pilgrim* Kamel's death, asking for the truth with all its pain. They wanted to know what had happened to him, to know the perpetrators and the possible punishment. Until that time, his mother has been waiting for the final report of what will happen after examining the body of the deceased, while, at this moment, Maya is still waiting for her husband for no apparent, convincing reason for Hamid. A reason we will discover in time. As we can find out all the reasons from our current location, from above the Holy *Tor* Mountain.

We will start watching the eternal play from its first chapter. I told her:

"The chapter of Adam's creation?" Hamidel was wondering.

"No, no, that is the first chapter of creation, a great chapter, which extends from eternity to forever, but we will begin with the first chapter that concerns your body only, concerning Hamid as a human being. The chapter that caused his father, Pilgrim Kamel, to enter conflicts with the conflicting forces and the power that exists in the Kingdom of Tablistan, where my human was, unfortunately, a crowned king. It is the chapter which followed by many successive events before the death of Hamid's father, Pilgrim Kamel."

"Death? Here you are admitting, Kingel."

Hamidel is always a constant, so I cleared: "I have not said whether or not he has been killed deliberately or unintentionally."

I invited her to go from this hour to second heaven, to remove the *Eternal Veil*. Therefore, she can see, "Republic of Arak" and what kind of disasters have happened there.

Raised by the word "Republic of Arak," she asked:

"Do we leave the Kingdom of Tablistan where we are now, and we go to Republic of Arak? Are you really going to take me there and that simple?"

"We will rise go up as I told you, and I will not re-explain much. We will go up to the second heaven, and you will find all the (there) behind the veil, we will sit in the Eternal Theater where *Mount Towa* is. The show will start from where we ask and we want, anytime and anywhere we want to follow it and watch its events and tragedies, sorrows before its joys."

"Isn't that impossible, imaginative and a kind of craziness?"

Hamid's soul still does not know that the dreams of human beings in the lowest heaven have no limits or horizons, nor the souls in the high heavens have any limitations; there is absolute time and absolute place. When the soul is inside a body, this mud body forces her to travel and move to see life and the worldly scenes at its current time. Those that resemble physical chapters of a theater in their real place and time, where man travels all land to realize it.

When the soul abandons the body, it is dislodged and descended only from the lowest heaven to the second heaven, the soul therefore becomes able to see everything, where she is.

I asked her if she had not understood the whole story yet. The worldly world is in fact changing in its time and place, and the souls remain in their heaven, looking at the panels and hovering around them, becoming in front of a contemporary eternal play, which has no past or future as you call it. All times are present and current. The souls only need to open or remove the veil to see what they want, no time limits it, no place to restrict it. There, we will see with exactly the absolute facts fixed as they are, as they occur unequivocally, not as others convey in vain. So, let's go to the second heaven, which, as I said, is not far away, we will sit on the holy mountain of Tur.

"The mountain of Tur! Isn't that found above the ground? Is it a physical worldly creature?" Hamidel wondered.

I said:

"No, it's not like that. The life of the world is a traditional symbolic school that simulates the greatest creation, and life is in all the high skies. Everything above the earth carries the symbolism of things that are difficult for the bodies to see, the House of God is a symbol of something else that you will see in the second heaven. The Tur (phase) is also another symbol. Even your body, O soul, is a symbolic and miniature image of the whole universe… Yes, the human body is the whole universe."

I returned to continue my talk:

"Let's start by watching the first theatrical show of the eternal play from above Tur Mount. We will remove the veil from there and see its most important characters. We will begin with the chapter of "Republic of Arak" as I told you. We will see from there Mr. Mahdi Al-Mualemi in the religious college founded by his ancestors in the land of Arak. A Religious College of Hussein, which is matched by the border of the conflict, a Religious College of Ali, and between them a conflict that will never end, not because it is mental, but because it represents the passions of the human soul, including jealousy and love of uniqueness and possession."

It was only a moment, and before Hamid gave attention, his soul, Hamidel, and I were together on the way to second heaven. There we will settle together in the chair in the Eternal Theatre. We will be above the holy mountain of Tur, above the chair guarded by the angels, to see from there with her own eyes how Mr. Mahdi Al-Mualemi began his story chapters in the Republic of Arak. Which ended, later, with the fate of Hamid's father in the Kingdom of Tablistan. We will begin the show of the first scene of the eternal play as soon as we arrive. I said, always remember that souls can see the panels of events as fixed as they are… Are you ready?

"No, I'm not, moments please."

"What else?"

"How did you leave the world in turn? And why did you go back near the body of Kamel, Hamid's father? Why did you go back to him there in the morgue?"

Since we were on the way to watch the play, I should remind Hamidel that I left the world, and I had left my body just a few days before Hamid's father left. I should assure her that the king refused the injustice to the people of The Land of Tablistan at all. If there were excesses, he was never aware of them, but those excesses and evils absolutely remain in his great responsibilities, as he was sitting on top of the pyramid of the government, ruling the land. He is certainly responsible even for tiny things. The king, in that era, never deviated from the truth. This is the way I knew and evaluated the events. He was a king on the land of Tablistan, a hereditary property and a great responsibility that he only had to accept, whether he liked it or not. I left him and your world in turn, only after he struggled a lot to receive acceptance and satisfaction from all people. I know, doubtless, that it was to meet God, and what was stuck between him and God Almighty, may be forgiven by the most merciful, but the debts of human beings are not interrupted, except by their pardoning them and overcoming. Listen, Hamidel, very carefully:

"God created the universe to show his power, God wanted to feel his greatness, so he created the universe. The souls chose their bodies to feel the theoretical value of them as well, and since I am the Soul of the king, and my name is now Kingel, I want to feel the value of being created as well and show my ability. I am thirsty for satisfaction and love, but I did not have the ability to return to the worldly lowest life again, so I wanted to feel that satisfaction by serving the people of Tablistan, including your human being, Hamid."

The Lord will not feel that he is a Creator if he does not create, and the Soul of the King will not feel its advantages if it does not lend a helping hand to the needy. Do you think I'm here by accident? Absolutely not. It is because, by my love, I have heard your pain and suffering, and the soul is tired searching for the truth. When Kamel was killed, the occasion was favorable. Kamel was a drop of dew that fell into the ocean and faded. After knowing his story, the whole ocean fell into his drop of dew. Then, he faded.

This is the bottom line. The soul of that dead person in the mortuary refrigerator does not want to leave me, flying freely. She has been chasing me in the heavens since I left her body. As soon as I left Heaven, her perched in front of me blaming as usual. I, therefore, knew that there is no escape from what I am in. Oh my God, as if I bear a matter of sins that I do not know anything about while in the world. But I am accountable for everything that is going on over the land of the Kingdom of Tablistan. Didn't those who represent me know that reaching the right things is easier than making mistakes?

"Oh, if I were one of the publics carrying only his weight. Oh, life of pride, you never end up."

As soon as I leave a heaven, I find the soul of Kamel, who will be lying in his morgue refrigerator, she chases me and stands in front of me, to disturb me and make me feel a lack of praise and reverence for the God Almighty. I have no choice but to respond. There is no doubt, as I am sure now, that the debts of the people are not exceeded by God if you are not forgiven by those who have been offended or oppressed. Although I do not know Hamid's father well, he knows me and asks me in front of his Creator. People are various, scattered and too many, but the ruler of every people on earth is only one, and I, unfortunately, was the soul of the king who sat in the chair of the Kingdom of Tablistan.

"I found the soul of Pilgrim Kamel really chasing me and roaming around me as if it were floating around the Muslim's *Kaba* in Mecca on earth. As if its buzz refuses to leave me." I asked her to forgive the sin that was made by those who represent me in this world, those I gave some minor tasks. I wish the king, that man, left the universe with its arrogance before leaving and abandoning him. But the soul of Pilgrim Kamel said:

"You must negotiate in the land and not Heaven, the blood money is there and not here. There is Hamid and his mother who has entrusted him to know what had happened to his father, and to take out the perpetrators. What a man's ignorance and selfishness, his problem is in his desire to know the facts, and he forgets that most of the facts are invisible. He must sense the facts and even if he does not see them, what is hidden from the eyes of the Son of Adam was greater and harsher.'

After I returned to the side of Kamel's body, waiting for its burying, I found Hamid, your body's soul, near him. I am ashamed of what I have done during my life, I wish I were oppressed and condemned in that sordid life, to enjoy absolute freedom here. I embrace the heavens unconditionally. I did not think that the actions of the officials whom I entrusted to serve the people have become an indefensible curse, even if I leave or escape to the second heaven or even the seventh.

As soon as I approached Hamid's father's body, I found you in the body of his son Hamid lying next to him, and I had to take the opportunity and talk with you as a soul. That will only happen in a dream. I approached Hamid sleeping next to his father's body, and I addressed you through his forelock, and here you are simply with me now. I have no desire to waste more time. Is it time for us to go to the second heaven and start immediately viewing the first scene?

"Yes."

"Let's go, and let's start quickly by following the first scene of "Arak Republic.""

(2)

After Hamidel kept a part of her to keep her body alive, she set off with me toward the second heaven, and we set off on a path parallel to the terrible isthmus tunnel, the tunnel in which souls travel from the lowest heaven to the second one. We were not allowed to go in, because it was only for the departing, not for visitors, for those who had died and left the world forever. We had flown parallel to it, as Hamidel's scrutiny increases, trying to explore and examine what is in it. It is a tunnel that resembles a spiral whirlwind that flows from the ground to the heaven, widens and sometimes narrows, in which some departing souls pass, reassuring, singing cheerfully in its spaciousness, while others suffer from its narrowness and unease. Every hostage of what has been gained in his worldly life. We were flying near it and in parallel, and we were witnessing the destabilization and trembling of souls in it, which fluctuated in its pitfalls and squeezed them into its straits. The isthmus tunnel began in a bright white color, but soon turned black.

The more work the deceased is bad, and the more they are overwhelmed by the passage they and become squeezed. We saw many situations, on the sides of this isthmus tunnel, the work of human beings is drawn on them, and every soul sees what it has done in its first life.

Hamidel seemed to realize that there were several breaks and stations in that great tunnel, and that every soul had to pass through it. We agreed to see the biggest of those stations whose names were written down for the departures to know: The Oasis of Truth, The River of Eternity, The Sea of Giving, The Horizon of Hope.

I passed with Hamidel in that heavenly way, and she kept turning in every direction, seeing another life, a life that was prevented from seeing because of staying or imprisoning in her body. She was flying behind me and almost stumbled upon her limbs from the horror of the great scene. Until we reached the first break, it was written on its highly written board: 'Oasis of Truth.'

We stopped to see her from afar, and Hamidel quickly realized what was going on inside it. Where the souls are overflowing with the absolute truth unconsciously;

"Why would you want to know the truth if the facts are harsh? Some truths let creatures down and hurt them." I asked Hamidel.

"That is to let Hamid's mother and Maya and those closest to them all feel the truth about what happened to Hamid's father and the truth that led to his death. They only hear what is said here and there, but they do not feel the pure truth; they still do not know that audible words are the most failed way to convey and express facts." She replied to me.

I talked with her insisting on the nearest arrival, the greatest eternal theatre over the Holy Mountain of Tur, where we will remove from there its jellied curtain by lifting the veil. We will see all the facts that we wish to know, we will see them as real, not as described or conveyed by others.

Not long after, we reached another break, with the name: The River of Eternity. There, souls feel the truth of their immortality and the impossibility of their death. Hamidel hastened to take advantage of the situation and asked me in her own way:

"If all heavens are your space, and they are the object of immortality, what brought you back to the lower heavens, and what kept you in the body of Hamid's father?"

Hamidel will realize later that souls want to glow and express themselves more and more, and you will know that the Creator does not give her or sell her in another body as an alternative. Therefore, she appears in the vision to serve others to get those joyous feelings and that's why I'm back in the darkness of the world. It is not a luxury of me at all, but to feel my ability to give and do good, to look for sophistication and ascension in the other life. I wanted in short to be a light in the darkness of the world, just as the flood of the Creator shows his ability and manifestations, so are the souls wanted to feel their values and abilities through this giving, so they visited their loved ones in a dream. That is why I returned to lower heaven.

Hamidel was silent and in her silence so much. We set off again in our line parallel to the Isthmus Tunnel. After another ascension, we found the last isthmus break, and it was written on its preserved board: The Sea of Giving, where pushing the affliction from the other is the pinnacle of giving.

"How can the soul here become a spirit of absolute giveaway?" I talked with Hamidel.

"Since I gave up my body, people have never stopped cursing the king as human, chasing him as if he were still living among them. It may not hurt me anymore, but it will inevitably cause the doer great harm, which may cause a black wall of hatred over his chest, making him live standing behind him, and I hate to be drowned twice on the trail."

"Paying the affliction about them from is a kind of giving." I told her.

"The people of the Kingdom of Tablistan believe that the ruler or king is the underlying cause of every crime. Every thief was poor, needed the sustenance of his day, and he didn't find it, so he stole, and every rich thief who didn't find a law a deterrent to him, he stole, too. And every adulterer had the doors open, she became a prostitute. Therefore, I became the only hidden reason behind every crime committed on the land of Tablistan. Is that justice? Those are their wishes and prayers which are never achieved if they are separated from the prayer of thanksgiving."

We crossed flew until we finally reached the Holy Mountain Tur. From there, the mountain and its valley seemed to have no horizons or limits. The *Durr Tree* raised on its right, shading the arrivals. From here, we'll see the whole eternal theatre, from eternity to forever, where all times have been and still are.

"A great Eternal Theater! She was wondering."

I replied with the same telepathy:

"Yes, existence was accessible, but it was (there), Hamidel, just like what the people of the world called the Big Bang, that explosion which happened there, and it became on the ground a long time later. For all of this, the presence, for the public, is complete only with the eye and the feeling.

Look now, human beings are walking in the scenes of the Eternal Theater and its chapters drawn with great accuracy, like a battalion of ants in its course and diligence, but some people ask for worldly life, so they change their diligence and destiny. They jump out of their desires to another different path. Then, the human falls into the quagmire of his miscalculation and choice. Some may thank for the grace and accept it, but some may deny it and covet it in others. Man never knows that his happiness's lies in his satisfaction and conviction in what he was destined for, not as what he was destined for himself and wished, and that his misfortunes will not come unless his passion prevails over his mind."

"Do you mean that every human being has two ways, one destined for him and the other purely of his will?"

"We have given him the way either to be thankful or faithless but unfortunately, as I have seen in this world, man's action is based on love or hatred, if he follows either of them, he will make the same mistake, because he is forced to repeat mistakes."

I wanted Hamidel to see from here other than what she saw in the world as there is no time or place to limit or define.

She soon expressed her desire to follow the first scene of the Eternal Play, to know first how the fate of Hamid's father changed, and his age passed, and then to see Maya's volatility and her relationship with the big event. Then, I became greedy and I hoped that the curse would stop there, and the debts of the worldly people will stop with it. We stood in front of the veil of the Eternal Theater, and we sat in the tarmac of seats specially designed for souls, between the two platforms of angels to the right, and the absolute selves to the left. We were ready to remove the veil from the theatrical scene that had happened after it was chosen by its doers. Then, we would remove the veil from the scene that was destined but rejected by the worldly people their desires, so their destiny was changed. We would also be able to see man's action, when he replaces his evil with his goodness.

I asked Hamidel to look up. As the worldly person looks at the top of the sky, the souls here so do, looking at the top of heavens. We found the luminous lights that is contaminated in some areas according to the sins of man. It is the Preserved Panel hanging in his horizon, that panel on which were written all knowledge, science, and names, and all the characters of absolute time and place, including all characters and places of the first chapter before the beginning of its presentation.

All the names appeared written on it. Together, we were able to know the characters of the first chapter of the eternal play. These were written:

Characters: Al-Mualemi, Faqih, Arak Leader, Al-Alawi, UN Envoy, Kamel.

Places: Arak Republic, Al-Mualemi House, Republic square

As soon as, Hamidel read the names on the Panel, she screamed, referring to the last:

"The last name is the name of Hamid's father, he is there, he is the one whom we came to know the secret of his command." Then, she became silent for a moment and continued: But the king has no presence, so where was your human being?

I said:

"You should know the truth at all, not as you want to understand it, let's start now following the first scene of the eternal play."

The First Eternal Scene

Mr. Mahdi Al-Mualemi is about to leave his house, heading across a narrow and winding corridor to the Husseini Seminary. He put his large black turban on his head, which he seemed to be lost in, wearing a transparent brown cloak on his shoulders, and letting the wind caress her behind him however she likes, fluttering behind him as a warrior' flag. His face, however, took the form of a scrawny triangle that corresponded to the thinness of his body, which concealed its features under the clothes of the clergy. He went to say goodbye to his family, his two wives and his children, and then he closed the door of his house about to go out, took some steps, but he stopped suddenly when found his uncle Mr. Al-Faqih and his companions coming toward him as if they had just finished a funeral.

His eyes widened as he was gazing at them, Al Mualemi gave his back to the door of his house and confronted Faqih and his companions on the way to him. He waited silently. Then, he began to accept and understand the sudden situation, and his uncle al-Faqih did not give him the opportunity to talk and preceded him:

"Peace be upon you; May God bless your morning."

"Peace be upon you too, welcome to our uncle Al Faqih, and welcome to his guests, I thank you for the surprise visit Uncle."

"Let us go inside your guest room, the matter is too dangerous."

Al-Mualemi returned into his house resourcefully, took off his brown cloak and kept his heavy turban over his head. Al Faqih and his companions followed him to the guest room. Al Faqih sat to the right of Mualemi, and two companions sat in front of him, while the others remained outside the house. They stayed silently waiting for the oldest to speak. Hot tea and water were brought to them in a hurry. Al Faqih then spoke:

"I introduce you first to my guests, Mr. Al-Alawi and Kamel, (visitors) coming from the Kingdom of Tablistan. I met them at the headquarters of the Al-Alawite Seminary a few days ago, we met and made some interests and agreements. Then, we all came to you in a hurry for different things. We will discuss some of them now and ask Allah Almighty to help us to achieve them, and then we, hopefully, will complete the rest of its procedures in the land of Burqan and the Kingdom of Tablistan. We will start the plan from here, from the Republic of Arak, and based on God willing, to complete it in the Kingdom of Tablistan."

"Are they religious issues? Say, I hear you."

"Yes, religion is undoubtedly a life, a trade that will not be ruined, but regarding our plan, it boils down to the first issue about the two seminaries, which is more important. We believe that the Husseini seminar must be fully independent of the Al-Alawite seminary. We have enough cracks and differences that have never ended, and different disputes all play on the chord of religion. You know that beliefs, such as customs, take shape with time. I was just there, in the Al-Alawite seminary, and it seems they want to humiliate the ruling regime. They don't want to confront the leader and his injustice and stand up to him, maybe they're afraid of being brutalized. They're afraid of his fist and his promise, and maybe, according to their doctrinal building, they're using *(taqiyya)* to avoid the reactions and madness of the Arak leader. Although I know that honesty is not always a successful way, I refuse the *(taqiyya)* and refuse to lie and be confused."

Mualemi was silent as was listening. His eyes turned to The Young Kamel, trying to check his features and dig them into his memory. As soon as Al-Faqih finished his brief introduction, Mualemi stood to address everyone, but it concerned the young Kamel in his speech:

"Do I know you? Have we ever met?"

"Oh my God, I don't know exactly, but everything is possible in this time." Kamel replied, moving his right palm on his chin:

"By God, he is only twenty-one years old, our master, and this is his first visit to the Republic of Arak, I mean, I don't think you have met." Al-Alawi intervened, explaining:

Mualemi stood changing the direction of the conversation, and in an unusual sharpness in the presence of his uncle Al Faqih, he put his right hand around his triangular beard, and took the strands of her hair, as usual if they had a big thing, pulled his brown robe *(besht)* lying next to him, and folded it with a quick lightning motion. He sat again and put the *besht* folded on his right, leaned on him, and said:

"You have your religion and so we do. We will not use *taqiyya* in the face of the oppression of the tyrant, the leader of Arak. This is the bottom line of the first order. As for us, we are not afraid to confront the oppressor, even if he is the leader of Arak. We have the best example in Imam Hussein, when, despite the few of his supporters, he faced injustice with its army and weapons."

He agrees with the thoughts, with whom Al-Faqih drew a smile on his face as he was looking at his companions. Said:

"This is exactly what we came for. When the first scene here is completed as planned, we will consider its implications, and if it is difficult for us and complicated, these two young men, Mr. Al-Alawi and young Kamel, will complete the plan from there, from the land of the Kingdom of Tablistan."

Then, Al Faqih stood up filled with anger, as if he remembered something important. He asked the audience to talk and explained that Arak Leader would rudely receive a United Nations envoy on the first day of the anniversary of his presidency of his ruling party. The leader will exploit the official and popular public presence to show the loyalty of the people to his person and to the ruling party. He already knew that those who would attend either from his own party, or from the army men before they leave the inflamed battlefields, or even from the public, who have attended with the influence of the desire, and the intimidation of the leader and his sword.

Al-Faqih then wondered:

"How can we then bring Al-Hussein on this occasion? And how can we say no in the face of the immoral oppressor, in the face of the Hitler of that era? How can we strive for injustice in Arak, Tablistan or any other country that is working hard to liberate?"

Mualemi nodded his head, explaining to Mr. Al-Faqih and his collaborators, and he was given the hugs, wherever this man speaks except for his words fell into the hearts of his audience, pointing his eyes directly to the pupils who looked at him, stitching them up, and keeping them in it until he planted himself in the same echo. Then, he reads that in the eyes of his followers, and these steps gradually pass on to all the attendees. There is no difference if he speaks in front of one person, a full family or even a crowd. The tendons of his throat make a voice that oscillates spontaneously between the heavy and the melodious.

His ability to cite and infer adds a major influence in the hearts of the recipients. It is a lord queen developed through training and practice, since he joined the study in the Husseini religious seminary before he reached adolescence. He soon completed his studies superior, and he was not yet twenty-five years old … Then he said:

"Leave the matter to me and trust all faith in Allah almighty and what I am doing."

"Won't we know the details of your plan and what you intend to do?"

"No, I just want you to make a whirlwind when I finish what I will be in, hoping that the conditions of resistance of the oppressor from Arak or beyond will be completed. I hope that the repercussions will continue until injustice and fear are removed from the entire region. I need these two men's promise to complete the road, and if I am arrested or killed, they must persevere and be patient at every obstacle. Patience, my beloved, is the amount of space between victory and loss."

They dated each other and swore that the upcoming meeting will be in the Republican Party Square in the center of the capital, on the third day of the party's annual celebrations, and in the presence of the official UN envoy, who will monitor the event and submit their recommendations to the relevant committees of the United Nations. At the end of this planned scene, the first eternal scene ends, and the eternal veil is descended from the Holy Mountain of Tur.

The Second Eternal Scene

Kingel, Hamidel and I were ready to follow the second scene. From here, the veil is lifted, as it was felled, from this great Eternal Theatre. The Republican Square which is known as Freedom Square appears. It was packed with large and compact crowds carrying pictures of the leader of varied sizes, rising alongside the flags of Arak republic. The roar of the crowd subsided after a request was broadcasted on loudspeakers. Arak, Leader, and the UN envoy entered surrounded by the heavily armed Republican Guards. Also, the head of Protocol, who worked hard for a month to complete the celebration, walked behind them.

The leader was not aware of what he had in store. He walked cheerfully like a peacock. He groaned in his steps as if he were playing it in a rhythm, not only turning around with his face, but turning like a machine with his full body, to spread his terror in the souls of his interlocutors.

As soon as the leader raised his right hand straight and outstretched forward, the crowd shouted and waved the colorful flags like a loud wave without an end.

Then, the republican anthem was played, and the audience started chanting the national anthem with one voice and rhythm. With that ceremony and its loudness, the huge and majestic festive scene reached its peak.

As soon as the republican anthem was over, the UN envoy spoke to the Leader who was waiting for the compliment in exchange

for the great welcome the guest received. He said:
"A massive party organization that has nothing wrong with a leader, in which the organizers have counted everything and focused on every stray and incoming. Although I know that the public is a herd that does not spare its leader and guide, it is here a distinct public presence, which is undoubtedly an effective populist, not a particular elitist as it is rumored. Freedom has been given to every attend."

The leader, with his intelligence and skill, understood the aim of the United Nations envoy. He requested the member of the Republican Guard who oversees organizing the affairs of the ceremony. He holds his left wrist by his strong fist, pulled him as the sheep is pulled, dragged him, and spoke whispering, as he was painting and making his smile like a tiger, while anger filled between his sides, and sparks were thrown between his teeth, and his thick eyebrows approached from each other. He bowed and said to him:

"You are too stupid."

"Sir, is there any failure of regulation or republican decrees? Is there even a slight flaw?"

"Listen to me, since I entered the Freedom Square with this guest, I found everything clean and accurate. The army, guards, and informants will shut up all people without any exception, while the audience spoke only with the republican anthem. This is really a failed organization of the celebration."

The Head of the Republic's Decrees was astonished. He muttered to himself: "If everything is complete, where are the defects?" Then, He asked the leader:

"Why, sir? You're saying that everything's in place, the system guys, the cleanliness, the security, the agriculture. All of them have carried out their roles to the fullest and on my direct and personal recommendation; there isn't even a single dust speck, not a yellow leaf for any tree lying on the ground, even the breath of the audience is under our control, sir; even the clothes of the audience we chose for them very carefully."

The leader pressed on the side of his right lip and his mouth was covered by his thick moustache after drooping on all his lips. He almost spilled their blood from the intensity of anger, then he said angrily:

"This organization is clearly human-made, I don't want that; I want my guest to see the making of God, to see everything natural, things must be kept incomplete, I want some leaves from the trees on the pavement here and there, I want some dust, some debris, some water, some public speeches, and speakers and not just the police, the army and the party ... This is how it will look normal in front of the guest; he will know that the people's love for their leader is divine and spiritual, do you understand? That's how he's going to report what he saw to his organization, to the United Nations, and the news will be broadcast on all the world's television channels. Do you get it, idiot, fool?"

The ceremony manager puts his hand on his mouth and speaks in a deep voice with a lot of fear and manners:

"I understand now, Mr. President, but I see the UN envoy smiling and satisfied."

"Oh, you're stupid that won't end either, he just smiles because he's a successful politician and not a fool like you, it's a mask, you should know: The more the politician smiles, the more he betrays, shall we wait his treachery? We're not going to let you both do that, okay? Do you understand? Now we want some attendees to be allowed to give a poem or speech in praise of the leader, praise the party and the country, all to avoid some of your follies that have will not end only with your execution or stoning."

The internal official announced through loudspeakers the opening of the participation through speeches and poems, classical and colloquial, to remember the achievements of the President Leader and the one ruling party, and to be sung by the audience and documented by history before the UN envoy himself.

Al Mualemi took advantage of the situation, as if the fate of heaven supports him, raised his right hand and advanced from the audience, so the organizers asked him what he intends and wants to do, and he said:

"I will have a poem that keeps history documented, suitable for this great occasion, to immortalize the president Leader and his guest, worthy and fits the audience."

The guard gave him the road on the previous recommendations of the Leader, which was accompanied by threats. Al Mualemi climbed to the wooden platform, covered from below to the top with Arak's flags. He gathered his cloak, remembered his uncle's advice: say your rhetorical words with reverence, and it will have a magical effect. Then he began to cast his poem:

> Tell the Leader if you stand to praise him,
> There is no difference between the curse and the pain.
> Leave the tyrant to the Creator,
> Isn't it enough for you to be satisfied?
> Oh, Leader, did you forget those who you had erased?
> Have you forgotten how many ribs you have broken?
> Oh, you pharaoh on us, must your hand be paralyzed,
> How many women have you widowed?
> You've spent your life of greed?
> How many newborns became orphans?

They will, all, revenge.
How many jails did you build?

Suddenly, Al Mualemi's voice was cut off from the loudspeakers. At the same moment, the assistants of Al-Faqih set a fire and made a bang on the other side of the crowd. Consequently, the attention shifted from the north platform to the other, and as the noise increased between the crowd, Al Mualemi threw himself into the crowd before he was reached by the Republican Guard, but his black turban helped them to distinguish him and facilitate his pursuit. As soon as he became aware of it, he threw it to the ground, and he removed his brown (cloak). The cloak fell on the ground and the audience stepped on it with their shoes. At that time, it got harder for the stalkers and Al Mualemi disappeared like a needle in a haystack. It was not easy for the guards to distinguish him among the waves of large crowds.

Al Mualemi slipped out of the crowd after he delivered his message perfectly, but he became pursued as a shadow by the Special Forces and the secret guard as well as the Republicans. As he is aware of all this, he went to the secret bunker, which was especially pre-prepared inside the old neighborhood, in anticipation of such circumstances. And there he was preceded by Al Faqih and Al Al-Alawi with the young Kamel. Therefore, will Kamel be a witness to all those momentous events? And will events rush him and take him to his end?

During the crisis, Al Mualemi and Al Faqih were in constant contact in various secret ways with their counterparts and supporters in the neighboring state of Burqan. They have different ties, social, family, religious and doctrinal as well.

The great escape to the neighboring Burqan was well arranged with great secrecy, while the rest of the wanted men, by organized smuggling methods, left to the Cedar Republic. The first mission ended after Al Mualemi delivered his direct message to all attendees, with the presence of the UN envoy and the international media.

I slowly asked for the curtain to be closed on the second scene of the eternal play, and here Hamidel wondered why of all this, as if she were rushing the next of events, she said as she was begging:

"Let's now follow the third scene until the end, I expect it will be full of excitement and suspense, although I do not understand the relationship of all this so far with Hamid's father, and whether that is the reason for what happened to him until his death."

"Events will come fast in the upcoming scenes, just wait, and you will know all that relationship with Hamid's father. But now we must get back to the morgue, where your sleeping body is next to your dead father's body."

"Why now, why the rush, why don't we stay so long?"

"The young Falah, the driver of the car of the dead, is now standing at the head of your body there. If you do not go back immediately, Falah will think that your body is dead, we're going to get into a lot of events which are out of our control. If his responsibly is taking out the body of Pilgrim Kamel, he will be required to take out your body too, and one calamity will become two."

After her first visit to the second heaven, Hamidel, who became eager to get out of her own format and her ground prison, desperately wanting to be free from what she was in? Talked:

"In fact, I want to leave that body now, it is certainly a good opportunity, I want to get rid of it now, life here is infinitely wide, while there, I'm in a tightness of existence and limitations, tightness of the body and materialism; I want my body to die now to get rid of it! I want the life of eternity that will come only through the gate of death."

"That is the will of God, if death comes, it is never an hour later or sooner."

The show has stopped now and is over, and it will not come back unless we lift the eternal veil again. Let's go back to world life now.

The veil of the eternal theatre was soon cast, announcing the end of the second eternal scene.

(3)

Hamid woke up to the sound of the driver Falah as they were alone in the morgue, patting him on his shoulder in fear and panic, moving his head right and left until he almost slapped him. He found his dead body, if it were not for some pulse coming from the depths of his heart, like waking up from a long coma. Had it not been for his lifelong experience of dealing with the dead and reading their face before their pulse, he would have thought at first glance that his companion had left life. He sensed the pulse with his thumb through Hamid's wrist, moved him as he patted and then hit his cheeks, then poured cold drinking water on his face.

Since only then, Hamid began to open his eyes slowly, and he could see the things in front of him blurry and limitless, and then gradually regained consciousness as he was looking at his friend's face and said:

"My Lord, where am I?"

He then turned to his friend asking him,

"Who are you?"

"Falah. I'm the driver. You forgot me?"

"Who brought you here, Falah?"

"Dear Hamid, get up please. Don't take us to the perdition, you're still in the morgue, we're not out of it yet."

"How come we haven't gotten out of it yet?"

Hamid put his hands over his head from the severity of pain and headaches, he sensed the weight of his body and the severity of his inactivity. He also realized his temperature and the rotation of his head, he seemed drunk, as if his center of balance became dysfunctional and deviating from his nature. He did not distinguish where he was and where he is now. He began to press above his ears and temples, as if he wanted to squeeze his head with both palms. All his limbs move and his body trembled. And then, he rubbed all his hair to express his annoyance and pain, I knew then that the most moving is the most disturbed inside himself, while the unsuspecting remains still. Hamid then wondered:

"What brought me here?"

"It's like sleeping took you and what you haven't woken up from so far, have you forgotten why you came to the morgue?"

Falah spoke to remind him, then helped him stand up for fear that the young man would stagger and fall on his face. While the refrigerator number five was still wide open, Falah extended his neck inside to see what was in it, and found the white cloth removed from the face of the body of the Pilgrim Kamel, and some parts of his chest appeared. He asked:

"Did you find what your mother recommended, Hamid? I mean, have you seen your father's chest? And did you see the wound I told you about?"

Hamid was in his body in the morgue talking with Falah with his tongue only, but he remained busy looking for me all over, that all his feelings are moving in the void. I feel him now and I see his eyes going in all directions, up and down, in front of him and behind him, and also on his sides. He became, in the concept of human beings and their definition, as possessors and maniacs. Then, he said in a loud voice that he barely heard Falah:

"Kingel must still be here in this atmosphere, I do not think she has left yet, she cannot leave me alone anymore, she knows my need for it, and she understands the need to atone for herself and what the King has done in his life."

"What are you talking about?" Falah asked him.

Hamid did not answer, and he did not care about what he said and became like a maniac peek all over the morgue, examining and searching, as if looking for a hair that moves and flies in the rest of the atmosphere.

Falah talked to him:

"Hamid, honestly, have you lost or forgotten anything? Your father's body is lying here in the fridge, not all over the morgue, it is not in the air nor on the ground! Focus with me please, that's enough, don't take us to a disaster, let us finish and walk please, don't bother us anymore, it's enough."

Hamid conducted what Falah wanted as an obedient machine without feelings nor emotions. He returned and examined his father's whole face and with utmost precision. The awe was removed from him and disappeared in its entirety. Then, he asked Falah to help him open the chest of the whole body, he wanted to take the opportunity that he got. He said:

"I want to see the hernia, or the wound stitched again, that's what my mother talked about, let me look at it, and see the seven stitches in my father's chest."

Falah stood stunned by Hamid's fate, he wondered:

"How has Hamid changed from fear to tranquility? Where did his confusion and panic go? Where is the influence of death and its sanctity on him? That's it, and it's simple. How did all this sudden audacity come to him?"

As soon as Falah turned to him, Hamid put his index directly on the wound and gradually wiped it as if he were away and dusted off him, and then explained:

"This is the wound my mother is talking about, this is the

mystery that took my father's life, what did they do to you, Dad? Who's responsible for all this? Did they keep your heart and guts inside, or did they take them out and maybe steal them?"

Then, he muttered to himself: "What got you to Arak, Dad? To its leader, to Al faqih and Al Mualemi?" Falah intervened and answered:

"Yes, yes. Hamid, you really need to know everything."

"But can we open the wound and skin and inspect all the organs and guts from the inside? Let us know what they did to the father's body from the inside, not just from the outside! They are criminals, they may have removed some organs and replaced them or sold them; I still don't know anything about all this."

"Neither do I, but this is exceedingly difficult, Hamid, this needs an experienced doctor, a real doctor" Falah answered him.

Then he looked closely in the eyes of his interlocutor, and he turned around him like a bee and said:

"Hamid, get this idea out of your mind, that's better for you, this is a complicated issue. It's impossible man. Don't drag us into a disaster, don't think about this story at all, this is a crime, another case that takes its owner beyond the sun, understand me carefully, don't involve me with you, don't make me regret my cooperation with you and your mother."

Falah pulled Hamid from his right hand toward the door, reminding him that the body should be buried in just a few days. He advised him to stay behind the door from inside the morgue and not to leave the place until the situation was clear outside, he preceded him outside, he checked the place and the nearby car park, and then returned quickly:

"Thank God, the road is clear, there is no one outside, yes, you can go out now, to come back at the same time tomorrow, without any delay, in the same way and without any change, we must be careful. And, from your head, cancel the idea of opening the wound."

Hamid left the morgue in a hurry and went straight to his car, and on the way, he was still looking for his stray, turning behind, left and right, before leaving. He turned around his car looking from top and down! I still realize that he wants to see me, yes, he wants to see nobody but I. But how come? He is wearing his body. He's still a prisoner in the dress of worldly life, and its cage? To see me, never try to use your five senses, Hamid. You must follow another method that only some of the knowledgeable know. Will he be aware of this alone and understand the story? Will he know the actual meaning of perception, or does he want plenty of time to understand all that truth?

After nearly half an hour on the worldly scale of time, Hamid returned home, entered to his mother as she was waiting for him in the hall of the house on the hottest of embers, she was wearing a loose black dress and hiding her entire body, but her face was no longer tired and exhausted. It became clear and seemed to her the effect of faith in god's judgment and destiny. A firm and reassuring faith that quickly manifests its features on the human face after every crisis, albeit prolonged. As soon as Hamid greeted her, she kissed him as she was waiting for his coming after a bitter long-term separation, and she brought him a remarkable eagerness, with a heart that almost jumped to him before she reached him with her body:

"Ha, have you seen your father's body, god's mercy on him?"

"Yeah, Mother, I saw him bluish in the morgue of the dead. They feared that the dead would resemble him, so they put a card bearing his name and date of death: Pilgrim Kamel Hamid.

Nationality: Tablawish. Age: forty three years. I also saw the wound in his chest, a long but healed hernia, not bleeding, and I saw all seven stitches there… But. Mom, where's Maya? I didn't see her, I didn't hear her, what's wrong?"

As soon as his mother heard the news of her husband's body, the tape of nostalgia and memories passed her, although the selective memory leads to madness. Her powers collapsed again until she went out, she fell to the ground gradually. Hamid took his mother's hand to the nearest chair in the small lounge, ran quickly into the kitchen and brought her a drink of water. She regained her breath and claimed herself, and her fear faded away. She sought refuge in God from the satanic devil, felt relieved, and then asked her son directly:

"What are we going to do now? And how to get the painful truth?"

"Mom, I cannot open the wound myself, and cannot use a doctor so that we become exposed. Thus, we get Falah, the driver in a situation that never comes out of it, it is in short, a legal issue, and our position with Falah is moral and we will not harm him. So, we are really worried about him. But. Mom, I'm sorry, but I asked you and you didn't answer, where's Maya and where's my son Kamel?"

She ignored his question again and returned the conversation to her husband's body lying in the hospital fridge. She said:

"We must get some way through which we know what happened to your father."

"Exactly, Mom, just wait, I want plenty of time, the most intractable things can't be solved but time, you know. I'll get you the news. But where's Maya now? I don't know why you don't answer me directly, and why I started to fear her, there's a strange inner feeling growing toward her, but, mum, at the same time, I don't deny that I love her and miss her so much, and I feel my shortcomings about her and our child."

"There is nothing new, Hamid. Your wife, as usual, is at her family home, she will come back soon, do not rush things, you were saying that time will answer your all questions. As soon as you get out, she leaves right after you… I don't know where she goes out, but I'm good to her."

He asked her to forget about Maya at that time, and to continue their conversation, but in her room after she lays on her bed to rest, so that no one would listen to their conversation, especially his wife, Maya, when she returned and at any time.

The bereaved mother mourning in a moan, speaking in a sad and deep voice. Hamid told her:

"Mother, where has your faith and contentment gone? I went to the morgue as you asked for, and from my tiredness, I closed my eyes, but I never expected to sleep there. I don't know how the whole tale went!"

"What tale? Well. Did you really sleep there?"

"Yes, I slept, Mother, and in a man visited me in a dream, I dreamed of who would show and tell me then whole truth, the truth of the wound on my father's chest, how my father died or was killed. I saw I saw the late king himself, Mom. Believe me, I spoke to him as if I had known him for an exceptionally long time. We became friends, he also wanted to show and tell me all the story, the whole truth, and with a sincere desire that I felt from him, he recommended me in return to pray for him with mercy, and to stop cursing him. Then, in that dream, we went to the Republic of Arak."

Hamid's mother looked at her son in a panic and wondered if what he saw in his sleep was a dream, a vision, or a troubled dream. The mother said:

"The vision is clear, my son, as crystal, and you need no one to explain it. This is what I know, it does not need interpreters nor specialists, and here you explain on your own everything you saw, and all that it says, they are the qualities of the honest vision, Hamid. Yes, your vision. Honest, and you must do what it says, and follow everything that is in it. It may take you to the right way, it will lead you to faith and belief, my son. Faith is the power that will make you an absolute slave to your dream and vision."

She then recalled her memories with her husband, Hamid's father, as she was discussing her son:

"But what does your vision say? Explain to me in more detail, I do not fully understand you, your father has only traveled once to Arak as I know, it's an exceptionally long time ago, after we got married directly, and for a brief time also, I was at the beginning of my pregnancy with you. He did not tell me much about his journey, or about those minute details, but it seems that the loss has affected you a lot, my son. May God bless you, my husband.

Hamid was talking to himself and nobody could hear him but me:

"Yes, I saw my father coming with Mr. Faqih and his Al Al-Alawi companion to Al Mualemi's home, my father was there speaking only in brief words and signs of tacit consent, as if he were robbed of power and will, helpless. In fact, I still remember Al Mualemi's visits to our house, it was not more than a year ago, and I also remember all his television episodes, and I compare them to what I saw there in the dream, there are many secrets and paradoxes, and we must know them. But…"

Then, he went to his mother asking:

"Mom, I want you to explain what my father told you about his visit to Arak, did he know Al Faqih and Al Mualemi there?"

"I don't remember everything, and I don't think he told me everything either, maybe your father was hiding something, or I, myself, forgot. I told you that his travel was a few months after we got married, and your father didn't want to say everything about his friend Al Mualemi. All I know is that they knew each other a long time ago, and years after they met, they met here again in Tablistan. It means they met after an exceptionally long breakup, and I do not know exactly whether they have been in contact during that time. Let us away from what I know and what I do not know, from what I remember and do not remember, and tell me more about your dream, yes, your dream, Hamid."

"There is not much, Mother, I just saw the king asking for prayers and forgiveness, and then he took me to a brief visit to the Republic of Arak.

She sighed as she repeated: "The King asks for forgiveness! This request means an implicit recognition of his mistakes and injustices in his life."

"Mother, do you think that God will fulfill our demands and prayers as we wish? I don't expect that. I don't think so at all, and I know that the soul of the king is aware of that too. So, I think, Mother, that the demands in the dream, as well as the demands and prayers of the souls, carrying other meaning than those that we understand, most of the prayers, mother, are certainly unanswered, and the soul of the King knows that for sure, why does it want to make sure that we stop cursing and damnation?"

I am pleased that Hamid did not tell his mother all the exact events, and those minute details that he had seen. He only gave her the outlines. He must be a mountain of silence, even if the silence is, in fact, a mountain carrying a volcano, but if Hamid's failed to carry those events, there is no point in seeing after that. I also liked that he started thinking in another way, thinking about what the people of the lowest heaven want, and what the people of the second heaven and the upper heavens want, as if he were walking at the beginning of the path of consciousness and perception, which is our distant demand. His mother approached him saying:

"You must return tomorrow to the morgue, Hamid, God will do something that was effective, you will reveal various things that you didn't think of God will bless your footsteps, and follow your way with Falah, that great man, he is your way to reach the truth."

It was only moments before he heard the key sound in the door. His wife, Maya, entered after a long wait, she searched for who maybe in the house, and when she found her husband at his mother's house, she gasped and came forward running to him in longing. Because love is a request based on choice, Hamid forgot his conflicting feelings, satisfied with himself, as if the recognition of tolerance and forgiveness and it confesses within yourself, letting others to feels it. He opened his arms and brought her into the depths of his chest and all of them got stuck in each other. Hamid regained all his soul and energies when he hugged Maya. She threw her cloak and her veil, and her hair tresses fell and covered all her lunar face, she kissed him and climbed his shoulders with her arms. He squeezed her shoulders from her waist spontaneously and she crumbled smoothly. His tears of sadness over the loss of his father mixed with tears of joy and meeting his beloved wife, he tried to enjoy his youth whenever the opportunity arises; sadness always comes late, Maya.

In the effect of this emotional scene, Hamid's mother left them for the hall of the house, Hamid, in turn, pulled himself into his room, holding Maya's hand as if dragging her to him, sitting in front of each. Her dark hair slipped on her head, and she became more feminine and whiter. Hamid asked her about her news and the conditions of her family and asked her to understand the painful and sad situation that has plagued the family since the death of his father, and in turn, Maya lay on her bed, buried her head between the pillows, and practiced her role successfully, not mastered by the non-expert, began the game of seduction where sex is the truest manifestation of love. But his heart was with me until that moment. He's looking for me with his mind and heart. Maya appreciated the situation with her intuition, she felt his deny, so she adjusted before turning the speech, and then said helping him to his misfortune:

"Those who have no good in their parents, there is no good in all the world. These are tough days, may God bless and helped you, I understand everything, Hamid, don't worry."

Hamid got up from his place and asked her permission saying:

"Maya, I must sleep early, I have a lot of outstanding things to finish tomorrow at the Capital Hospital and in the Ministry of Health."

"I get you, my love, I will go out of the room, to the office room or the lounge. Do sleep, baby. But don't forget to dream about me. She winked at him with her right eye, filled her chest balloon with air and then said,

"Don't forget to dream about me, just me."

"I dream of you, you alone! God willing.2

Then, he muttered:

"Currently, I don't want to see anyone but the king himself. And what does Al Mualemi hide in Arak?"

Hamid waited until the end of the evening, which seemed to

him to be one of the longest summers. He was very worried, and you never worry unless you dig up the past or fear the future. He spent his time between what happened to his father, and what Kingel told him.

Finally, after a long wait, the middle of the night came in a heavy, slow state, and Hamid fell into drowsiness. And it is time to meet and contact. I approached him and extended my ether to his forehead and between his eyes, his soul heard the knocks on his forelock, so she responded and approached welcoming happily, as she was waiting for ages; and after she pulled his mind and ordered his body to relax, Hamidel came saying:

"Is it time to show another scene from the eternal play?"

"Yes, come on fast, I do not want the life of lowest heaven, let's go together to the second heaven, and remove the veil from the third scene, the scene of events in the land of Burqan as I promised you earlier, there we will see what has never been considered." I spoke.

(4)

Here, Hamidel feels the kindness and greets me happily as she flies next to me to the second heaven again, flying while its spectrum expands to its greatest extent, and then intensifying its water ether, which is almost dew, once again to express her feelings, and soon happiness is drew on its light shape.

At the same time, some darkness of world life has thrown its sins on its distant sides, showing its sprawling limbs in its blackish colored versus the bright white, which is basically its spiritual spectrum, as if to say that your story is your image, whoever you are, it's yours.

After several meetings, in which I examined My Being, and The Being of Hamidel, the souls consist of darkness and whiteness, as if all creation is based on dualities and contradictions! Her whiteness flies her to heavens for perfection, while her human sins with her black spots weighed on her on the underside, dragging her to the lower heavens with her never-ending follies and wit.

Hamidel relaxed happily, looking at the Durr Tree underneath in the Holy valley of Towa, landed on the holy Mountain of Tur, which is in the form of a light flood, which had already been prepared as a theater to see the chapters and scenes of the eternal life, in which all events are presented, since the beginning of creation until its end. As I have repeatedly said, we, the souls, must come here only after leaving and disposing of our bodies.

We have to remove the veil from what we want to see, it is the story of eternal creation, from the first creation to the limits of the courtyard, that is the eternal tale, Tales of all creation, tales of souls after wearing various human beings bodies, those different and contradictory human bodies and even their suffering in getting rid of them, tales of war that have always raged between good and evil since immemorial time, between the black and white… between the soul and body.

I started to feel Hamidel's desire and her relentless attempts to get rid of her body. This will become more once she climbs to come here to the second heaven, where she finds the deep meanings of a vast life. That freedom which gives her a new life, a life that is more extensive than all the decorations and temptations of the worldly life, a happier life in which creation does not need mind, because the mind alone is unable to bring happiness, even if it is not absolute!

Hamidel settled, by my side, wondering:

"Which eternal scenes to remove their veil now, and through which we complete following the life of Kamel and Mr. Al-Mualemi?"

"The state of Burqan, my dear, as I said."

Then, because of her unbridled desire, we settled on the holy mountain of Tur, which is now in its theatrical form. We will lift the veil from there and will begin another performance of the eternal play.

The Third Eternal Scene

Characters: Al Mualemi, Kamel, Al-Alawi, Al Wajih, Sheikh Al Ataba, Dherar, the Prince.

Location: Desert and Landmarks of Burqan, Awareness Society, Government Headquarters.

The veil of Eternal Theater was removed in response to the common spiritual desire. The desert of Burqan country was clearly visible, smooth, and semi-flat with its sand. Its towering and diverse architectural features bear witness to the existence of its human being and his success in exploiting what the God has given. From afar, a giant flat hill has emerged occupying a large area of the country, and although it is in a yellow desert almost dead, it looks from far away to a greasy, shiny black, as if the whole hill were swimming in a flowing and moving oil pond. The picture is gradually getting closer and clearer, even as the suburbs, streets, and alleys of Burqan have clearly emerged. A café on a busy commercial street has clearly emerged: markets and meetings made by the Burqan man himself and accumulated throughout history. Blesses to its creator and keeper, its markets, many merchants, and customers are always moving around. As Burqan announced with a collective voice: it is the peoples, not the governments, who build their own destinies and create their own history.

Only there, in that traditional market, we saw our demand that we trace, we saw Mr. Mahdi Al-Mualemi sitting next to a cleric from Burqan, and on his right Kamel, Hamid's father, who is still a strong young man, and on his left, sitting their comrade Mr. Al-Alawi. Suddenly, a businessman, called Al Wajih, is coming to where they are. He is a well-known businessman in Burqan. As if they were marching to an inevitable encounter!

Al Wajih gets in wearing a traditional dress known to the Burqan people as *Deshdasha*, a loose cloth dress, the body moves freely as if swimming in its own miniature space, descends his scarf from the right on his shoulder, and twists the other side on the shoulder. On his right arm, Al-Wajih carries his golden embroidered cloak (besht) and he has also carefully folded it. He did not even forget to carry with him a luxurious yellow amber rosary, whose lobes are chopped up whenever manipulated by the fingers of its experienced owner.

The cleric, known locally as the Sheikh Atabah, stands with him wearing his white turban; t. the audience stands with him to receive Al Wajih who shakes them individually, and his expressive smile fills the face, which has been dominated by dry rivers of time; barren grooves and wrinkles were painted on his face, and the Sheikh of Atabah himself introduced all the attendees:

"Mr. Al-Wajih, one of the dignitaries of Burqan, known for his trade, religion and political role in the country, and his will before his projects attest to his faith and the whites of his outstretched hands."

Al Wajih interrupts him as he denounces the two qualities that have been attached to him:

"There is no need to mention the details, and do not over-praise, Sheikh, so you offend the turban, let all the works be pure to God, integrity is the greatest dignity, and it is better not to engage in matters of religion or politics."

He laughed in a deep voice as he was saying: Let's talk about culture instead of politics.

Al-Mualemi interrupted him while raising his right hand to express his intervention: "In fact, I agree with what Al-Wajih went to. We usually talk about politics more than culture because politics is a revolution for the public, while the culture is a revolution for special."

Sheikh Atabah smiles, makes a shame as he hides his laugh beneath his teeth. Then, he continues: "This is Mr. Mehdi Al-Mualemi, who comes from nearby Arak, and he is rich in definition. As he is well known to you, he was forced to flee with his uncle Faqih and some of their comrades to the Cedar Republic; they fled from the oppression and tyranny of Arak leader. As you know, the dirty hand of the leader pursued Al Faqih there, that's why Al-Mualemi and some of his companions came here. We belong to God and to him we shall return."

"Sudden death prevents you from having pre-death troubles." Al Mualemi expressed his opinion briefly.

Then, Sheikh Al Atabah continued to talk:

"Well done, sir, even with the help of traitors, the men of the leader could not follow your footsteps, sir. The hand of God protects you and show you the way. They could not, thank God, assassinate you by the bullets of professional snipers, and that is the mercy of God too. Al-Mualemi has nothing but to take care of the security and hospitality of the State of Burqan."

"We have all heard and surprised by the assassination of Al Faqih in Cedar Republic, it is harmful, it is a great human loss, we ask God to make him in the rank of martyrs and believers, we belong to God and to Him we shall return."

Shaikh Al Atabah completes his mission of identifying the audience:

"These brothers in front of you are Al-Alawi and young

Kamel, both are from the Kingdom of Tablistan, they were in another car accompanying Al Faqih at the time of his assassination, who were also mistaken by sniper bullets, and may not have cared. They were lucky and perhaps waiting for another fate. They were the guests of the Deceased in the Republic of Arak, and they accompanied him to the Republic of Cedars. They are now also dear guests of the State of Burqan and will return in a few days to their homes in the Kingdom of Tablistan, in the hope that God will do something that was of his will."

The two men shook hands with Al Wajih and the rest of the audience, and walked away, smiling, sitting the opposite side, wishing to know what the meeting would bring as soon as possible.

Al Mualemi and Sheikh Al Atabah approached and sat to the right and left of Al Wajih, who asked them what they intended to do during the stay of Al Mualemi and his companions there in Al-Burqan, explaining the role that Mr. Al Mualemi can play in the service of Burqan community, and for the prosperity of humanity.

Al-Wajih said, addressing Al Mualemi:

"I find that before we start working, we must host you in our humble home, and you must accept, and there is no room for rejection; there you will feel that you are among your relatives and friends. We will be really honored by your presence as well. You will be more familiar with the people of Burqan and quickly; I hope you find acceptance and welcome on their chests, which I really expect."

"We don't want to burden you, gentleman. Al Mualemi answered with a flat tone, neither rejection nor acceptance seemed behind it."

"We are honored and hospitable to you, and it is our duty to honor the guest."

Everyone moved directly to the Palace of Al-Wajih, they moved while Al Mualemi was holding the left hand of Kamel as if asking him to stay by his side always and wishing to give him a sense and perhaps linking their destiny to each other.

There, in the Palace of Al-Wajih, they were greeted by the butler, who was lined up with his assistants, at the entrance to the palace. Al Wajih welcomed all his guests and took them to the hall of the palace which is called diwaniya. Al-Mualemi walked down the aisle next to Al-Wajih, while Kamel walked behind him as a shadow, and the rest walked behind them, Then, all of them sat in the diwaniya of al-Wajih, where Al-Wajih usually holds his weekly council, and the public attends, considering their needs, before starting religious or weekly speeches called the USUAL or A'deh.

Al-Mualemi entered the Diwaniyah and found Al Wajih sitting proudly in his seat. He put the images of the Prince of Burqan, his crown prince, and the founding Shaikh, behind him. Pictures carrying glamorous gold bows, while raising Burqan's flag on a parallel gold mast.

Al-Wajih let Al-Mualemi and Kamel sit on his right. When Al Mualemi raised his head to the opposite wall, he found a large picture with a wide silver frame, lined with a dozen men sitting regularly, in old traditional Arab clothes, green turbans and black robes. They were beautifully bright faces. All the characters looked similar and wearing the same, except for one of them, only one of them was an exception. Al Mualemi approached the breathtaking and effective picture, took a long look, and meditated on its characters. Then he asked Al Wajih:

"Who are these people who look in the image of the

shimmering moons for their goodness and beauty? When you think of them, you notice the splendor of their good intentions. He's creative who drew and photographed them."

"Oh sir, you certainly know them very well. They are all, with no doubts, the saintly Imams, the twelve Imams, and no one else."

Al Mualemi looked toward Kamel, he didn't smile nor grieve, he never seemed to be affected. Then, he asked him,

"Are you sure you know them?"

Kamel was confused, he nodded and suddenly shook his head.

Al Mualemi turned to Al Wajih asking him:

"Is there anyone who saw and drew them? Or did he only draw them out of his mind?"

"Not quite, sir, and it is never hidden from you, but draw through those who are honored to see them in vision and dream." Al Mualemi returned to his seat on the right of Al-Wajih, took a glass of water and got a quick sip, thank God, and praised him a lot and said:

"Vision and dream. Whoever saw us had seen us, that's what you want to say, brother, is that part of traditional and famous? We build stories and author novels based on vision. Isn't that just pure madness?"

Everyone was silent, as if the bird had descended on their heads. Al Mualemi asked Al Wajih as if he had been lurking in the eye and wanted to sign it:

"Why do people comment on these pictures knowing that they are never true? Some of them are visions, dreams, or pipe dreams as they claim, and they may all be illusions… Yes, absolutely illusions."

The confusion seemed to be apparent, Al Wajih put his face

between his palms wiping his chin while he was thinking about it, it did not occur to him that there are those who dare to ask this kind of question, and do not give to what is said in the main and traditional sources. People are controlled by inherited issues, until everything with time became sacred... Said:

"In fact, I have never thought about this before, I took the matter in good faith, but it is, as is always rumored, a ritual of God, yes, the rituals of God. As for Quran saying, 'and those who glorify god's rites are those who strengthen the hearts.' We are always celebrating the anniversary of their death as also a sacred rite of the day."

Al Mualemi listened to the justification of his host, and then directed his eyes to Kamel as if he were recommending the need to listen and think before making judgments. Said:

"To allow me, Mr. Al Wajih, to say something that everyone may know!"

"Go ahead, go ahead."

"We, attach the images of Imams in the houses unconsciously and we have never seen them; this is to preserve the imagined images of them within us, and to preserve them from falling to keep them in our imagination as we get closer to forgetting them by word or deed. We are also continuing to inherit beliefs and ideas, and the current and accelerating changes are grappling with them, so most societies are usually hit by clashes and general chaos, and about the rituals of grief imposed by certain religions and sects as the closest way to God, and they have greatly preferred it to joy as well. I see man, in that issue, has conquered his soul before his body. Dear brothers, infection, not mental argument, is responsible for spreading any idea, because most of us tend to say the idea and not what the idea itself says."

"So, there is no harm in hanging and maintaining their pictures, why complicated things, sir, which are amazingly simple? We do not need to discuss the assumptions and axioms."

Al Mualemi pointed the arrows of his eyes directly into Al-Wajih's eyes, stitching them and specializing him in speaking and in a heavy loud voice rather than what he uses in passing conversations, as if he had had a speech in front of a crowd they are looking forward. That tone provoked Hamidel sitting next to me as if she recalled the speech of Al Mualemi, as he was casting his fiery poem in front of the Leader of Arak, the one from which Al Mualemi sought the chase, and then created that historical religious discourse, and after a while, Al Faqih was assassinated, what awaits him in this situation, and he used the same method to influence the recipient?

He breathed deeply, as if he had relaxed in his abundant chair, whose sides were full of his body. He suddenly became ready to listen to the cosmic secrets Al Mualemi:

"You are respected, honored brothers, the simple people are in constant need of ready-made ideas, and sincere faith does not need to be imagined at all. You should, from deep inside, practice the act of truth, not chasing its image nor imagination. These images benefit the public to keep them behind the religious pattern, and behind the religious discourse, but those specials, as you one of them sir, is indispensable, indispensable to all this customary tradition. Because you are special, you must take them out of your sight to keep them in your mind, to follow them by heart not eye. The depiction of legends or the discussion of their biography does not actually lift them up, but eliminates them, and undoubtedly takes them away from holiness."

Al Mualemi's heavy speech left its echo in the chest of his escort, Kamel, and Al Wajih as well, who was captured by the core of the speech.

Al Wajih relaxed astonishingly in his seat, unable to pronounce a word, while the stature of Al Mualemi rose, and he knows that prestige is a prerequisite for persuasion. Ana a man maybe imitated for the sake of his prestige. Then, he answered him simply and briefly:

"You have what you want, sir."

The word (sir) satisfied Al Mualemi's heart and made him happy. He found the effect of his speech in the heart of Al Wajih; and that he broke into his heart with the magic of speech. Since then, he has known that Al Wajih has become soft as a flexible vase that the Al Mualemi forms as he pleases and whenever he wants, but he has shown more fear and humility, where humility is elevated.

He cast his eyes to the ground and missed as an ascetic in silence and calmness. In turn, Al-Wajih was impressed by Al Mualemi, his faith, and his humble appearance, and Kamel was really attracted to his escort until he took possession of it. The speech threw Al Mualemi and his prestige into the chest of the whole, Al Wajih, Kamel and all the audience. Therefore, I always emphasize, as a self-contained soul, that I do not fall under the influence of any human being. I emphasize that speech is a kind of attraction and magic practiced by someone or a literary work on human souls, which are then astonished and respected… Al-Wajih then spoke to Al Mualemi:

"Sir, no one in the region denies the severity of your influence and charm in rhetoric and persuasion, so I find that you will play a major role in the service of the Awareness fund that we established a few years ago, in terms of highlighting its financial capacity and economic impact, and in terms of instilling religious values in the Barqan community, this awareness fund has not played its role yet, and we still do not know why. We are always at your service and the service of religion and people."

Al Mualemi answered him as he was still bent back and looked to the ground in a vulgar humility up to the point of reverence. At that moment, Al-Wajih recalled Al Mualemi's fame, his sure name, religious and militant history. Then he said:

"Mr. Al-Mualemi, we will put the situation clearly in your hands, and you have to determine the best way to work, we have worked in the Awareness Fund for a few years to this day, and we have not been able to reach our desired goals, goals that serve the community; we are still covering the repeated financial deficits, where the participants do not pay their contribution fees, and they only pay the legal fifth and the handouts to the jurists and their representatives, as if our institution does not serve the society in which we are! We have also not been able to obtain a State budget for the Fund, to play its hoped-for social roles."

Al Mualemi asked Al-Wajih a pencil and a white paper, which he began to write down and he said:

"We must identify and write down the goals that we want to achieve progressively, to start with the easiest to reach the higher and more complex goals, and if there is an unintended human error, we must wipe it and cancel it, not correct it. Therefore, to be as assertive as this pencil, write down your steps in all your life, and then wipe out what you have done wrong without the slightest attention or reinstatement."

After Al Mualemi finished his instructions, he asked Al-Wajih to set him the goals and visions hoped for… He saw the audience all, thought a little and then said:

"That our public pay their contributions willingly and without the influence of anyone, that we get the legitimate right of the fifth, that the State co-finance this Awareness Fund, that we serve society to the fullest of our energies and ambitions, and that we please and thank God before and after."

Al-Wajih stopped listing his goals, and Al Mualemi added on him:

"Excuse me Mr. Al Wajih to firstly remind you of the following: do not ask a question if you know its answer, because then you are willing to brag, not to inquire, and I would be happy to add some objectives to those you have mentioned recently: to build an economic, religious entity, which is socially independent, based solely on contributions and assistance. Then, it can recycle its own income, so that it becomes independent income-free. It means we build an independent foundation that serves the people of Burqan and all the countries of the region, they are all brothers in humanity and religion as well. And we are allied also with the possible governments of the region, to strengthen our thorn here, to get the full right of the Imam, and to build force capable of overthrowing the Leader of Arak, the Arab Hitler. We must establish the desired and promised state, so that this state will overthrow Satan, who is in every human being, and in every land that God has given to his human slave."

Al Wajih replied to him:

"We are at your disposal, sir, you must plan and manage, and we must implement it."

Just two days after that historic meeting, al-Wajih set up his weekly council. Poor and needy people used to come first as usual, asking Al Wajih and taking his gifts with pleasure, and then leaving. Then, the religious scholars came, headed by Sheikh Al Atabah. One of them gave a weekly, lamentable speech. Some of them shed tears, cry, chant the name of the absent and rush him, as if the hot bath were a physical and spiritual necessity, taking them to relax. Then, they ate and left quickly.

Later, the luxury class comes, the class of traders, businessmen and honor, they come only before midnight, they eat, drink, and laugh. They backbite about others. They make some verbal deals, agreements, and interests, and then they end their meeting happily before leaving.

Al Mualemi asked Al Wajih: Where is your place in all this great council?

"Head of council, of course, sir, and in this particular chair, I hope that you will be at the leadership of the Council this time, sir, and there is no harm or wonder if I take your place or your seat."

A few days later, it is the deadline and promised day. Needy and poor people came first, they waited in a lane to speak, or to get dinner and gifts assigned to them. But nothing of that happened or was about to happen, they were sitting in the last row of the council, at the door of *Diwaniyah* exactly, and none of them dared to go to the first rows of the council. Al Mualemi. went and sat between them and next to the entrance, he was wearing normal clothes like theirs. So, Al Mualemi sat near those poor and needy people, interacted with them in their places. As soon as they lost hope they decided to leave, but Al Mualemi asked them to stay until the end of the council, where the dinner would be this time at the end of the time.

A few minutes later, Burqan's clerics and their preachers came in, the first of them was Sheikh Al Atabah with his light red beard. They sat on both sides of diwaniyah, which began to be completed packed by attendees. Sheikh Al Atabah observed the heavy attendance on this extraordinary day, after Al-Mualemi's presence and the prestige was well known all over Burqan.

Sheikh Al Atabah asked for permission, by his eyes, to begin the oratory, but al-Wajih pointed to him the side of Al Mualemi sitting near the entrance of diwaniyah, to ask for permission from him. Sheikh Al Atabah went to him, Al Mualemi and Kamel stood to him respectfully, and invited him to sit next to them. The Sheikh was embarrassed looking at Al Wajih who pointed to him with his hand agreeing and gave him a sign of approval and acceptance. Al-Mualemi asked Sheikh Al-Ataba about the content of his sermon tonight and said:

"The role of the public in the time of the Imam's absence."

Al Mualemi remembered the picture with the wide silver frame, the one hanging in diwaniyah and looking at it, and then Sheikh Al Atabah asked:

"What is their role except waiting?"

"Fighting and recommending the soul…" He answered quickly.

As soon as Al-Mualemi shook his hand and gave him the blessing and actual approval, Al Wajih, and the businessmen of Burqan began to flock, as if they were only waiting for a signal from him. Everyone stood up to them, shaking hands and greeting. They started with Al Mualemi himself, who greeted them without, as usual, giving an impression of what was going on inside him, no smiles, no sadness, no happiness, equal feelings, and face features. Diwaniyah was fully occupied by attendees so that some notables were forced to sit in the center of Diwaniyah, after Al-Wajih announced the start of the weekly religious lecture. Sheikh Al Atabah came forward with some verses and adages, as if he were aware of the need for people to have a hot psychological bath that would loosen them and make them obedient, accepting what would be said and to be thrown at them. He then spoke about the foundations and characteristics of self-fighting and its recommendation in the time of the great absence of the Imam.

When Sheikh Al Atabah finished his verses and his lamentation, Al-Wajih directly introduced Al Mualemi to the audience, and asked, in a mumbling form, that Mr. Al Mualemi would ascend to the pulpit; so, the rest of the audience stood supporting. Poor and needy people were really happy once he left them as if he were representing them. In turn, the rest were forced to stand affected by the situation and the influence of the voice of the masses. When Al Mualemi progressed on his way to the pulpit to deliver his first speech, he was followed by Kamel who glorified him. He gazed in all eyes and said:

"Sheikh Al Atabah has spoken thankfully about the significant role of self-fighting and its recommendation, and about its effects on the normal human being, and that, as you are aware, it is a loose words and general topics that are useless, unless they are accompanied by action. There is no self-fighting or self-jihad except by restraining the soul and resisting its desires, and the soul in turn does not approve except via giving, where charity is zakat for money, and you must collect favors through charity, where the collection of wealth comes from attention to trivial things. To achieve all of this, dear brothers, I dedicate myself to the generous attendants with three steps to follow. First, the stage of self-awareness and understanding of religion in its natural form. Then, the stage of personal commitment, and finally, the stage of social action, which also results naturally in political action. Gentlemen, many of us believe that they have moved beyond the first step, which is the stage of self-awareness and understanding of religion, and most of us are now committed to the instructions of religion in its broad outlines at the very least, and they don't know that religion is a public affair in which everyone speaks, and social work remains as private as cultural that only the conscious elite understands. Therefore, we now have only the stage of social action, where the symbiotic value among us is. Therefore, we, gentlemen, invite you to see the Fund of the Islamic Awareness Fund, which you created yourself a few years ago, that symbiotic fund, which is still empty of your active participation and contributions, and many of those present here are still providing helping hands to their needy brothers, who seen as if they were begging. We must, dear brothers, take serious active fraternity and work that has been going on since this hour. Your contributions have been below expectations over all those years that have passed, and I declare it honestly, and from this rostrum: The fund-raisers of the Awareness Fund will print the names of the largest funders on its wings and halls in honor and in memory of their illuminating works."

While he was followed and encouraged by Kamel's eyes, Al Mualemi, with the blessing of Al Wajih and nobles, mobilized his abilities in the rhetoric and urged to give, and called for the donation for the benefit of the Awareness Fund, and soon the prides of the people increased. Many presents were donated unexpectedly. The impact extended to the outside of the council. Then, the documentary speech of Al Mualemi spread all over Burqan. It was received by public before private. It was only a bit more than a month when the awareness Fund was about to get full. Thus, planning became an essential requirement to deal with the money that pours into it. At that time, Al-Mualemi met with Al-Wajih and some dignitaries and deeply discussed the situation, after which they decided on various matters:

"There is no specific limit for the doing of good things, including material contributions, because it is a good thing that prevails and reflects the spirit of giving to all the people of Burqan. Therefore, the funds must not be accumulated, but disposed of in their proper legitimate channels for their beneficiaries, whether they are in the State of Burqan or the Kingdom of Tablistan, and even the Republic of Arak, Cedar Republic, and others."

"How are we going to spend it in Tablistan, for example? There are governmental legal issues and religious implications that must be kept in mind and coordinated."

"We will transform it to strengthen the role played by the Husseini Awareness Fund in Tablistan, and through these two men, Mr. Al-Alawi, and the brother-friend Kamel, will be a kind of cooperation and fraternity. From here and there, we will achieve many foreseeable goals, fraternity, and community cooperation, to the ultimate goal of overthrowing the leader of the Arak Republic and spreading justice and well-being in the region."

After that, Al-Wajih explains that if it is about good things everywhere as ordered by various religions, the Amir of Burqan and his government will also be the first participants and contributors. The man's intuition was swift, honest, and real.

At that moment, Al-Wajih suggested that he should address the Emir of Burqan if he has a popular acceptance and resonance in the public opinion, success is usually depending on relations more than achievements, and if he wishes to get rid of the Leader of Arak and the dangers he represents for the security of his country. Said:

"I find it useful to send a letter directly to the Prince's (Amir) Office, explaining our objectives, Sir, and I am sure that we will find the Prince at the forefront of charitable deeds."

As soon as the suggestion reached the Amir of Burqan through official channels, he delegated some of the closest people to study the subject of the Islamic Awareness Fund and its stated objectives. After that, he quickly appointed donations and official assistance. The Amir, himself, ordered to meet the necessary needs of mosques and *matems*.

With the reputation of Al Mualemi across the border, especially regarding his knowledge, pride, and prestige, he becomes famous, and his status rises, until another detailed day comes that will never be forgotten.

One of the religious scholars came to negotiate with Al Mualemi who accepted and suggested that the meeting should be in the Council of Al Wajih, and that the meeting should take place during the weekly (usual) council.

After the religious lecture held once again by Sheikh Al Atabah, the Persian representative came forward and asked the audience to speak:

"Good evening gentlemen, I have come officially as a delegate and representative of a number of jurists in Persia, carrying a letter through which Mr. Al-Mualemi informed the wish of our imitator and three others, that Islamic desire to appoint Mr. Mahdi Al-Mualemi as the agent of the four jurists, provided that he has the absolute authority and right to dispose of the funds of the Imam's right, and in the funds of the charity, the fifth and all donations and all the assistance."

The people of Al-Burqan received this news as if it were a blessed religious recommendation for the safety of their religious orientation and its rightness, setting the legitimate responsibilities in their natural context. Thus, the race to pay handouts, donations and assistance became a goal for all.

In a parallel scene, which occurs above the Eternal Theater,and occurs the evening after the following day. As soon as Al Mualemi goes down from the awareness tribune, Al Wajih, and the rest behind him shake his hand, Then, Al Wajih invited everyone to have dinner together. From that point, Al Mualemi's reputation rises the sky of Burqan step by step.

There is no reason that shows how he influenced people but by the religious admiration he had instilled in the hearts of his followers. He was always concerned about the expected danger coming from Republic of Arak, and from the traitorous agents of its leader planted in State of Burqan.

In another minor scene, Al-Mualemi received a local delegate on an official mission, he asked Al-Wajih to be the only attendee of the meeting; Without any introductions, the official envoy expressed the official desire of the State of Burqan and its Amir.

"The high command conveys to you its sincere greetings, and let you know its blessing of the good steps that you follow for the benefit of the people of Burqan, as it emphasizes the provision and harnessing its potential to destabilize the unjust regime there in the Republic of Arak. That enemy is an official and popular demand, even we know it's simply confused dreams, but we can achieve it with perseverance and hard work, even that difficulties prevent us from working together, but we want to harness and use all the potential to achieve that goal, albeit far-reaching, to get rid of that enemy is a formal and popular demand."

Al Mualemi nodded his head as proof of approval and said:

"This is proof of your success; it is a manifestation of failure not to have enemies!"

He then looked at Al Wajih, who in turn questioned:

"Does Mr. Al-Mualemi not wish to meet the Prince of Burqan himself?"

Al Mualemi locked his smile and forced her to stay inside,

because he knew exactly what was behind the question. He feared that the prince would fall under the influence of Al Mualemi's appeal and charm in the speech.

After minutes of silence that were enough to accommodate the whole situation, the envoy corrected the whole situation, organized his papers, and arranged them on the table, as the bewildered arranges his own thoughts and concerns. He took a deep breath and gave that space required to talk, he said:

"The Government of Burqan, and some representatives of the Amiri Council, authorized by Amir himself, invite you to attend an important meeting, which will be held next week at the Palace of Government. will be held in the government building itself."

The envoy waited again for the definitive answer, waited for Al Mualemi's decision to carry it, and return it to his officials. Al Mualemi used the weapon of silence and waiting. So, Al Wajih was confused between the approval or rejection, and confused the audience. Consent means embarking on a mysterious, long, and irreversible path, and rejection means that Al Mualemi leaves the Burqan land without completing the dream project. As usual, Al Mualemi asked for a piece of paper and a pen, asked permission to sit at the side table in the office, and then, he commented on the white paper. When he finished, he placed the paper in a white envelope bearing the Burqan logo, closed it with some saliva, handed it over to the royal envoy, and asked him to deliver it, without being seen, to those who carried it on this arduous mission.

The delegate returned with recommendations, and he returned with Al Mualemi's comments to his leadership and he did not know what the envelope was hiding. There, he told the officials all the details and everything Al Mualemi had done. The officials then understood that there was a secret, or something planned by Al Mualemi and planned to be implemented, and that would only be in the interest of the desired goal. When the meeting was over, the delegate returned with a second envelope to Al Mualemi, who also asked him to wait.

In the afternoon of that day, Al-Mualemi and Al-Wajih came in the company of the official envoy to the government headquarters, they came on time, and as planned and confirmed in that envelope, the guards lined up his welcoming him in a formal military march, which surprised and shocked Al Mualemi. They let him in but asked Al Wajih to wait outside the meeting room to preserve the confidentiality of the mission. Al Wajih agreed to hide his rage and curiosity. The head of the protocol took Al Mualemi to the meeting room, where he was welcomed by three advisors, they all were waiting for the arrival of the Amir himself.

Hamidel and I moved, we saw the next events to the right of the Eternal Theater From here, the Prince, who called locally Amir, came in slow steps, smiling to all, instilling confidence in those he meets; the presents stood to him respectfully. The Prince presided over the meeting himself, and began by welcoming Mr. Al-Mualemi warmly, then gave the speech and his management to the state's foreign security official, who was at the top of his elegance in his local dress, and then spoke in turn:

"His Highness the Prince, as you know, looks forward to getting rid of the Leader of Arak, who calls himself the believer leader, and we know very well the difficulty and impossibility of that mission, but we also know about your strained relationship with this tyrant, and we are fully aware of what happened to you personally and some of your relatives, and we also know what happened to the members of the Husseini seminary there from successive assassinations, as well as the injustices of our neighbor in Arak. We are aware of the danger that lies ahead in our country. Therefore, we extend our hands to cooperate with you toward that goal, albeit far-reaching and difficult to achieve. We want to know exactly what steps you are drawing, and we are offering you as much help as possible."

Al Mualemi started straightening the arrows of his eyes, and stuck them in the three advisers before dropping them in the prince's own eye, and when he felt the bigness of that step and its weight and even danger, he removed his eyes to the general faces of the neck before saying:

"The believer leader! This is a despicable method in which the Arak leader wants his people to kneel psychologically, and I see that for the ruler to control his own people, he must be (God fearing) a God, and if he cannot; he must lead his people to obey that God, which is what the leader literally does! Now, our first goal is to create resistance from within Arak, and since we know the regime's brutality and its power there, we have begun to form organized cells from Cedar Republic. And as you know, the tyrant regime has pursued us there, and we have been tracked even in the alleys of the capital, and so my uncle, Al faqih, was assassinated. May Mercy of God be upon him, and I have since been forced to leave that country, and it was only the bosom of the lovers and faithful in the state of Burqan a safe place to turn to. Thus, here I am among you now, I put my palm in your hands, to work together to get rid of the tyrant era, from the leader of Arak. Agreements and discussions on how to make resistance in all its aspects took place in Arak's neighboring countries. And from here, riskiness has begun, and you must be careful.

Al-Mualemi explained:

"We must plant the seeds of resistance in the neighboring countries, we should start with the smaller and nearer countries, including Burqan itself, Coast state and Tablistan. If we can form the required mass base, then our common goal will not be impossible and far from being achieved. We must be aware that the grains of sand make a mountain, and that the same mountain may be dropped by one ant if it has the required time, we must believe in what we are doing, and work for it day and night."

One of the advisers, aware of the approval of the Amir, said implicitly:

"We are very willing to finance your political and economic approach, we will do what you want voluntarily."

Al-Mualemi stressed his role and his group and the readiness of the sleeper cells, those belonging to them in Cedar Republic, and other cells in the Kingdom of Tablistan and the Coast, and that they need a lot of political and military support, and a lot of hard work and preparation waiting for the right hour, to inflict damage on the leader of Arak.

It was only a few weeks later that Al-Alawi and Kamel left Burqan for the Kingdom of Tablistan, but these weeks were enough to awaken the eyes. The news grew through the agents and spies to reach the Leader of Arak himself. He knew about the presence of Al Mualemi and his steady activity in the State of Burqan, they transmitted his audio and video recordings, and analyzed what beyond. But the Leader's regime was not sure, until that time, of the close relationship between the Prince himself and Mr. Al-Mualemi, so he used his spread eyes and arms in Burqan. Therefore, he sent his delegates on a threatening official visit to the state. The oral message came in this way:

"Mr. Leader and President of Arak, informs you of his greetings, and alerts you to a danger lurking in Arak before the Burqan. The danger is represented by a dangerous criminal named Mr. Mehdi Al-Mualemi living in Burqan, he is engaged in hostile activities to the Republic of Arak. To preserve the historical relations between the two countries, bilateral relations, and the ties between us, we strongly ask you to hand it over to Mr. Mahdi Al-Mualemi. In the words of the briefest and unequivocally explained: The State of Burqan must hand over Al Mualemi to Arak, if you refrain from doing so, there is no way for us but to invade and fight, so that we can uproot our enemy from your land and with our hands."

The advisers soon informed their Amir of Arak's Leader brief message; he called on them to act and to prevent the evils and madness of the Arak's Leader, who had threatened to invade the country on every occasion, and to keep relations with Al Mualemi under top confidential. One of the advisers in Burqan suggested that they tell Arak's leader about the Al Mualemi's secret departure from their lands, before another letter from the Leader arrives, mentioning that Burqan had kept him under house arrest before he was expelled from the country. So that they would make sure that they informed all issues concerning Al-Mualemi.

The difficulty was who would tell Al-Mualemi of Amir's sudden decision, and the senior state officials met with him earlier and gave him assurances and charters that would make him work comfortably in security. The foreign security officer was chosen to declare the new matter with Al-Mualemi and to show him the Leader's message.

This time, in his entire uniform, the man went to the headquarters of the Awareness Society, and there the receptionists were stunned by this guest, who wasn't expected. He told them that he wanted to meet Mr. Al-Mualemi. Some of them were confused and their teeth were stammering, while others stuttered, all wishing that their master and boss would not be harmed. The official understood what the employees had become:

"Dear brothers, there is nothing to fear for Al Mualemi. I came carrying an official letter. Could you please tell him?"

A staff member set off for the internal office, where Al-Mualemi was accompanied by some of his close consultants, proposing to him some influential figures in Kingdom of Tablistan and neighboring countries to write them a detailed report on the political and religious situation there. The staff member interrupted them by saying:

"Sir, there is a security man asking to meet you, and he seems to have a big position and a bigger job."

"Why are you so scared and confused? Don't worry, brother, God is the best safer and he is the most merciful of all merciful."

He replied:

"The official seems to have come on a dangerous mission. Let him come in."

Al-Mualemi received his guest in his office, welcomed him and said:

"We met a few days ago at the government meeting, didn't we? You're the same government delegate, and I think you, through your uniform, you're the head of general intelligence."

"Yes, sir, I am Dherar, head of general intelligence. I am sorry, I have come to inform you of an official decision of the State."

Al Mualemi read what roams in the chest of his guest and was able with his intelligence to gather the evidence and approach the order that brought him. He sat him on his right and then left his office and progressed sitting in front of him, they exchanged greetings again, and then urged him to speak without hesitation, but the matter remained in the chest of the guest and could not reveal it. Al Mualemi gave him a drink of water and asked him to wait in his place until he felt comfortable. Moments later, the guest said:

"Sir, I want to talk directly, but for your majesty and your charm is the ability to mute the speech in my chest and the chest of everyone who comes to you. Sir. I'm sorry to tell you that you must leave the State of Burqan."

"He's the leader of Arak." Mr. Al-Mualemi responded directly.

"Sir, which is the case, as your intuition tells you. And I'm afraid for you."

Al Mualemi's mouth widened as if he wanted to smile and said:

"You are a believer, brother, do not be afraid, a religious is more afraid of making mistakes, and who is afraid of something, falls into it. Beware of fear and get away from it. Just find me a safe way out."

"Sir, if the Prince himself had ordered me, I would have had one of our officers smuggle you, but if master Al Mualemi, himself, has told me, I can only drive you, myself, to Kingdom of Tablistan. I do not want you to travel alone, the difficulties are an emergency, I will give you a passport valid for one trip, and I will be on the same trip there, and I promise to carry out your orders without discussion, because the leader of Arak is like a fire that throws flames in all sides."

Al Mualemi replied: Forget the hell of Arak and think about what can happen suddenly, looking at the fire shows you its flames and meditating on it protects you from it. You must meditate on the whole situation to avoid the Leader of Arak.

The head of intelligence's eyes widened as Al Mualemi was silent, and the silence of what could be spoken is more eloquent.

On the voices of the leader's threats, Al Mualemi leaves the state of Burqan with his escort Dherar… The veil of the Eternal Theater is cast, and the third scene of the eternal play ends, waiting for what will happen before Pilgrim Kamel's death.

(5)

I was wondering of what Hamidel became, and I can see how much enjoyment is felt from the aura surrounding it, it is the soul that is always motivated and bouncing, which extends its jellies to what looks like spilled milk whenever it goes to the high heavens, to take the furthest possible range for it, and soon after, the first part joins the last one, it increases in density and becomes smaller in similar movement to the celestial comets, and so on.

After a long while of meditation as she was watching the third eternal scene, which tells the story of Al Mualemi, his friend Kamel and the rest in the state of Burqan, suddenly happened something which was not in mind. The calamity came which scares those alive, and the general human beings on the ground escape away from it.

A dark and great smoke object appeared from above the great theater, stretched horizontally, almost hanging from both sides of the Eternal Theater despite its greatness. It's all contained or it's under its wings, devour it from below to the maximum. Then, that smoky self-became a semi-liquid, condensed state, as this unparalleled creature approached us, which soon changed its shape in turn into a dark red spherical shape, it. Looked rough-cut, sharp looking frightens the looker in the first heaven and above.

When Hamidel saw it, she shuddered, her limbs shook, and the threads and lines of the light halo that formed her were conflicting; so, she approached the limit of sticking, trembling, and terrified of this huge scene:

"What is this giant object that forms as it's coming to our way? It's like he pacifies me, and he sees only me. He has no eyes as the human beings of the world or the creatures of the earth, and I cannot talk to him as I communicate with you now by telepathy, but I feel him as someone who sees me for who I am, and does not look at anyone else, as if he is asking for me!"

I said, calming down, and creating intimacy between them and other creatures:

"He is Azrael, the Angel of Death, in his volatile form when he sets off on his official missions from the high heavens to lowers; to carry out his duties without any boredom. He doesn't care about the people of the world at all never cares about their howling, he never talks to bodies, but telepathies with all souls which they do what he wants voluntarily. Once a soul is certain that her body is unable to carry her, Azrael sets off her side, helping and freeing her from the shackles of that mud-body, and rejoices if she realizes her decent work. He holds the earth and its human beings from bottom to bottom, even if the number of creatures is high and swells, as if he were playing with them and practicing his favorite hobby, and only feels the value of his existence and the purpose of his creation as he performs his great mission, a solemn message that frees lives from the constraints of human and non-human bodies."

Hamidel was astonished after that introduction, so frightened that she almost reduced the intensity of the panic, seeing the role of the Angel of Death, Azrael, embodied in front of her, and from a purely heavenly perspective, she was not familiar with before, and then wondered:

"If this Azrael serves the interests of the souls on earth in the lower heaven, what does he do here in the second heaven, why does he mean me now? What does this terrifying Angel want, and he knows that his first job is only there, on the earth's heaven and water where the world is?"

I smiled as I was about to make fun of her; because. Hamidel is very much like her human being, the body is a reflection of his soul between his two sides, and when she found my smile, she wondered how I knew many things of the unseen, she should know that I was completely separated from my body, while she was still attached to her mud body; the more you get rid of your clay, the closer you get to God, the more you see with insight. Then I said:

"Just wait, I will now ask him before you fell, and your dewy material turns into small atoms scattered in the sky like light."

"Don't you fear the King of Death as I fear him, Soul of the King? she asks me."

"How can I fear Azrael who has completed all his tasks with me in the worldly life? He has, thankfully, delighted me with his distinguished services, he has moved me from the narrowness of the body to the spaciousness of the universe that you see now, he comforted me when he separated me from my body, and what is left with me now has no other role? There is really no life, no death, no sadness, no joy. The departure of one of them only makes you feel the impact of the other. Human beings in the world are usually afraid of the unseen and ignorant, it happens gradually, and therefore they do not feel it. Death is only a transit channel for a wider and more spacious life as you see it now, it is the life of no-time and no-here in the seven heavens. I am now reassured and happy whenever I see him. He has done me great favor after I have tasted eternal life, and as soon as I see him, I expect another birth of a soul that is liberated from its muddy body. The human being sees Azrael as a calamity and a tragedy in his first life, while their souls see him in the second life as a good omen and a promise of happiness, which takes him and through him to the seven heavens. I will now leave you a little bit to meet him and ask about what he wants and intends to do."

I returned to Hamidel a few minutes later, and her situation worsened and turned on, and her radiant aura became darkened in a gradual concession that was almost extinguished with him. I did not know for sure that the fear of the unknown is a curse that infects the soul as well as human beings.

She trembled and shuddered from her place, asking astonishingly:

"What does Azrael want from me?"

He says categorically and unequivocally:

"The remaining soul in your body there, in the world, is almost getting away with it, if you are late for your body to return, the mind will be disrupted, and Azrael will be demanding and justified that your worldly age will be destroyed. He will get out, from your body, what is left of your soul in a glance, he is going to squeeze your soul totally. I do recommend you let him rid you of that muddy body, and to destroy your worldly age, it is an irreplaceable opportunity, it's a unique opportunity. Therefore, you can understand the meaning of eternity while being here, in the high heavens. Do remember that human beings are eternal, have not emerged by birth and will not end with death."

Hamidel rose from her place, gathered all her limbs, collected all her borders, reduced to the shortest extent, intensified to its small size, and reduced, turned similarly to ether, and decided to return quickly to the lower heaven. She threw her mass to the earth where her body lying there disputing in small death. She fell there like a comet. She went in between its eyebrows and got him quickly; she went back into her body. She said while in her body, talking and willing our dialogue not to be disturbed:

"You minded me, and you urged me to break away from this limited life, but now that I remember what I have come for; I do not want to leave the world without completing my goal, man, as you say, does not die unless he loses the desire to live, and I am still willing to do it, I followed the journey of Pilgrim Kamel with Mr. Al-Mualemi from the Republic of Arak, and then State of Burqan, and now that he is on his way home in the Kingdom of Tablistan; I came close to knowing the full truth, and the reasons for his death, the threads approached each other and I became able to solve the enigma, and I began to know the story that my mother wants to know as well."

Hamidel returns to her heavy dress in the world, so that she can recover herself and work her mind, bringing life to the body lying on the bed. I was watching her wearing it slowly after she had settled into the forelock of the body and penetrated the forehead and the point between the eyebrows, which point from which I had already come out, and the one I used to visit and talk with her through. I landed near her body, in the space of her body, where howling began to float, shouting was rising, and the obsessions were getting fiercer in the air. I stood meditating on the conditions and horrors of human beings, all misfortunes of human beings are illusions they make themselves, the product of what they had done. Here you find the illusion of separation and its pains.

Hamid's mother sat at her head, scattering her hair, almost breaking her pocket for fear of losing him, and in pain of recurrence loss recently got her husband, Pilgrim Kamel. As for Maya, Hamid's wife and the repository of his pain, it is another human tale, a rebellious tale, I would like to recount its details to let Hamidel sees its chapters as it came, and as it will come, because her story carries with it a world full of wonders that characterize human beings, a case of gathering the contradictory at the same time, honesty and lies, loyalty and betrayal, good and evil.

Maya sat next to Hamid's legs, controlling herself and sobbing, slapping her cheeks with compassion, afraid to be widowed and having only one child, she was wondering: "Isn't the desire for family stability one of the most important reasons for a woman's marriage?" Crying on oneself and self-consolation on an incoming unknown you don't know, these people delirious me and I, from height, watching their actions and scrutinizing their feelings.

Hamidel settled down and released her body, which was absent from human consciousness. His heart rate accelerated upwards, and his breath was harmonious. As soon as his mother poured some water on his face, and read some verses, he grew up and brought life to his whole body as the wasteland lived.

Sleepiness and drowsiness moved away from Hamid, and after he closed his eyes, he opened them slowly, then expanded as much as possible. The audience imagined that Hamid was surprised by his command, and they did not know that himself had taken the greatest extent during his sleep after its last ascent. Maya meditated as she witnessed his color changes and transforms, so she screamed at him suddenly:

"Hamid, my love, God bless you, don't leave me a widow alone with our child, I still have a child, and I am still young, don't go, don't leave alone if you love me."

His mother patted him on his shoulder and forehead with

tenderness, addressing him faithfully:

"May God protect you, my son, we are beside you, may God bless you the whole life, O, generous Lord."

Hamid closed his eyes, and then began to open them gradually, he differed for the center of the whole universe. The center of the whole universe differed for him, so the center of his ethnocidal differed regarding to his place and new position. His body is on the ground among his loved ones, and the center of his soul is still stuck in second heaven, and between them, his mind is still exhausted, suspending his disposition and whereabouts. He said, putting his hand on his forehead, as if he were keeping away from him a severe headache:

"Where am I now?"

"You are among your family and loved ones, dear son." His mother answered him.

"You are in my heart, my love." Maya explained as if she was in a race to show emotion.

"I mean I'm not in Burqan, and I'm not on my way to Tablistan?" He asked.

"Oh my God, he is feverish, the boy began to hallucinate." His mother screamed again.

They both helped him to sit down, and he leveled between them, one smelt him and the other kisses and hugs him, while he was saying in a quiet voice as if he were talking to me alone, nobody listens but me:

"So, these are the secrets of the fever and delirium that we hear about. I'm not in Burqan and I'm not on my way to Tablistan."

"Where is my father, where is Pilgrim Kamel?" He said loudly.

The mother screamed regretting her luck:

"Losing his father hurts him very much. He is in the mercy of God, my son, your father has gone to his Lord, as you know, he left to his Creator a few days ago."

Maya put her palms on his forehead saying: "My love, we are all passing away, but God remains with majesty and honor."

Hamid felt a heavy headache and almost closed his eyes; he asked for a cold drink of water. He sipped and saturated, until he began to distinguish between the two places, and realized the difference between the places of the lower and second heaven, and soon he began to look for me in the atmosphere like a dog gasping. I was watching him, but it is impossible for him to see me; bodies use their eyes only to look and can't insight unless they abandon all five senses and replace them with others, no one will feel Hamid's desire but me.

The mother was confused again, seeing her baby in the room, as if looking for a lost bird from here or there. Then she said:

"My son has been touched by madness, Oh my God."

She hit her cheek, so Maya collapsed in front of her, screaming:

"Hamid, Hamid. Don't leave me alone, please. I don't want to be alone with your mother!"

As a natural consequence when a person feels helpless and unable to explain something, he throws that heavy burden on the unseen, and on those who oversee everything.

The mother ignored what Maya had just said and read some Qur'anic verses around Hamid's head who was absent-minded, while I was sure he was still distraught, looking for me all over, but he's gradually regaining his equilibrium. He understands he is on the ground and between his family. The mother attributed the safety of her son and his speedy recovery to the influence of the Qur'anic verses that were read on his ears, while I, myself, know that Hamid regained the center of his equilibrium and balance. Moments ago, he thought that he was in the second heaven, and in a noticeably brief time, he found himself in the lower heaven, and between his family. Unless of his hardness, his family would have continued to know him as crazy or possessed in fact, it would be only around the center of his equilibrium, which is the Eternal Theater that swims there over Jabal Al-Tur Holy Mountain, next to the Valley of Tuwa and the Durr Tree in the second heaven.

Hamid woke up the next morning, recovered and returned to his world with different feelings, and no doubt the feelings of man are born of his thoughts. His mother and wife Maya were sleeping on the floor around his bed. As soon as he got up, his mother did so at the same moment. Maya remained in a deep sleep. He asked his mother: Weren't you asleep, Mom?

"How do I sleep, and Hamid is not stable in his normal state?"

His mother was right, the mother may not heed the sound of thunder while she is asleep, but she will not lose sight of the voice of her newborn or the movement of her unborn child, it seems clear that human beings sleep only for things that do not concern them. Hamid turned to the place and said:

"Where's Maya?"

"To the right of your bed. She's tired and asleep."

"Excuse me, Mom, please forgive me, I have worried you so much."

"It's all right, son. But tell me what happened to you?"

I always kept an eye on Hamid's hardness and ability to

retain the details and peculiarities of the apparition, the details of that journey in which his soul accompanied me to the second heaven, and how I wished to finish my heavenly high message to show him the greatest thing that was hidden from him, to preach and follow the path of good ness in his worldly life. If Hamid tells what he saw in the apparition, I will be cut off from him forever, the souls of second heaven are very selective about cooperating with the souls of the first heaven. She knows her choice and can't connect any but privates, t. to achieve a higher message, they select those who have the power and wisdom to absorb beyond the apparition, where wisdom then requires apparition. Hamid regained his strength, standing holding his mother's hand by the wrist, asking her to remain silent and not to wake Maya.

They went out on tiptoes to the hall of the house whispering; they got their breakfast which was some brown bread and milk that Um Hamid hastily prepared. When she returned to sit next to him, she urged him to talk with her looks and gestures; but Hamid's desire came first to interrogate his mother instinctively, he realizes that people tend to instincts when calamities end:

"Mother, you must remember very well, when my father returned from Burqan to Tablistan?"

"Why is this question, what makes this question appropriate? I don't find it meaningful, my son, but if you wish, I remember that we talked about it already, a few months after our marriage, your father traveled with one of his friends to the Republic of Arak, I was pregnant with you, and from there he left the Cedar Republic with his friend, and they did not stay long. Then, they left the State of Burqan, he did not delay, he returned home here in the Kingdom of Tablistan, all of that was shortly after our marriage. When your father returned, Hamid was a little boy. While you are now head of a family, and you have a child you call Kamel after your father. You must imagine all those years that have passed, your father did not give me a lot of details about his movements, and he did not speak other than the general lines, but I remember that they sent him to prison on suspicion of belonging to…"

"Put him in jail suspiciously, and for what pertinence? Say what you know, Mom."

"The events that prevailed at the time required the state to classify people as loyalists of power, or outsiders based on their religious doctrine, their regions and even their different ideology, at that time, your father wrote slogans classified as political."

"Slogans? My father used to write slogans"! Hamid wondered.

"He was writing on the walls: The leader of Arak falls. Falling… These slogans take the doer directly to prison, on charges of spreading hatred and terrorism."

I intervened myself then, and I referred to Hamidel to stop the chat between Hamid and his mother, which is useless. If Hamid looks ahead and away from his steps, he will find that doctrine is a disease that puts a black cloud on the heart that prevents vision and keeps serenity and purity away from his heart.

If Hamid listens to the diseases of the doctrine and its repercussions, he will put a cloud on his forelock, and a membrane above his heart. Therefore, it will be difficult for me to reach him again. Hamidel instructed.

Hamid's mind to change the direction of his whole talk. He said in a normally simplified way:

"Mom, how would you describe your relationship with Maya? What do you see? Will my happiness extend with her for a long time?"

The mother was surprised by Hamid's question and the way he changed the whole conversation, moving from doctrine and thought to love and marital relationship, perhaps because love is originally the opposite of doctrine!

But she preferred, for her part, to change her discussion with him until he settled and calm down:

"You and Maya are not the same in everything, Hamid, and not different in everything. I think that this situation between you is enough for you to have a happy life. Similarity in everything is a problem, and so are differences. But you only know the good of things as shown."

"Isn't love between us enough to live a happy life?"

"Hamid, your father used to say: Love is not happiness itself, but it is only one way of happiness, love blooms hearts but hearts cannot bloom love. I think that love may mature but it may also die after marriage, because we do not know the volatility of hearts or what goes on in chests!"

"Seems you want me only to marry her, you don't prefer to have another baby, you might not want us to involve others."

"It is your choice, consider what you want, and what you want is the will of heaven."

Hamid went to the window and looked at the distant horizon telling himself: Heaven, heaven, as if my mother was pointing up there where the second heaven or what above, as if asking to remove the veil from another chapter of the eternal play, as if she would like to read the horoscope from here, and I wanted, with her, to see the truth from there, where the truth in the second heaven is absolute, telling us about reality, albeit bitter, the reality that passed us or is still hidden.

Hamid felt a hand and chest hugging him from behind, hot breasts injected the rest of his back with a widespread heat, a warm kiss from behind his neck gave him powerful energy that never subsides. He turned behind inhaling the smell of a breast… he said:

"All this love, Maya, take me to you, beloved."

Maya hid her face between her hair and Hamid's chest, and then she missed one of her dreams, so Hamid chose not to wake her up from him. He hugged her but looking around, so he could see me even by accident, and when he couldn't, he gave up and closed his eyes, too, I whispered him directly:

"Once a woman hides her face between her hair and your chest, as if she were hiding from you to you."

He woke up in a hurry, rising, searching for me, he wanted me. Therefore, he forgot about Maya and suddenly opened his arms; he noticed nothing but Maya falling to the ground from his arms and chest. The woman was angry at his disgraceful act; she screamed at him; he realized his unintended mistake. So, he holds her again, he asked for her consent, so she was spoiled and shewed her will… He evaluated the emptiness of the place and did not find his mother; she had already left the lounge since Maya woke up and came to her husband a few minutes ago. The mother read what would be, she left between grumbling and contentment.

Hamid became fond of Maya; he flooded her more than what she wanted and needed. As soon as he finished what she needed and satisfied her passion, he kissed her and went to bathe in a hurry. Then, he came with his wife and his face shone, filled with joy and clear confidence. While Maya's face became rosy with a smart breath, as if satisfied breaths could be seen. Hamid asked

Maya to stay alone with his mother. He walked into his mother room, kissed her head whispering in her ear after Maya went out:

"Mother, I want to go to the morgue this evening to complete the rest of the procedures."

"Let it be tomorrow morning, Hamid."

"You know, Mom, I can't stay by my father's body until ten p.m., there is Falah waiting for me with his recommendations, and he wants us to take the body and bury it as soon as possible. I don't know exactly what's going to happen, but I'll tell you everything."

Maya wore her clothes elegantly. He came toward her hugging and smelling. He realizes that the pinnacle of love is to inhale the smell of your beloved from her clothes. After he finished his worshipping, he asked her to go out with him. She held his hand and they went out together. He drove her to her father's house where she wished to spend most of her time, and outside the door of their house, he printed another kiss on her forehead and he said:

"The kiss of loved ones does not go off, goodbye Maya."

"Goodbye."

(6)

Hamid drove his car fast to the public parking lot of the Capital hospital, it was 9:15 p.m. and it was still too early to meet Falah, enter the morgue and examine his father's body if possible. Otherwise, he must wait for the UNSEEN that has no logic nor explanation. Hamid turned off the engine of the car and moved the chair back, he laid down for a few minutes to relax, his father's file still worried him, the calamity of his death, the story of his meeting with Mr. Al-Mualemi from Arak to Tablistan, but... Maya's kisses take up more space emerge in and come to his memory against his will, and the last bed battle tape passes on his imagination, the events of a cumbersome battle that needs her knight to rest and relax to regain even some of his powers; he closed his eyes like who dreams and desires a goal that can be invested and reached.

I was waiting for that decisive moment; I was able to reach his forehead at the speed of lightning, and his eyelids were weighed directly until his eyes were closed by force and without feeling, and soon, his consciousness and awareness of what was around him was interrupted and disconnected, as I crept into his forelock between his eyebrows, that point of separation that any man can realize with his finger if he starts it with a large circular motion, decreasing to the center[2]. I found his thoughts still hanging on Maya, and he is still astonished by her last battles!

I feared that Maya would go on and suddenly produce a

---

[2] As you are doing right now.

confused dream or chimera! Then, Hamid will be very confused about the whole situation, and he will not be able to distinguish between his reality, the apparition and chimera.

I rushed it, and took his soul from his forelock, I pulled her to accompany me to the usual Eternal Theater in the second heaven, Hamidel did not hesitate and did not show any resistance even for a moment in accepting the expected invitation, she expressed her pleasure without words, because she is aware that the pictures of words are independent of their meanings, and then she came in a full mass but some of herself in the body drowned in his sleep behind the seat of the white car.

There, on the mountain of Al-Tur, opposite the sacred Durr Tree that separates the mountain from Wadi Towa, we will remove the veil from the Eternal Theater in the same way you know. We will see in the fourth eternal scene what happened to Mr. Al-Mualemi, and what happened to Al-Alawi and Kamel, Hamid's father, in the Kingdom of Tablistan.

We will also recall that Al-Alawi and Kamel moved quickly to Tablistan, while al-Mualemi remained in Burqan for several years. It was enough to have a wide mass base, and to support the Awareness Fund to be independent. Hamidel will find also that Kamel has given birth to his eldest child and named him Hamid. The body she wanted to pick herself and to wear since his mother's belly had a created embryo.

You will also know that Al-Mualemi will meet his closest friend in Tablistan after a long worldly separation, but they will meet feeling that they have only been separated for an hour! We will see the most influential and decisive chapters in the life of Pilgrim Kamel.

On our way to the Eternal Theater , she said:

"I want first and strongly, to see the scene of my life until its conclusion with Maya, did you not say last time that the future had happened, and its chapters were complete just like the past, but that human beings have no access to it, and they can only see its present time? You said, and you confirm that all the time has happened, but the Creator has singled out human beings by examining and living the moment he lives only there in the lower heaven. Now we are in the second heaven, free souls, and freedom from the body gives you a spiritual energy that almost limps you to the third heaven and beyond. We can now overcome the power of time; so, we step back and jump on it another step forward how we want. It is a purely heavenly gift, surpassed by only spirits! Let's take advantage of it now and see what happened and everything that will happen! You just must be normal while other lives push you to transcend nature."

I am now sure that Hamid's soul has truly absorbed me, she knew the meanings of the temporal dimension of eternal life, that which was there and has not yet reached us. It is similar, as I mentioned what people called the beginning of creation through what they called the Big Bang, that event occurred long ago but did not reach them for an exceptionally long time, everything has happened, but unfortunately, existence is not complete in the general human beings except with the eye and the rest of the five senses. Without these five senses, human beings are helpless to deal with time. Once Hamidel competed her questions, she said:

"How will Maya be with Hamid after she has other children, and how will she build an independent family? There is love and passion for her. There are many warnings and future messages always reach him as signals from his mother and… From you, the Soul of the King."

"We're going to postpone the scene of the Kingdom of

Tablistan after the Maya scene, based on your will." I spoke.

All the events of the world are happening here as we are sure. We only must lift that veil at times or let it back. To see everything, we will remove the veil in this scene from a future that has happened, and Hamid has not seen it in the worldly heaven yet, he thinks it is in a future that has not yet occurred! In fact, we have no difference between watching scenes about Hamid's father or those of Maya or even others; All are the same, here we are sitting fast to enjoy the new show.

At this magical eternal moment, I wanted Hamid's Soul to know other creatures as well as the King of Death in advance; perhaps Hamid finds something similar in his world. I wanted someone to share with us, to be honest and impartial, to stay away from all feelings and emotions and to be stripped of them, to provide advice without affecting the circumstances of the events, no emotions, no hatred, no backbiting, or envy. He never speaks to us but is pure and logical.

Hamid's soul was shocked and said: Are there any human beings here or souls that have not been completely separated from their bodies?

I replied wondering:

"Are human beings normally neutral? But in any case, there are no human beings except in the lower heaven, since the first creation of Adam, the father of humankind. The upper heavens are full of souls, angels and… and with other creatures, but they are all inhuman, Adam is not their father. Therefore, don't you notice that today's human being strives to discover life like his own on different planets?"

I didn't finish my sentence until Hamid's Soul interrupted me with a high whistle:

"The demons! Do you want to share with us a demon or devil? Is that really what you want?"

How can I change those souls during their short visits to

second heaven, before they return to their mud and nasty nature there? I said:

"Never a demon. O soul, we are now in the second heaven, and separated souls may cross those heavens above them, climbing via ascent, and transcending according to their degrees from the third heaven to the seventh, continued praising and glorifying. However, here we can address absolute values, which are in their first form when they materialize, this characteristic is difficult to exist and even impossible in the lower heaven."

"Absolute values? Do those values take specific forms? And how can they materialize?"

I smiled at Hamidel's interventions, which reflect her inner turmoil, neither is a soul in the lower heaven nor is it all in the second, hanging between them and subject to their influence both at the same time. I said:

"Absolute values are the amount of worldly moral virtues, and when they turn to the second heaven, they are embodied and become different forms, what concerns us in this eternal place is to invite the Pure Mind to be your reference and criterion when things are mixed up, when you argue with me as usual, and when it is difficult for you to distinguish between right and wrong because of the effects of the emotional organ of the living creature."

She replied:

"I don't need it much here, everything is clear and obvious, my need for it grows when I wear my clay body there on the ground, because the mind does not see the world as it is a reality, while the soul looks at its reality. I need it there when I become a witness to the constant conflicts between the mind and the body, which is dominated by desires and driven by how you want, and he knows nothing about which ways he chooses! It's exceedingly difficult, but the most impossible things are the most influential things. For all that, I now realize that human beings return their decisions to the unseen and the coincidence to get rid of the burden of the future, they do what is known as (the lottery) perhaps the chance is truer than their intuition and be better than a thousand dates!"

She has long been relaxed and happy in a state of conflict with herself before she continues: the needs of the body usually overcome the human mind as I have grasped the reality of creation now, I am sure from here that emotion is always stronger than the logical of mind. I explained to her, that there is no need for the soul to address the pure mind if it is completely separated from her body, it is enough for him that he does not sleep but only has a lower level of awareness. But the soul can appeal to the pure mind while being there in the world, man can summon the pure mind but if he conquers and stops all the accumulations of his memory, and all his emotions, but I think the impossibility and difficulty but rarely, there is no action that happened to man except by his choice, enough of his thinking, opinions and perceptions. Therefore, I will summon Pure Mind to accompany you, or you may find someone like him whenever you decide to return to the first heaven of the world.

I will now call him to follow the events of your story with Maya, and he will not give you a judgment or an answer unless you wish, remember that love always happens without reason, while hate only happens for obvious reasons. Pure Mind came in the form of a giant human brain, which is uncovered by a human skull which limits his horizons, he became luminous and transparent, its colors change according to the rightness or errors of any act! And if you gaze at it now, you can see the other side of the universe.

Pure Mind came and leveled at our request, came from the opposite side from which the King of Death came in one of the previous scenes. He took his seat on the Holy Mountain of Turr, which is specially designed to accommodate the events of the Eternal Theater and its guests. Together, we began to follow Maya's scene from behind the great eternal veil.

The Fourth Eternal Scene

Characters: Hamid, Maya, Pure Mind, Kingel, Hamidel.
Places: One of the educational institutions in the Kingdom of Tablistan.
The eternal veil is raised to the top, and Hamid's name appears as the first of the characters written on the Legend Board. Hamidel jumps and screams in unusual astonishment:
"I see me from here." Then she said sadly: "But it's not me!"
"He is your human being but not you, your worldly image only, you are a pure soul, but Hamid, the man, is a soul, a body of clay, and a mind that links between them. If the body submits him to his will, takes him to his world, drags him to the inferiority, and if the soul subjects him to her will, she took him to the top and the highest limit."
"Yes, I am aware of that now."
"Not enough, my dear, you must reach the stage of perception, it is the height of awareness, to recognize your awareness. well done, O soul."
I sat her down to watch Hamid meeting Maya for the first time in a private educational institution. Hamid enters the small educational institution, where their eyes meet directly. They became familiar without a date. Their eyes speak without words whenever Hamid enters or exits that institution, He sometimes delays, he hates to abide by time and clock, as if he knew that there is no time at all. He is disturbed by side talk when it is about others and not self; he finds it a waste of time and energy. He

became in favor of getting to work only on time.

Maya was watching him when he spoke to her or others, and she realized that half of his side conversations were directed at her.

She knows him very well by time, wishing him in secret, while he wishes her in his bed like most men of the East, and she used to talk with herself:

"It is you, Hamid, it is the promise that I have been waiting for, the other half, seven typical years that separate our ages, there is nobody but you, Hamid, it is you the destiny that I wait." Hamidel looked at me, and I nodded to her asking, but in terms of Pure Mind who agreed to accompany us as we watched and eagerly follow the fourth eternal scene, there is more neutrality.

She went to his side; he telepathized without the need for words as the people of the world do:

"Didn't you hear what Maya said?"

"Is it you, only you, Hamid, it means Hamid the human, it is the destiny to be expected?"

The communication of the Pure Mind through telepathy also came a flowing from its light mass, and without the knowing the responsible organ for issuing those feelings and thoughts, as if the language of communication is undoubtedly based with flashes of telepathy, like the movement of meteors and meteorites in their paths, and like asteroids in their orbits. It is indeed a heavenly creature that works according to equal flashes and is different from that of the worldly mind that works according to blue and red flashes. When a man gets angry, his red flashes blaze and vice versa. Pure Mind telepathized with Hamidel, and he never said a word to her:

"You should know that sexual relationship is the pinnacle of autism with the other, because it gives the human joy, strength, energy, and confidence… Don't count on it because it doesn't last long. Pure Mind telepathized with Hamidel so she understood what meant. She really knew what Hamid was thinking when he met Maya, and she knew what Maya herself wanted."

But she went on my part, asking:

"It's like he realizes everything, everything! How did the Pure Mind know what I was just hiding and thinking about, and I hadn't spoken yet?"

I did not answer her, but telepathy came back again from the Pure Mind himself:

"I know the truth of human thoughts and their nature, and I know what Hamid knows and everything that is on his mind, if you ask for my help, I will put the whole truth in your hands here, but there on earth, man does not want the truth itself, keeping it rational, as he sees it only and from the angle of his vision."

The words of the Pure Mind provoked Hamidel, and she argued with him:

"Aren't you at the top of your happiness and you realize the truth from falsehood, and good from evil? "

He answered her while I was listening to their dialogue:

"I stand at the top of the consciousness stage. So, I am aware of the reality of everything, but I am unable to reach absolute serenity, there is no root for total happiness; happiness does not reside behind sanity, happiness is felt by man when he makes mistakes and corrects himself; there is no happiness if we are forced to do absolute right."

Hamidel took her face away from Pure Mind, and asked us to go back to follow Maya's scene… Her manager at the educational institution soon asked her to call Hamid asking about what makes the alleged daily delay, and how he did not like side talk with co-workers. Maya took the opportunity to achieve her goals and to jump over the barrier of the first threshold, to capture Hamid Kamel and achieve the desired dream.

She said:

"Hello, Mr. Hamid, the director asked about you."

"It doesn't matter, let him ask as he wants, but I am incredibly happy to hear your voice, thank you and to those who asked you to call, but, without the word Mister, please. Is that possible?"

"Possible, Mister. but I called as the manager asked first."

"Mister, again, and then?"

"So, did I."

"I am on the way, the time is not yet, Miss Maya, and as you know, I do not come in time, even minutes, I like to start on time, and leave as soon as it is over, clear, Miss Maya?"

"No need to say Miss Maya, please, but someone wants to talk with you, there are some people who like to sit with you, chat you… But I apologize if I bothered you indeed."

"Okay, okay, no problem, I always wait for your call… Remember that. Goodbye."

From that moment on, and that call which Heaven and Maya wanted, contacts between them continued beyond official time. Hamid started by inviting her to dinner, then a café, and then… Thus, the stones of the border between them gradually fell. Then, they discussed the similarities and stressed the common altogether.

After that, the conversations began to continue the telephone and tended toward personal and private matters a lot. Thus, they met according to a written fate they had never expected, but it was a will and a fact that had already occurred in eternal life, and they didn't feel anything but in the present of the world!

The more calls between them are made, the more Maya's

heart is attached to her colleague. So, she fell into the illusion of the so-called love; she wished him to her heart more and more, maybe she feels her completed feminine, and fulfills the wish of motherhood through him, he is undoubtedly a man who many would like to be with him.

The series of events continued until Maya was able to achieve her goals and ambitions, she easily dropped Hamid Kamel in her trawl, and engulfed him from all sides. The differences between them were not a barrier that was difficult to jump on, and their tongue says: Love melts mountains of problems, not just minor differences. By the time, Maya became aware that Hamid was undoubtedly the man of her dreams. Then, they began to develop a common plan for a beautiful velvet life, decorated with money and children.

Hamidel looks at the brief scene of the eternal play. As the show continued, she wondered:

"Are human relationships formed and twisted as simple as this? All families are created like this, without any complexity or effort, but they also disintegrate quickly as well."

"Why don't you also ask Pure Mind this time?2 I suggested,

Hamidel settled with him, and he understood her intention and said:

"More than that O soul, states and human civilizations on earth have the simple same style; Because human never build up their relationships at all, they only see and endorse them. In fact, there is no action that has happened to you except by your choice and within your absolute consent, enough your thinking, opinions, and perceptions about that event. You should also know that if one of them succeeds, others will fight him directly, and if the same person fails, they will be happy to do so. But man's thinking about what he likes to be, and his hard work will achieve the desired goal, even of haters and disbelievers. Once this is achieved, he must cling to it; he must change his actions and behaviors to match his thoughts, and to capture his dream… This is what Maya wanted specifically, and disintegration only occurs if the love of control comes, because it is the basis of the problems between the lover and his mirror."

I have always been pleased with the conversation I used with Pure Mind, and if it weren't for the purpose for which I took Hamidel, I would never have changed the direction of talking to him. I said with a telepathy with him too: but as human civilizations in their origins, in their rise and fall, let's see what happens to Hamid and Maya in a few years later, let's follow the eternal scene, which we are accelerating and has in fact happened for many years.

We jump over some scenes, fold some of them like a record fold. Then, we stand up, and Maya is now thirty-eight years old, and she finds herself fast as a mother who has a teenage ornery boy. Maya then struggles to achieve herself so that her youth will not be kidnapped, and to keep her family with the least number of sacrifices or losses that make it difficult for her to reach her goals and achieve her dreams. At the same time, she must remain a mother and cancel many of her wishes and give to her son. She must also abide by what is required of her sacred bond of married life… Or to break the shackles by force and be free from it forever, and to seek achieving herself, and being well known. In the end, she concludes getting rid of that (non) sacred ligament, and from Hamid himself, is an urgent necessity for me to survive, and to be satisfied and convinced of the least damage.

I look at Hamidel's side and find her at the height of frustration and pessimism, begging her to talk so she says:

"Do human beings build their relationships so easily and end them more easily?"

Pure Mind interrupting the dialogue: yes, so he must not put a full stop at the end of his friendships or whole relationships.

Then, I commented on the words of the Pure Mind: "That is your life of the world, Soul, have you had enough now? Or do we have to continue the rest of the eternal scene, or do we go to Al Mualemi and see how his friendships and relationships have become in the Kingdom of Tablistan and throughout the region?"

Hamidel's limbs became darker as an expression of her deep frustration. She answered:

"Let's leave for the Kingdom of Tablistan, but on the promise of returning to the scene of Maya and beyond!"

The veil is closed and the fourth scene of the eternal play ends and comes what after it. Let's go on.

The Fifth Eternal Scene

Personalities: Al Mualemi, Dherar, Pilgrim Kamel, Al-Alawi, Minister of Finance, Minister of Information.

Location: Kingdom of Tablistan's Airport.

We raise the veil as usual, to begin another chapter in the life of Mr. Al-Mualemi, through which there appear to be many repercussions on the lives of those close to him, the two friends will meet after a long worldly period, the two friends did not see each other but remained in full psychological contact. In this scene, we are interested in following Al Mualemi in Tablistan, and searching together with Hamidel about his relationship with Hamid's father, who has shown the features of the obsolescence of time and became old. He is called Pilgrim Kamel. We have seen the pilgrim's relationship with Al Mualemi since its inception in Arak and Cedar Republic, and how Kamel left Al-Burqan by choice while Al Mualemi forced to. We will also see how the relation crystallized and increased between them, as they are now in the Kingdom of Tablistan. They meet in the official departments and then under the family of Pilgrim Kamel.

From there, the new scene begins, and Al-Mualemi's plane lands at Tablistan International Airport. After turning behind him to find a man who follows him with his eyes and keeps a steady distance between them that does not arouse anyone's curiosity, Dherar waits while Al Mualemi crosses with the travelers, and finds himself exception in terms of his religious dress, while Dherar wears his local dress as in Burqan. Al Mualemi is standing worried in front of the passport stamp officer with his eyes straying between Dherar and the employee. The passport, which is now officially in his possession, bears the logo of the State of Burqan, but is valid for a single trip only, will the Government of Tablistan allow him to stay, even if he will not be able to return to Burqan? Al-Mualemi became concerned about the issue of the passport that he is now carrying and is afraid that there will be a generalization on his image by the Arak regime and its leader, after this generalization became distributed to all the countries of the region, including Tablistan itself, remembering Dherar as he is behind him to solve any emergency crisis. So, he settled down now.

He asks his God to be kind to his condition as he was so kind to his prophet Moses and to get him out of his fear. The staff soon asked him:

"Where are you coming from?"

"Burqan."

"A Transit or permanent residence?"

"A short visit to friends, and the stay may be prolonged and if good hospitality."

The employee focused on the computer in front of him and Al Mualemi's face. Then, the employee asked him to wait, he called the shift official employee who arrived quickly. The employee showed him passport and then the data from the computer. The official raised his head while Al Mualemi kept looking at Dherar. The official recommended him:

"Don't forget to follow the official procedures while you are in the Kingdom of Tablistan, abide by the law, have fun, sir, goodbye."

Al Mualemi felt relieved, went in a straight line, and looked only in front of him for the luggage claim area, realizing that

Dherar is behind him and may God guide his footsteps. He waited to pick up his bag from the luggage claim, avoiding looking at civilian and military security soldiers deployed in the arrivals area. He was watching them from the edges of his eyes only and without his eyeballs meeting one of them, as if fleeing from them to them. He took his bag and waited for a few moments waiting for the opportunity to leave, and then he entered himself among five other arrivals, inserted himself among them, walking with them in a hurry and usual speed with the arrivals, until he reached the reception hall of the foreign travelers, looked behind and in front of him but did not find Dherar, Whispered to himself:

"The man has completed the task to the fullest as promised.

Then his soul felt relieved, he thanked God very much and praised him for his good management, looking for someone waiting his arrival, or for someone who might still be lurking."

"Thank God, nobody."

Suddenly, a person is patting on his shoulder from behind. Al Mualemi freezes in his place and even electrifies, and takes a deep breath, he turned around his side; he found Mister Al-Alawi, invaded by white hairs, remembering his first encounter in the Husseini seminary in Arak and later in Burqan, he hugged him with a reassuring joy.

As soon as he opened his eyes while hugging Al-Alawi, he saw pilgrim Kamel and his beard was also filled with whiteness. Al Mualemi knew that the will would be extinguished with aging, but he was overwhelmed by happiness. He moved to Kamel hugging and welcoming him, asking him about the last time they met, about his health and his family, to which Kamel replied:

"Thank God, everything is fine, and we last met one minute ago."

They laughed and the Al-Alawi stood watching them,

recalling the past, seeing the amount of happiness painted on the face of Al Mualemi and his companion Pilgrim Kamel, and then he welcomed the great guest of Tablistan:

"Welcome to the Kingdom of Tablistan, my dear."

"Thank you, my dear, that's your kindness and generosity."

Al-Alawi turned to the third of them to introduce him to Al Mualemi.

"This is my older brother, a minister of state, who will appeal to you very much."

Al Mualemi returned to his steadiness so that no emotional expressions appear on his face when he meets any stranger, they shook hands without a smile or frown, so that person cannot know or read anything about him.

Then, the minister said in an official way as he was tightening the hand of Al Mualemi: It is an honor to meet you, Mister. Thank God for your safety.

He replied:

"It is our pleasure indeed."

The minister replied, while he was avoiding looking directly into Al Mualemi's eyes, trying to protect her, and not wanting to know the reasons for his feelings. The prestige didn't you see this? discuss its causes, loses its value.

"It's like I already know you or I have met you somewhere, but I'm sure that I have already seen you, I feel that I have seen all this situation! But I don't remember exactly where, and he started asking himself: Where, where did you see this gentleman, man?"

Hamidel got close to me, asking:

"Have they ever met?"

But I said, "You have to ask Pure Mind." Who answered almost automatically:

"A minute of patience lifts you from ignorance to knowledge."

She felt so pleased and invited her to return to the Eternal Theater now. We continue: Al-Alawi: Look at our fourth now, to our friend who never waits, he is a very practical man, he carried Al Mualemi's bag ahead of us and urged us to walk behind him to the parking lot.

Al Mualemi turned to Pilgrim Kamel, and he was happy, and a rare giggle came out of him to express the sincerity of his feelings toward that man of confidence:

"My dear, Kamel, I miss you very much, you trusted man."

"For which Kamel do you miss specifically? Kamel of Arak, Kamel of Cedar Republic, Kamel of Burqan or Kamel of Tablistan?" The pilgrim asked him as he rushed in his footsteps.

"All of them represent you, my dear Kamel, you are a group of integrated attributes, met in a complete human being called Kamel, the love of God almighty gave me his friendship."

Al Alawi takes them all to his GMC vehicle, that dark red four-wheel drive, and then Alawi's brother, the minister talks:

Minister:

- Will my brother, Al Alawi, allow me to invite Mr. MahdiAl-Mualemi to lunch at our house, the invitation will of course be open to all, but in honor of our generous guest?

Al Mualemi:

"Oh my God, I have no desire to be a heavy guest on you from the first day, if you can only excuse me, let me breathe and rest."

The Minister smiling:

"We will be happy to have you, all of you loved ones," wishing Mr. Al-Mualemi a pleasant and lasting stay in his second country, in the Kingdom of Tablistan.

Al Mualemi:

"Hospitality is deeply rooted in the hearts of Tablistan."

In opposite to the Eternal Theater, where Hamidel and I took our seats next to Pure Mind, Hamidel renews her troubles, asking me if we can follow the movement of Al Mualemi and his hosts, and not to stop. I told her:

"There is no need for us to chase them, I remind you always and ever: worldly life is a play, the one that you witness is always happening and verification. In short words, it is all the time, all the things and events on the earth happening here at the same time, all depend on the time of lifting of the veil in front of you; after all that, the time of the show becomes the past, the present and the future, all combined at once, with no time and no place. Is it difficult for you to comprehend that? Maybe it's because you haven't completely separated from your body, so it's going to be hard for all human beings, even if they watch or read these eternal scenes, it's going to be hard for them to absorb, understand and work with!"

I went back to her illustrating: this is life in the second heaven, while that worldly life on Earth, in which human beings only can see the time of their present, their current time. They can only recall their past, as memory, without seeing it, and then forget most of it. They do not remember it unless they write it as history. They expect an uncertain future, which is also a reality, and they are ignorantly looking for an elixir of life! I hope you don't miss it again. We do not see here, in the eternal theatre, those many performances that take place simultaneously on the right of the stage near the Durr tree, which represents the future on the scale of the human mind, the events on the left of the stage, which we do not see either, while it is what humans call the past. I repeat to you, Hamidel: the time to lift the veil gives us the labels of worldly temporal events. Therefore, it would be natural and obvious to realize that events, sounds, light and everything on earth do not go to waste, even if man cannot see it in a holistic way, but the souls here are able to gather it, and to see those observations and scenes, do you now want to know what Pure Mind says about that?

Hamidel turned to him, she telepathized with him, listened to her, and suddenly said:

"Forty years is considered as one hundred years or three hundred, they're all less than an hour. It is the law of true consciousness for human beings, the law of consciousness that exists in the Seven Heavens, the law of infinity: each number for the end is zero, and all that is below zero remains zero as well."

I have now listened to the voice of Pure Mind, and we have no time but to ask to see what we want, to recover, preach or be alert. Let's go back to behind the veil now. Therefore, Hamidel is getting ready, she sits on the holy chair under the Durr tree, and the eternal scene continues as it really had happened in worldly life.

The minister appears slowly in his council, slightly thinner and slightly taller than his younger brother Mr. Al Alawi. The minister wears a white dress and brown cloak (Besht), folded part of it under his left arm. The minister moves toward his brother, Al Alawi, and behind them Al Mualemi and Pilgrim Kamel. He welcomes them in exaggerated joy, and starts the spontaneous dialogue among the audience:

The Minister:
"You are welcome to your family and brothers, since I have heard that you are here in the Kingdom of Tablistan, and I know that it is a great blessing that God has given us. In fact, I would like to

look for a suitable home in the heart of the capital, where you can carry out your missionary awareness activities and direct them to all people, without racial, sectarian, or even religious discrimination, which I would like to present to the government through the endowments department, so that you can officially take your stay in Tablistan aside and play your awareness role under the light. Knowing the officials here, I find that you will have a good and fantastic opportunity, the Government of Tablistan wants to remove those delicate barriers between all communities and religions. Hey, what do you think?"

Al Mualemi, in half-smile that does not reflect his happiness, says:

"Dear, all religions are similar tissues, if you sew them well, you will make one robe that suits and warms all humanity."

The minister remained silent and relaxed in his seat, and the three attendees looked at him, as his eyes widened, and his mouth opened. After digesting what he had heard well, the minister said:

"I will introduce you soon, even as soon as possible to the Minister of Information, he is an educated and enlightened man, you will like him very much. What do you think?"

Al Alawi is over lapping: so, Al Mualemi will not play his required awareness role! It's going to be a very formal role.

"That means you're planning, Minister, and this is your system."

He said it with a laugh and addressed his speech to his brother; all the audience laughed, but Al Mualemi kept silently, and as if looking away, meditating said:

"Gentlemen, the role of man in this life is to spread public awareness; to work against deviant currents wherever they are. Among them are the growing left-wing currents and others, which are spreading throughout the Kingdom of Tablistan."

Al Alawi confirmed his words:

"Yes, in the face of the state of the widespread left-wing tide in the Kingdom, you brought it briefly, God bless you."

The Minister:

"Very nice, you must be familiar with the growing left-wing currents, the left tide that is hitting the country these days. Oh Mister, does it matter if you temporarily moved away from the pulpit of the mosque or the condolence council and release your thought through the pulpit of the homeland?"

"The Platform of the Homeland?" Al Mualemi wondering.

Al Alawi raised his fist and moderate in his session:

"You are deeply welcome by everyone, Mister Al Mualemi, I welcome and reward you for the pulpit of religion, Kamel embraces you to his chest as a brother, friend, and silencer of secrets, and you are now in the hospitality of my brother the Minister, who is clearly caring for you, I may be jealous of that, and he takes you to an official position that may be high."

"By the way. What Ministry are you in?" Al Mualemi asks the Minister,

At his session, the Minister rested his hands over the arch of his full belly and said: Finance. I'm the Minister of Finance... I will introduce you to the Minister of Information, whom we spoke about moments ago, and from there, we will see what your awareness role can be opposite to the left tide, the tide that has come to destroy the pillars and customs of our society.

Al Alawi got up and clapped his palms, as if he were ending their dialogue and agreements: dinner is ready, come on everybody, you are all welcome.

As for me, I turned to my right, where Hamidel was sitting, and behind her Pure Mind is settled in complete silence and a deep serenity that almost I forgot him. I told her:

"Would you like to see the rest of the subsequent events?"

"Of course, we must invest all the time."

The eternal veil is still raised, and another chapter appeared in the office of the Minister of Information which is heavily guarded. He is a forty year old man full of body and face, shaved with hair on all sides, his body filling all his abundant seat, he barely budging in it, and behind him a library full of various books, periodicals and various volumes of sources and references. The Minister of Information stands for his visitors with a great welcome from behind his desk.

Minister of Information:

"Welcome to all of you, we are honored by your presence, gentlemen."

The Minister:

"This is our guest, Mr. Mahdi Al Mualemi of the Republic of Arak, the man I spoke to you about yesterday on the telephone, and whom you have heard a lot about, and this is his friend and escort Pilgrim Kamel."

Hamidel shivered in her place and said:

"Hamid's father knew Ministers too! Oh my God, where are we going to get with you, Pilgrim? Will his meetings reach the king himself? Did his body meet yours? It's as if things are now becoming more apparent, as if the criminal is hiding behind them."

Hamidel looked on my side, and she pointed out:

"But who killed him, could he be...? But she hasn't accused my human being yet!"

The Minister of Information's speech brought back Hamidel to her silence and to the influential eternal scene, explaining and illustrating:

"In fact, the Government and the kingdom's senior men

believe that there is a widespread left-wing tide in the Kingdom, which is on an upward trend, which is more dangerous than the extremism of the usual religious tide. The Government sees the possibility of benefiting from your experiences and capabilities to face this abhorrent tide, we want to strike it in the killing, and you represent religion, which is the best spear to stab. The government will help you on your good activities to reduce this strange tide from our kingdom, it is a danger like war, trying to bring down religion before the state, and we must line up in his face and confront him together, we must fight this arrogant and deviant current."

Al Mualemi conveys his eyes from the whole to the Minister:
"Let the Minister allow me to express my opinion freely, I am a cleric in the first place, but the shame is of us, as Government and people. It is shameful and illogical to go back to the clerics, to know their opinion on political issues and their endless affair. I think that is to abolish ourselves, implicitly in recognition of our inability to face every political crisis."

The Minister's face reddened and he stood up:
"It is not really a political crisis but a religious and social crisis, I think the state made a mistake when it sent its young people to study at the universities of left-wing countries, those that deny all religions, yes, it was a big strategic mistake, and the state should make up for that mistake."

Al Mualemi twisting his white-striped beard strands:
"That was a big mistake. But you're repeating the same mistake. Man makes the same mistakes when he acts according to the thoughts of others, you refer security issues to the clerics!"

The Minister sat in his chair again, knocking his pen at the desk: I understand that Al Mualemi refuses to cooperate with the

Kingdom of Tablistan in this regard!

I turned to Hamidel, seduced by the talk, drooled its saliva, and drowned with the characters in minute details. But she said:

"Al Mualemi now throws the ball in the government's net and asks them, and on their tongues, to beg him for help."

I smiled and asked her to return to the eternal scene:

Al Mualemi:

"Serving religion is a duty for every Muslim, wherever and whenever he is, and the love and service of the homeland from the foundations of the religion. I can speak in this regard only from a religious point of view, I hope not to be involved in the policy of the Kingdom."

Minister of Information:

"Yes, yes, the Ministry of Information will provide you with a television space where your religious awareness program is shown weekly, so that your speeches are to the public and not class as planned, in the condolence council or mosque, and since you separate religion from politics and you are a cleric; It is not harmful if you talk about the people of the left from a purely religious point of view, people are afraid of the forces attributed to religion, and religious passion tends to describe the rejectionists as enemies. Master, if you want state help to achieve your goals, we will give you a hand, we are adopting your reform project."

The Minister of Finance breathed deeply:

"Finally, our master agreed. As I promised you, Minister, Al Mualemi will be our effective face to confront these cultural diseases and to maintain security and rules in the Kingdom."

Hamidel interrupts me as he strongly satisfied:

"From here, I find the first way for Hamid's father to penetrate the official channels of the kingdom unconsciously, hosted by official meetings, and his specialty as an accompanying companion of Mr. Al Mualemi."

"We will get to the truth if we run after it."

There, in the lower heaven, and in his white Camry car, Hamid's body is still relaxed behind his seat, it's time and the alarm has been ringing for a long time without hearing or turning to him. How can he have heard it and his soul is still present in second heaven?

I told Hamidel who is next to me:

"Hamid is too late to visit his father's body in the morgue because you're now here."

"I'll be right back right now even if I don't want to. She said as she gathered her limbs and collected her lights."

At the end of the scene of the first meeting between Al Mualemi and the officials of the Kingdom of Tablistan, the fifth eternal scene ends, and the veil is down above the holy Mountain of Turr, ending with a scene and starting other tales that have no endings!

Chapter 2
The Theatre of Perception

You think you're a minor luminary and in you, the biggest world is folded.

Imam Ali

(7)

Hamid woke up behind the steering wheel of his car, hitting it with the head repeatedly, almost breaking his head to get rid of the pain which hits after each visit and storming he made with me to the second heaven. That is the habit of his fragile body and its nature with suffering when I ask him to accompany me to my world, where we are in the infinite space of the universe, in which his soul reaches the level of consciousness, when we are above the holy mountain of the Turr and between the End and Durr trees, which both greatness shade the Valley of Tuwa. I have never felt sorry for him because of his pain because I am confident that with time he will get used to that kind of buzz, and I am very much aware that repeated buzz transfers you to the tinnitus of bees. His apparition and the journey of his soul, Hamidel, to the high heavens continue to affect him and exhaust his body, which has not yet adapted to him. He began to recall what happened to him in a voice closer to howling and screaming, as if he were arguing himself and discussing it, but wrestling it in a battle that will not end and go away, as if he is now feeling more than ever, that he carries among himself more than one living being or creature, every latent being tries to pull him to his ego. Hamid has a mind and a soul, past and future, a dream, and a reality, but he doesn't know that the pinnacle of realism is to dream that you dream, which is generally known to human beings as perception.

His soul became conscious whenever it departed to the

second heaven, flying, enjoying and controlling his mind, but controlling it without the need for the body to implement, jumping on it, marginalizing and smashing him, but when he is on earth, where Hamidel returns to the lower heaven, she intends to do good as she has motivated, while his body remains driven by desires and is captive to it, and between the soul and the body, Hamid's mind is bewildered without purpose or decision and lost in the empty space.

In the end, the body can only submit to the sound of its passion and desires; he scares his mind and disrupts it, while his soul remains independent and hidden. It may be infected and hurt with diseases of resentment, blame and envy, so she can only watch what the body does with sorrow and pain on him… that is the human being! His tongue pronounced, but Hamid did not know to whom he was speaking at that time.

There, in the second heaven, the father is now accompanied by Al Mualemi in the Kingdom of Tablistan, while Maya is in her future, and less than two decades later, she became a teenager's mother. She will have stayed with her family, installed in her place, doing her duty, and denying herself. Therefore, I know, at this moment, the end of the two stories, and I imagine their conclusion with me completely, this father will die in this world, and he will end up in the morgue of the dead, a violated body in the capital hospital. Maya will end up leaving me and destroying my family for something that will be unknown for a while, and my life will be ruined after we have a boy, that's after we will be a close-up family. One of the two things, my father's death, was achieved here and there, in the lower and second heavens, and our mission is to find out how the circumstances of his death or murder occurred. Maya's tragedy and bitterness have already been achieved there and will certainly come true here. Maya will become like spilled water, I cannot touch or collect its limbs, bring it back to his glass, and can collect water or cry on it? I had explicitly warned about it there and all the consequences that would be here, how long will the situation be? And how will we end up here, and what is our future? Do I listen to what I saw there and lie about what's going on here? Or do I listen and follow what I see now here on this earth?... oh, damn you, Maya, my black destiny, which chose me until suffering, you are my absolute pain! What a lie and folly that we call love illogically, it is undoubtedly the greatest trick, I am now certain that love is the greatest form of deception.

While Hamid was still raving outside his worldly consciousness, he struck his fist with regret on the steering wheel and with great force, as if he were scaring his luck for what was (not) yet happening. He woke up with alarm; he shouted from the pain coming from his wrist, joined his right to the top of his belly button, and began to wipe on it with his left hand, may the intensity of the pain decrease and fade, a spontaneous movement ordered by the mind to return the part to all, instead of falling apart the rest of the whole body. Hamid returned home in pain, and when he opened the door with his left and pushed it with his leg, his inevitable destiny was waiting for him, he found his wife Maya waiting for him as if fate had gathered his strength and his illusion to wait for him and to be lurking on the hottest embers! He became confused between two things, does he continue to love her and adoration as the reality of the world tells him, or does he do what the reality of the apparition tells him after he has seen the unseen? He became very confused between them, hanging between two things that bitter.

She came in a black, glossy, and transparent shirt, which appears more than covers, and, as usual in her charm, she wishes him to hug her in terms of desire to melt between his palms, to lift her from her slender waist; so, her top crumbles, her beneath dangles sliding and fluttering. Hamid was able to read the noise of her desire from her lips when their two existing corners were released, he also read her anxiety from her narrowed eyes when she fell asleep. He waited, and unhopefully expected him, put the rest of his hand on her circular chest, he kept the distance of his arm a rigid comma between them, and then he spun his face off. Maya was lost between his love and hatred for her, so can a man love someone who used to hate? Taking a space of time… He got the answer: Of course, even the sinner loves the one who loved and helped him, feelings toward human beings always return like an echo toward us. Then she asked him:

"What is wrong with you, Hamid? Your situation changes as soon as you get out and come back, this is our whole story with you, you are being too moody."

He was trying at that time to find me and to get help him with a convincing answer to something new for him, he didn't use to and never expected. But, by current time, he knows that I can only address him through apparition. That apparition where souls only telepathy and man speak with universal and absolute values. If he wants telepathy by another means, he must find an alternative way to reach that stage of unseen detection without the need for an apparition; he must be deeply satisfied with himself even for a few seconds, keeping all diseases away from his soul and reaching for absolute happiness. It is the alternative means of apparition to complete the task I started with him, and to help him! He turned around talking to himself:

"So, as Kingel said earlier, I can address absolute values,

including Pure Mind, instead of them, while I am on the ground! To discover his existence while I am here in lower heaven! Where are you Oh mind, and how will you reach you?"

I instructed him to remember the commandment thrown at him at the top:

"Any human being can find and realize the whole universe in himself within him and without visiting the high heavens. The whole universe is within you man, if you know yourself, you will reveal yourself, you will reach the total serenity. You will reach, from your inner, the great universe, you must find your inner heaven as you found the lower and second heaven. You will also find all values there beside Pure Mind, but you will not be able to see the universe, and to reveal or consult the mind unless you are stripped of all your emotions, from all your past experiences, from all your future wishes, from all your mental illnesses, you have to extinguish the fire of human desires that usually raging in the chests of human beings and never extinguished, and remember that the magnitude of your pain at first is equal to the size of your happiness in the end. What a difficult and perhaps impossible mission, and they will only be rewarded to the special and all those who have great luck! But Hamid became aware of the value of the attempt and its feasibility."

A voice came from within him like a tinnitus, I was standing behind him:

"But it remains a possible mission, meditate the whole creation, in the whole universe, and you will recover, Hamid, yes you will. Remember that the revelation himself did not come down on a prophet except when he was at the top of the stages of meditation, think about self-serenity, and you will be able to achieve the highest degree of meditation. If you reach the stage of cognition, then the absolute values may manifest in front of you, you may find them in all things. You no longer need to move to the second heaven to see the universe from there. when you realize yourself and your inner heaven, you will find the whole universe firmly in you, the whole universe with its galaxies and its heavens, with its stars, planets, and orbits, because man is the core of the universe, the nectar of the universe."

Then, another voice came to break his mind, a voice coming from outside his body, it is Maya's voice:

"You repel me from you and keep me away, and I am not as stupid as you expect, stay with the second or third woman, how you like; she may accept you and be useful."

She collected her clothes, got dressed, gathered her needs hastily, carried her baby and went to her parents' house. Therefore, Hamid sat alone meditating on her case, and she was walking to her estimated end not long ago! Then he said,

"It's like I've seen all this situation before, like what's happening now has already happened to me. It may have happened to me since later as well, why the situations in front of us are repeated and we cannot determine where and when they are?"

Maya left the place, and as the place was leaving Hamid, he was still meditating at the same point where she was standing, he forgot the world and its horrors, and she forgot him as well. Here he sees the apparition that we have shown him to come true and easily from where he did not count... From that state of contemplation and serenity, Hamid set off to his sovereignty where his inner heaven was. He was not alarmed by what was happening, the man believed in fate and destiny, and his heart was full of serenity and light, he knew that adoring was a mixture of love and separation. He sat on his favorite sofa facing the lampshades and behind it the balcony of the living room, which arms opened wide into the sky, through which the air and even the birds cross. Hamid immersed himself silently, swimming in the sovereignty of his heavens, and almost saw from there what was impossible in his eyes. He found himself there and he left life, his breath swayed, and his frequencies became like rhythm: (Bot/To, Boot/Too, Booot/Tooo). He dropped his eyelids on his eye's pupil and closed them, and soon after, he set off within all his space. He realized himself there in the mystery of his depths, he found the same orbits of the universe that were in the second heaven, and with the same atomic movements… He found them all in a miniature theatre because a human being is the core of the universe. Therefore, this scene of perception is like the eternal scenes to which his soul was previously transmitted! From his depths, the first scene of perception was born.

The voice of Pure Mind came to him for the first time, commenting on Maya's situation and what she had become. He formed in a form of a giant mind drawn on celestial bodies, through which he addressed Hamid as he fixed in Hamid's inner heaven:

"Hamid, there is no contradiction between the choice of the Lord and the choice of the servant, the Lord has chosen for his servant what the servant had chosen exactly for himself, so that god's fate and destiny became accurately the same of the slave's freedom and choice."

Hamidel listened carefully and then suddenly interrupted pure mind:

2So, there are things in the world, we don't have to run after them, or we must look for solutions, time is the best way to cure them, for all that, Hamid let Maya do what she intends and what she wants; he maybe reaches the real reasons for her action and crime one day... fatal eternal reasons or self-awareness."

Maya left while waiting for Hamid to remain captive to the love of her body and his desires, and to return to ask for her consent, listen to her and conduct automatically what is meant. He, in turn, looks at the same thing, but sees beyond that and beyond the horizons; he realizes that when a woman refuses to shine her moon in her husband's sky, she will shine in another sky, albeit cloudy. Hamid is now in the dilemma of his future, which he saw in the two heavens, the interior and the second, and between the reality of rejecting the inevitable destiny, and bringing his family together and preserving them. Between these two things, Hamid remained bewildered, relaxed, thinking, meditating... I have already given him access to the optimal means, one that brings him to the stage of total abstraction, enabling him to realize absolute values, to speak to Pure Mind and others whenever he requests and moves to the scene of perception. He can practice these steps after trying them once. These steps require impartiality before reaching the degree of total serenity.

I telepathized with his soul:

"You, Hamid, first have serenity and imagination, then meditation, it's the long silence that cracks the lips, later, you'll reach the stage of transfiguration and the scene of perception."

During all that happened on that enormous perceptual evening, Hamid's mother was sitting in her room not listening to what was going on, but she heard what happened against her will. She came out immediately after Maya's departure to find her son sitting, with his back cornered vertically on the sofa of the house hall, looking at the lampshades installed in front of the balcony while the stillness seduced a bird; it sat on Hamid's head as if he had become inanimate. Hamid's mother stepped in horror so the bird flew away.

"I know that the inanimate does not stop praising, and that is why the bird came on Hamid's head."

She stood in front of her son, saw his eyes falling and almost closed, and he stole hearing to his deep breath, and found the space between his inhalation and his exhalation in a steady breadth, and endured an ascending rhythm. His chest filled completely with air, and then breathed him into the sky deliberately. His lips are about to close with his inhalation, and he makes a sound closer to the b-sound, and then he exhales his breath from his lungs to another sound close to the t-sound. (Bot/Tu, Boot/Too, Boot/Tooo…). She watched him, so she could realize now what he was looking at and what he was seeing. Nothing but the balcony overlooking the blue sky and the clouds going on. She waved her palm in front of his eyes hoping to open them. He let her down. He did not stop what he used to do. His mother approached him more and patted him on his shoulder tenderly, so he turned to her as the sleeper turned awake. He said in amazement that the fear of the breadth of his mother's eyes was widening:

"Mom, how long have you been here?"

"What's wrong? I was around you a few minutes ago, and you're not here."

"Really?"

"Yeh, but what matters now is, move and ask for your wife's consent, willingly, and bring her home, don't create a problem from scratch."

Hamid stayed in silence, where silence is another way of realization. He gazed directly into his mother's eyes, dipping them, but he was unable to tell her everything, so he spoke to himself and addressed her.

"Willing one of us could hear him: I am Kingel or the voice of Pure Mind. Nobody but us flying in his inner heaven."

"O, Hamid, don't desire whom left you." Pure Mind addressed him.

Hamid raised his eyes to his mother and said,

"Why would I want her then? She's leaving me in the future, she's going to leave me after we have a son and our son grows up, why don't I take the chance and get rid of her now? Why don't I change my fate with these hands? Can't the act of cognition be associated with work? Facing the scourge is better than waiting for him."

"Isn't it, Mom?" His voice suddenly rose.

"Yes, right, my son, go and bring your wife back, this is better for everyone, for you, for her and for your child."

"Do you see it like this, Mom? That's the way it is, then. We must obey the mother in any case."

Between his mother's desire and his love for his family, Hamid forgot his inevitable destiny, which he had already been told, and he forgot what he warned of in the scene of the perception. He rose from his place and performed ablutions, and then he started the Qur'an telling his mother:

"I will ask Allah almighty about Maya, and God has the will to choose, matters are to God before and after, and we do nothing but follow and submission to Allah. His mother agreed with him, worried about her son's troubles, from his problem with Maya and the misfortune of his father's death."

He read some Qur'anic verses secretly as if he had muttered them, and read verses of sincerity loudly, prayed on the Prophet, his god, and his companions, then closed his eyes. Then, he opened the Holy Quran and put his finger on one of his pages and fixed it on one of its verses. He opened his eyes and read the pointed verse referring to his mother who was standing in a solemn silence:

"In the name of Allah, the most merciful, it seemed to them what they were hiding before, and if they responded, they would have returned to what they had done, and they are liars."

"We are entrusted to God, Mother, the verse is clear and does not need interpreters or experts in speech science." He spoke.

Hamid then asked his mother to prepare to accompany him, but she suggested to him to maintain the confidentiality of family relations and their privacy, and stressed the disadvantages of involving others, even those who are relatives, she said:

"Let it be between you and Maya only, the wider the circle, the harder it is to manage."

The next morning, Hamid set off for Maya family's home, it was only half an hour away from his home. She went out on Tuesday afternoon, and he came after Wednesday's dinner prayer. He knocked on the door, her father greeted him with his distinguished sound of pronouncing (R). He put his Arabic scarf on his head however, he welcomed Hamid with half a smile and invited him to his council as so called majlis, and in the presence of his eldest son, he spoke blamably and grumbly:

"Maya has been here for more than two days, and you have not asked about her and your son since Tuesday, you just came now!"

"I wanted her to calm down and reassure herself."

"I know what happened between you, why didn't you solve that problem?"

"By God I know nothing, I did not understand why she left our house since beginning, I have not understood anything yet, I swear by God."

"If you don't know why your wife left, it means maybe you don't know how to relax her in bed."

"Oh My God, please my uncle, may God rest your soul, change this subject, and hurry up Maya, send her my apologies and I will carry out her requests and her best wishes."

Hamid hit, with his fist, on his forehead deliberately and forcibly, his pain increased, but he hit that point between his eyebrows on the forelock, the one I was passing through to him, and I wish he would say to that man:

"Don't you know that sex is only interesting in its beginnings, and then it goes toward imagination to accomplish the task?"

Maya's father sensed something to poke, then relaxed on his chair, rubbing his coarse and short white chin hair, adjusting his position his scarf position:

"Maya left a few minutes ago, and she had never expected you to come to her."

"Okay, where is she now?"

"We do not ask our daughters where they go or where they came from, we trust our upbringings, your wife is a mature mother, not nice to ask where you go."

Hamid was stunned while listening to Maya's father's comments, it's like references to what the previous eternal scenes talked about. He had nothing but to ask him to bring her back to her husband's house. The man refused to change what Hamid asked for and said to him: "Come tomorrow at the same time, discuss with her, return her to your house, and keep your family safe.

Hamid returned home, greeted by his mother, eagerly asking what had happened, to which he replied:

"Nothing, Mom, nothing ever."

"And the love that was between you?" She spoke.

He replied, repeating what he had previously listened to: from your experience, you know, Mom, love can accommodate two before marriage, but He rarely can after marriage, that's my brief story with Maya. Don't worry, Mom, Maya will be back tomorrow, God willing, she doesn't want to die; separation is rational death, as they told me.

Hamid's mother went out to her room and sat on the woolen carpet in his room, he sat on it and put his right hand on his left thigh, and his left on the right thigh, putting his hands open up, he began to look at the sky and its stars through his balcony, expelling bad thoughts from his mind, focusing with his eyes on one of the bright stars, gazed at it, silence started to talk between them, and she began to see him from afar as if coming from the second heaven. Whenever his breath is in tune with the same rhythmic sound (bot/too, boot/too, booot/tooo), he misses where he is. He moved through to that star and its surrounding orbits, he moved himself there, taking advantage of the instructions I gave. He found the star and everything around it became inside him, he absorbed the celestial bodies and their orbits. From there, he felt serenity, and began to address those who could listen to him, all the sounds became indifferent and do not distract him from what he is now, all of which are in harmony with his great self… Said:

"Why is all this happening?"

He imagined the shape of Pure Mind which he had previously seen; the sound came our off him:

"The human act is based on two: love or awe. Maya loved to be a mother, so she married you, Maya was afraid that her star would get dim, or get old, so she destroyed her family. Then, she will love what she destroyed and be familiar with, and then she will rebuild what she destroyed on her own, etc. Only foolish woman who destroys herself to prove the other's fault. This is how man is forced to repeat his experience because he only follows his feelings."

The star, in which he stared, has increased its luster, its flash lit up his inner space as if Pure Mind were talking through it. Hamid wondered: What do I do as a partner in life?

The sound came from the flash:

"In short, you can't love the other if you don't love yourself first, your success or your failure is not what your partner does, but your reaction to it. You should always ask yourself: Who you are and what you want."

Hamid and Pure Mind telepathized:

"How can I ask if I have not tried yet?"

He felt the response quickly where there is no need for words if feelings speak:

"Didn't you get angry and negative feeling at Maya since first?"

He answered automatically:

"Yeah, yes."

The light flashed waited and turned blue then he said,

"It was enough, Hamid, yeah that was enough."

"I am not wise enough to know that." Hamidel spoke.

"So, I told you from the beginning that man he who decides all his own life, no one forces him, no one imposes on him. He should not call what is a calamity, because man grows and learns from these experiences, and he can invest them in his own good." He replied to her.

Hamid breathed aloud to his exhalation and inhalation (boot/Tooo) as he was listening to his talker:

"How did you build your relationship with Maya? You had

to build it on the right foundations, not to eliminate loneliness, to be sexually discharged, to be bored, to address an earlier mistake, …It's not one of those reasons at all, is it?"

"No, never. not at all, I married her for nothing but love, just love."

The flash from the star changed to red, as if she denounced what Hamid said in his argument. she asked:

"What is love in humans? In short, I give you what I have and give me what you have! Your love and Maya were, without a doubt, just a trade. A swap which was built on something that could be invested between you, and once she got what she wanted, the necessity of that relationship was no longer necessary before the discomfort and the phase of hatred crystallized. You, Hamid, feel that you are nothing without Maya, while you were an important thing, but your patience ran out of weight because of the sexual energy driving you. After forty, a person begins his relationship waiting for the worst, because your partner does not believe in or agree with your new goals. Maya's love grows for you as she loves herself increasingly."

"Do you mean to take guarantees on each other when writing the marriage contract?"

"No, no, guarantees lose married life of its value, you must not see your partner as an opposite and contrary to you, accept problems and difficulties and consider them a divine gift. For example, money distress in the family drives you to work hard to succeed, and that makes you feel the value of money, and so on. You will find that you have more than you really have. You will be incredibly happy if you feel that Maya is big in your eyes, she will realize that and give you something bigger, you should praise and compliment Hamid… Give up your ego there, and your values will rise here."

Hamid woke up from his meditations to the noise of the phone, but he seemed contented and satisfied. The feelings of reassurance seemed to be drawn to his life. He replied:

"Hello, yes."

Maya's father said:

"Listen, Hamid, I talked to Maya, you must come back to take her now, keep her safe in your eyes, I mean you must meet her requests and demands. Women are under mind and religion."

Hamid didn't waste a lot of time, and he said goodbye to his mother and went directly to where Maya and his child were, he entered to her smiling, knowing and even aware of the secrets of human problems, that meditation overtook him with another perceptive scene, and in a conversation with Pure Mind, a talk that kept him away from sins and gave him a lot of gifts. Therefore, Hamid now looks at his problem with Maya with a lot of disdain…He said to her:

"You are welcome, I'll do my best to satisfy you, May God help me to make you happy always."

Maya entered her home and Hamid's mother greeted her with a broad smile and a big hug, while Hamid stayed silently watching the event. Maya greeted her mother-in-law coolly and entered her room with the feeling of the victorious conqueror, Hamid followed her and sat opposite her while she was on the side of her bed, she said:

"You must allow me twice a week to take out my freedom and without questioning, yes, I want to share your life with you, but I must live my freedom and independence, isn't it right? This is my decision, and my words are clear."

Hamid listened to her as she made her demands while he kept remembering his dialogue with Pure Mind during the perceptive scene, he said:

"In your recent crisis, Hamid, don't blame anyone, everything in you is created for you, and it has gone the way you wanted, rearrange your life, never regret any mistake, don't regret doing it, every mistake you consider now may become right later, and every situation is a lesson and a heavenly gift."

Hamid nodded with a smile on that quiet voice; Maya took his consent and was willingly satisfied. Hamid left the room telling her that he wanted to go to the coast where he was alone, she didn't say anything.

He left and Maya came out with her victory, raising her right fist:

"Yes, yes, I will finally live the way I prefer, I finally got my freedom, I love you Hamid a lot once you are like this, listening and executing as I was first met you at the educational institute."

She then turned around:

"But I find his situation turning up and down, he's always happy and smiling, what's the secret to this smile and calmness? And did he go to the coast? Why would he want to be alone and not oppose my wishes? And he didn't ask me either? Why did he choose not to pay attention, and what is the secret?"

Suspicion spread throughout the whole of Maya. She waited for two hours thinking about something, and without hesitation, she called her husband:

"Hello honey, Hamid, where are you? You must come back now, I'm tired, and maybe I need you to take me to the health center, don't be late, honey."

Hamid returned quickly at her will, gave a brief greeting, changed his clothes, and sat in front of the TV waiting for a doctor's visit, and the more she gazed at him, the more she found him smiling and satisfied, she became angry and said:

"Tomorrow, after sunset prayer, I will go visit my friend."

He smiled at her, nodded his head, remembered the most

important thing in his dialogue with Pure Mind where wisdom comes from, and then he said to her,

"Take your time, you are a wise wife and mother, do whatever you want, we do not watch our wives."

Maya was happy with her victory over Hamid as if the hidden conflict between them had ended and she said to herself:

"Oh, Hamid, if you just know where I will go tomorrow, you might kill me, you will. But what is the story of his happiness and his constant smile, he bothers me once nervous and scares me once happy; I must know the reason, if he refuses, I will kill him."

After listening to the voice of Pure Mind, Hamid began to remember him every time he is alone:

"It is normal, if man loves, he builds. Then, he destroys what he built, he rebuilds what has been destroyed, and so on. Everything has two different poles, but if they are similar, they will destroy each other. As for your wife Maya, she destroys what she has built because of the great love she has given, and she destroys it out of great fear as well, equal to his severity. You, Hamid, must decide the image you want to be, and if you want to be exactly that one, you must give up some things or add others to it."

Maya rose from her place, screamed at him but Hamid remained smiling satisfied:

"If you love me, you must prove it."

"How?"

"Fulfill those promises that preceded our marriage, and change your behavior with me, yes. Trust me in everything, and don't keep asking me."

Hamid pinched his sharp nose silently as he smelled a strange smell that ravaged the place. I knocked on his heart to tell him: The smell of betrayal is like the smell of a passing barbecue, both of which we realize without the need to know its source, while promises, they increase before marriage painfully until each imago that it is the absolute happiness.

Maya pinched him on his nose as well, asking him,
"Ha, what do you say?"
"Do whatever you want, Maya, whatever, up to you… He answered her."

(8)

Maya returned from her family home, but Hamid became bored alone throughout his life, dressed in grief over the passing of his father and his mother's deep sadness, and the pain increased with Maya's situation and of their child. He came to his bed driven by thoughts and different illusions: "Who killed my father? What does the king have to do with his departure? And why would Maya turn around for no good reason? Is there a relationship between my father, the King and Maya?"

Thoughts and ideas disturbed his mind even after midnight, he left his bed sneakily, and he sees separate sleep as a necessity for many couples. Head to the lounge and take his place facing the balcony from which he overlooks the sky. He sat relaxed on the same couch, thinking about the bird he did not feel, considering what happened to him and what would happen. Recall the tape of previous events, and a tape of what could happen in the future until the two tapes met in his mind. It's the current moment, the moment between the two tapes, the shortest point on the eternal timeline. Hamid reduced all time at the shortest possible point, tried to confine the widen sky in front of him to the smallest point as well. He absorbed the Eternal Theater that he used to visit, and as usual, he relaxed and breathed deeply (bot/to, boot/too, booot/tooo). He got the rhythm and found those stars and orbits had been reduced to his depths, the light moved with its flashes in his head, then the negative red flashes began to shrink, and the number of positive blue flashes increased, the movement of stars turned into something like the movement of electronic energy in his brain. I was watching all this scene while he was in perfect serenity, thinking and meditating. If you look at the universe, you will dream and dream, and if you look inside yourself, you will realize, because the depth of man is the root, and the universe is the extension. Hamid realized the similarity of the absolute universe from the depth of human being. Hamid was able to realize the Eternal Theater within him, even if his soul did not pass on to there. I don't need to wait for him to fall asleep, because he's now able to see it in himself. I got the opportunity and entered through his forelock fast… I was greeted by his soul, Hamidel, which was between joy and sadness.

She said:

"Where have you been all this time? I've been through the pain from every point of view."

"Soul, I wanted to see how Hamid's experiences in dealing with the events of life, did your body's perfect the workmanship?" I spoke.

And he knows now that too much pain teaches your patience. Yes, Hamidel, pain always knocks on the door of man, if he opens to him, disease will enter. But there is no necessity to take you up to second heaven anymore. We will find the universe in our current body. We will settle over the image of the holy Mountain of Turr, and from within Hamid We will remove the veil of perception as we removed the eternal veil there. Immediately, Hamid's mind stepped down, and Hamidel became the dominant figure in the rest of the situation.

It was easy then to see what was written on the legend board, and to present the scenes of the Theater of Perception.

The First Perception Scene

Personalities: Al Mualemi, Minister of Finance, Minister of Information, Minister of Defense, Pilgrim Kamel, Hamid's Mother, Hamid, Maya, Shawzan.

Places: Kingdom of Tablistan, Minister's Office, Kamel's House, Al-Mualem's Apartment, Capital Funeral Council.

The Minister of Finance, the Minister of Information, accompanied by Al Mualemi and his friend Pilgrim Kamel, are together welcomed by the director of the Office of the Minister of Defense, he stands in respect of his visitors. He receives them with pleasure in his formal uniform, while his chest rises like a peacock. He asks them politely to wait until the Minister of Defense ends his regular meeting with some senior security officials and ministry of defense officers. After the meeting, which quickly broke out inside, the Minister of Defense, accompanying those he had just met to the office of his office director, and there he meets with his visitors, who knows some but not all, shakes hands with the ministers of finance and information, and then Mr. Mahdi Al Mualemi, who became known in the Kingdom of Tablistan after the presentation of his weekly awareness program (My Success) on the local television channel. He presents Pilgrim Kamel, who seemed a shadow of his companion, to confirm that a man follows his friend's religion. The minister raised his eyebrows and asked his friends via gesture:

"Who is this?"

As soon as he shook hands with Mr. Al Mualemi, he looked at his black turban, where his friend head is lost inside it, and his semi-worn brown cloak.

Then, he said:

"You are Mr. Mahdi Al Mualemi, without a doubt, the presenter (My Success), that weekly television program, I was honored to meet you our master, people have always talked about you and praised you, especially these two ministers, and I have always wished to meet you for a long time. As usual, when Al Mualemi exercises his hobby of reading his talk errand through his eyes, he tries to gaze at his eyes and enters to his depth, and then reads some of his qualities."

At the same time, he keeps his facial expressions fixed, neutral, silent, lost between frowning and smiling, grabbing his hand with a handshake before answering him:

"Peace be upon you and god's mercy, I am happy to meet you, Minister."

Before the security officers and officers left, the Minister of Defense invested the situation, to interduce Al Mualemi to them individually. Hence then, a specific man came forward, he is of a medium stature, wide-shouldered, wide-handed, and a big scar on his right cheek, it looks like a dry, stiff river… The minister presents him to Al Mualemi, proud of his presence.

"This is Mr. Ahmed Al-Shawzan, the Director of General Intelligence." He turns to the other side: "This is Mr. Al Mualemi, a well-known thinker and orator, and the presenter of the famous program 'My Success.'"

Al Shawzan grabs Al Mualemi's palm, handshakes and keeps his face sulky until his cheeks were red as if it were flaming.

The two men stood shaking hands but in a spontaneous

challenge between them, as if they had met for decades. Al Mualemi pulled his hand from the grip of the Shawzan urging him to shake hands with his closet friend Pilgrim Kamel. Kamel's hand sank in the palm of his talker, and he remained silent, informing him that silence is the shadow of politeness.

Al Shawzan didn't know anything about these two men, even he is an expert in reading the depth of people, and giving a first impression, usually honest, reflecting what was going on in their own circles.

Al-Shawzan spoke to Kamel:

"As for you, I've certainly met you. Remind me when and where?"

Pilgrim Kamel said:

"I don't remember. But everything's possible these days. We may meet."

Al-Shawzan and the other officers left the Defense Minister's office after that mysterious encounter, keeping eyes on the two men, and while his sense of security still feels uncomfortable toward them, he wished them as Sidon they would not get away! Then, a flash of cruelty appeared in his eyes for few moments, as the beam suddenly faded from the wolf's eye, then he left.

After that situation, which was printed by Shawzan in Al Mualemi and his friend Pilgrim Kamel, all the guests entered the luxury office, led by the Minister of Defense himself, entering a deep longitudinal room, where a brown table with gilded sides, and from behind, there were two flags bearing the flag of the Kingdom of Tablistan and the emblem of the Ministry of Defense. On the right and left of the office, two leather sofas were placed, on which the ministers sat opposite Al Mualemi and Kamel. After the usual formal courtesies between friends and acquaintances, most of the conversation moved and focused on Mr. Al Mualemi. The Minister of Defense, carrying a pen, knocking on his velvet desk, said:

"I became a follower of your awareness program, Master, and I liked those enlightened ideas that you put forward, your speech is modern and logical."

"We are honored and pleased with your opinion, Minister." Al Mualemi said.

"In fact, in the previous meeting with officials here, we were talking about the role of security and intelligence officers in countering the rampant leftist tide in Tablistan, and we all agreed that we cannot use excessive force with the outlaws in the name of the left and its hostile slogans, even if it touches the leaders of neighboring countries, they are focusing their slogans on Arak, often writing: (The leader of Arak falls). These slogans, by their very nature, affect the national security of the Kingdom. Despite all this, we naturally agree that the excesses of the law and the infringement of national security cannot be eliminated unless we address the extremist ideology, which is based on the hearts of the so-called leftists."

The two ministers endorse the previous statement and praise it, while all of them are now waiting for what Al Mualemi will say, but Kamel started to pat the thigh of his friend, urging him, and encouraging him, and Al Mualemi said:

"On this solemn occasion, Minister, and in the presence of the two respected ministers, and the friend Pilgrim Kamel, I am pleased to present you this book entitled *'The Struggle.'* In it, I put what I could from my political vision in government, and I also put in it a lot of security and defense theories, most of which I have recovered and developed through the book (Rhetorical Approach) of Imam Ali, may God bless him. I am now confident that his Excellency the Minister will inform it by himself and with all scrutiny, and I am then fully prepared to discuss what the book said when the Minister requests that."

Al Mualemi stood asking for permission, took his book out from under his cloak and gave it to the minister who received the book as an unexpected gift, held it with both hands, as if he was receiving a valuable gift, read a summary on its back cover, and then looked at the drawings on its front cover, before browsing the book smiling:

"I will start reading your valuable gift from tonight, Master, and I hope you will have time to visit me here on Monday morning next week."

"I will visit you after that Monday afternoon prayer."

"We'll meet, but. If I like what's going on in the book, I'll pass on some of your theories to the king himself. Do you mind so?"

Al Mualemi spoke slightly and didn't answer him to prove, to the minister, that silence prevents man from wasting his energy, so the minister stood, and everyone followed him as a kind of respect, he went to the door, so everyone understood what that meant. Everyone left the office of the Minister of Defense, who accompanied them with his office manager to the outside door, and he confirms the meeting with Al Mualemi next week.

"Where is Pilgrim Kamel from all this?" asked Hamideil, who is next to me, seeing the whole universe in Hamid's body. His presence is only a formality; And why did he fall victim to these absurd relationships?

"We have heard Al Mualemi repeat the saying that man is in the religion of his friend. And Now I recommend you just wait, fates show each other. Let's see what Al Mualemi will do when he returns to his home, or when Pilgrim Kamel receives him later at his home." I said:

After the meeting between Al Mualemi and Kamel with the Minister of Defense, the veil of the theater of perception was brought down from the right side, before being lifted from the opposite side, in which the Minister of Information seemed to leave for his car, while the rest boarded all in the car of Alawi, and the Minister of Finance delivered them to their homes but took Al Mualemi to the house of Pilgrim Kamel at his will. Kamel knocked on the door, which was opened by his Hamid's wife, Maya, carrying her child on the side of her buttocks, which stands out as a slope sculpted by torrents with great care. Al Mualemi kept his eyes to the ground to prevent sedition; Kamel said:

"This is my son Hamid's wife, and this is their beautiful child, he is called Kamel, in the name of his grandfather."

Without raising his head, Al Mualemi said:

"He will have a decent position like his grandfather had, with a word and a will that will not be extinguished."

Then, he addressed Maya:

"We are honored to you, my daughter."

"Okay, raise up your head while welcoming." Maya said as she addressed him.

Maya left them and her mother-in-law welcomed their guest, who was told about her by her husband earlier, and whom she saw repeatedly on the local TV channel. Kamel introduced them:

"This is the gift of heaven, your sister, my wife Hamid's mother."

Al Mualemi smiled and said:

"This is our sister, who was chosen by Kamel after a long search and effort, and he refused to marry one of the women of Arak, who remained faithful waiting for his destiny to be satisfied with him, and here I am meeting your destiny, Kamel, after all these years."

Pilgrim Kamel laughed and raised his voice calling for Hamid who hastily came in his pajamas, greeted Al Mualemi warmly, kissed him between his eyebrows.

Al Mualemi stood silently, meditating on Hamid's face, staring at him, then raising his hand and putting it on Hamid's head, and pulling it down to his forehead, until he stopped his index finger on that point between his eyebrows, as if he saw me there and wanted to meet me, rubbing it with his slab lightly and then saying: people could be read via their faces, son.

I listened to Hamidel telepathizing while she was next to me: "Does Al Mualemi know exactly where we are now?"

"No. No one in the world knows the secrets of heavens, not Al Mualemi nor anyone else can understand what the Soul is and where it is, unless it is the soul itself, no one understands you but you." I spoke.

He took his entire guest to the guest room and Hamid returned to his wife in her room, where he found her tying her right tresses up, while the left part fell on her face and her slender waist, like a velvet curtain dangling. She was upset:

"Why does your father bring his guests home here? Enough burrowing we live in. There is no privacy in it, the house is missing mice yet!"

Hamid asked his wife to lower her voice, there is a generous guest, and they have a duty to honor and respect him, but she continued:

"Your father, your mother, you and me and this child, how does this house carry us? Then his guests come to us? O Lord, God, save this house from existence, or get rid of it as soon as possible, I pray and beg you O Lord."

Hamid couldn't bear what Maya was saying, he said goodbye to his father and his guest and left the house without waiting for the shared dinner prepared by his mother.

The dialogue between the two friends continued, and Al Mualemi began to explain the whole way of dealing with the top of the state and warned him not to appear weak in front of them: do not inflate the prestige of your interlocutor, whether he is a minister or even a king.

After having a light dinner prepared by Hamid's mother hastily, Al Mualemi sensed waves of anger floating in the atmosphere of the house, inspired by its meanings, and soon heard Maya from inside her room saying in a bold voice:

"Go to her, go for it, go irreversibly."

"I apologize for what Maya said, she is like this if she is angry, but she is particularly good. And by the way, I don't find you sad or upset about what she said, weird!"

"Kamel. He, who knows where the world is going, is never sad, the one who knows the creativity of revenge, who ignores and improves to the one who abused him, who uses abuse for his own good. The revelation of worries eases them. Maya has not said anything bad, in short, that is the mid-life crisis that is ravaging her."

Al Mualemi said that and left the house; and the veil of perception was cast on another part of the scene of perception, and lifted elsewhere, while Hamidel is eager to learn more…

On the promised Monday, Al Mualemi arrived at the minister's office as planned, taken by the director of the minister's office with a moustache that fills half his face, took him straight inside, and there the Minister received his guest Mr. Al Mualemi at the entrance more warmly than the previous one, welcomed him and sat opposite as usual on the black sofas. The

Minister spoke after he had finished the preamble to the costly welcome, which his job forced him to master:

"I've finished reading half of your book or more."

"How did you find it? I hope it's good for you."

"Sir, we can put the chapters of this book in special episodes that you will present in your weekly program, My Success, after agreeing with officials in the Ministry of Information, and as I know about the strong relationship you have with the Minister of Information, the approval will almost certainly happen. Master, if you allow me to get out of the book, I know you're being pursued by the leader of Arak Republic to this hour, isn't it? The Prince of Burqan gave you a pass document that is valid only for one trip, and therefore, I have put the whole matter to the high command, which has shown its willingness to grant you the nationality of the Kingdom of Tablistan, to be one of its honorable citizens, to you the rights and duties as the rest of its people here. What do you think?"

Al Mualemi did not show a good reaction to the Minister's words and offer, but he stuck to his composure and hid his surprise and his overwhelming happiness as well. He said: We are honored by your decision and your generosity.

So, I have proposed this to the higher authorities, and then you will be honored to meet our redeemed King, who I hope will imitate you as a loyal state man, and for our part, we also propose to appoint you as adviser to the Ministry of Defense, and we will bring the matter to our king to decide, and therefore, you will have your own office, near my office. In fact, since now, we want to build the army of the Kingdom of Tablistan in accordance with modern regulations and laws, and in accordance with the principles set out in your book *'The Struggle,'* we are always honored by the fruitful cooperation between us.

Al Mualemi removed his black turban from behind and

dropped it on the front of his forehead, from which nothing visible was left, he said:

"As you wish, Al Mualemi serves religion from any position that raises human dignity and protects humanity."

The brief meeting ended, and the minister offered to his guest that one of the ministry drivers would drive him to his residence, but Al Mualemi said:

"My friend, Kamel, is my driver and my close friend, and he is now waiting for me in his Datsun car outside."

Al Mualemi stood by the Minister and left the office, and his tongue was tied preventing him to talk and comment, Al Mualemi went up alongside his friend Kamel, who did not understand what happened to his friend, but let him take his breath and regain his strength. He realizes that it is only a matter of time before Al Mualemi reveals everything that has happened in the Minister's office. As soon as they arrived at Al Mualemi's house, he changed his clothes, went to the couch in the middle of the hall and lay down on it, and Pilgrim Kamel sat away from him, waiting to tell him what had happened in the minister's office. It wasn't long waiting once he said:

"Sit next to me, I have decided, as you know, since my first meeting with you in Arak, that I would marry you to another good woman who completes half of your religion while you are there, and I could not do so. But you surprised me by insisting on fulfilling Hamid's mother wish to remain the first and last, and you took her as a good mother; And here I recommend you, I remind you, Kamel, not to disclose what we have in between, whether it's your son or wife, even if it's…"

A full jump from his place, Kamel saying:

"Don't you trust your friend?"

" All confidence, I do trust you Kamel, but it is the care and seriousness of the situation, brother, they have handed me the whole neck of Tablistan, and I will be able to strangle her or give her new life whenever I want. The king will receive me soon, and will offer me the nationality, and I will be given The leadership of the Ministry of Defense and the army as a consultant, and this will enable me to conduct things in the best interests of our higher objectives, our objectives that we have carried on our backs for ages, our goals and dreams that we agreed upon a long time ago in the Husseini seminary in the Republic of Arak. Don't you remember? You are a part of me, Kamel, and you will stay with me for a long time here at my home. We will no longer have visits to your home except in the presence of your whole family, we do not want to raise doubts inside or outside the family. We will work carefully to achieve our goal, the goal I hold with these hands."

"What about the projects we worked on together? Isn't it hard to achieve? He asked him full."

"Dear Kamel, you can achieve everything you like if you want and work hard. I do not hide the need for the awareness fund in Tablistan to be an extension of its counterpart in the State of Burqan, and to be funded by the State itself here; in order to have a broad public base capable of achieving goals and exerting influence, some are socially trained, others are politically and the most important group will be trained militarily abroad, and we will restore them and bring them back to us when needed."

Al Mualemi sipped from the teacup slowly and asked his friend: Do you want to know what happened in my meeting with the Minister of Defense?

Because Kamel knows that Al Mualemi will go through everything whenever he wants, he understands that friendship is a skill and cohabitation is cleverness. He replied:

"I don't want to."

"That's good, then I will change the conversation to the memory of my uncle Al-Faqih, may God rest his soul."

"It is the beautiful past, he was assassinated by the criminal of Arak, God damn, and your uncle, my brother, left for the paradise of the Mole, God willing."

"Brother, the past is never more beautiful than the present, we say the beautiful past because the world of memories is easier than the world of dreams. Nor should you curse your enemy, brother, because he pushed you to stay in your way and stick to your principles. The presence of enemies is the best proof of your success, and the best motivation to complete your tasks."

Al Mualemi went on to talk about his uncle and elaborated on it a lot, as if he were recounting a novel of success. The dialogue branched away from the most important symbols of his family, until the talk became a kind of pride, to remember after each sentence saying: He who is humble for God, God raise him. Then he went on:

"My grandfather was a religious warrior, who stood up to Britain to deter its desire to monopolize tobacco and market it, and my other grandfather was the giant who called for jihad against them all. For all of this, my ancestors must get more opportunities in the Kingdom of Tablistan and elsewhere. They represent a great jurisprudence, and perhaps a knowledge that will emerge the peoples of the region from blind obedience to self-reflection. Our project in Tablistan should not depend on the areas of advocacy, guidance, and discourse. They're all gone, Kamel. You should know that the biggest worldly punishment is to bury all your loved ones and keep breathing on your own."

"You mean a change in…"

Al Mualemi didn't give time his friend to complete his conclusion. He continued his speech as he headed all to Kamel:

"We must strive to build man culturally and politically, then God will eliminate his fate. As I told you, we should call here the most knowledgeable jurisprudence, my grandfathers have the priority to be followed."

The talk of pride continued, until Pilgrim Kamel felt sleepy, and spent that night with his friend. He woke up early on the phone, a call from a friend in the Cedar Republic, the voice came surprised:

"We are to God and we shall return to Him, today one of the great jurists has left, he has left this world the reference and the great jurist, Sayyid Al-Hakim."

After hearing the full content of the call, Kamel said to his friend lying on the sofa: As if you know the unseen, Master, yesterday you talked about the jurisprudence of the knowledge and the obligation to imitate him, and here is Mr. Al Hakim passed away this morning! And here's the arena is totally empty but your grandfather!

The news was widespread on the same day, and the funeral ceremony was held in the capital's largest Council, funded by the Awareness Fund, attended by large and different audiences, who expressed their sorrows, and presented the relics of the deceased in various forms, in the form of poems and prose speeches.

On the third day of mourning for the passing of the late Sayyid Al-Hakim, one of the clerics came as a naive orator in tribute to him, knowing that the skill of making grief is a trade that will never be fulfilled. He must use it as best as he can, he said during his speech: After the passing of Mr. Al-Hakim next to His Lord, you people should imitate the most efficient, not the most informed. May the most efficient be closer to knowing people's interests and needs.

Al Mualemi was next to Kamel, and they were in the memorial council, and he pulled his friend from his right and he said: This is a temptation will be used to fire all, let's now go home and prepare for the TV episode that I will present tomorrow.

Hamidel turned out to denounce the end of the first perception scene; I told her:

"Al Mualemi was distinct by his rhetorical power and his

ability to convince, as he has shown his intelligence and intuition. Everyone has seen his knowledge and depth in Islamic and Western philosophy and thought as well, these are the features of the prominent leadership, all crystallized in his person, but he focused a lot on the religious aspect in the Kingdom of Tablistan."

Hamidel wondering:

"Was the religious side responsible for the death of Pilgrim Kamel, for the death of my father? And about what else will happen to Maya."

Let's watch this in the second scene of the perception theater. The veil is lifted with the end of the great scene, and Hamidel remains motivated to see what the next scene will bring.

(9)

Because of grief and frustration that engulfed Hamid, and the desire for revenge that has come above his control, until he knows who is responsible for the death of his father, and because of the constant of anger that control his relationship with Maya, it has become difficult for his soul to cross the gate of the heavens or to penetrate her heavenly orbits, as evidenced in the previous scene. It became impossible for his soul to accompany me, and I can no longer take her upstairs.

I found an alternative way to accompany his soul to the high heavens. After Hamid realized that by knowing himself, he would reach the same conclusion, we got the way to ascent into his inner heavens, and from there we will know the whole universe.

She greeted me with grief, asking me if I wanted to see another eternal scene, but that also became impossible. The diseases have weighed heavily on Hamidel. The desire to avenge the one who killed Kamel is tiring her, a weight that makes souls paralyzed in the journey of the High Heavens. it has become impossible but visiting her inner heavens.

When the opportunity arose again, I came to his body and got into him from the entrance center in his forelock. Hamidel welcomed me happily:

"I have been waiting for you, Kingel, and the task is not over, is it the desire to express the biography of kings in the world, or do you miss the love of possession?"

I did not want to tell her that if the kings are infected with what they have, then the ownership does not have the equivalent of a grain of mustard. She must realize that on her own, to know that what man owns is ephemeral and permanent, a divine gift that is meant to be swallowed up, a valuable gift that was given before it is recovered. Man will not take more than his need.

Hamidel has insisted so much that she leaves to the second heaven for one last time, wishing to meet Pure mind and consult him on assorted topics, because it is difficult for her to understand and realize the worldly events.

I showed her my conditional consent, and I asked her to cure all her diseases firstly, those diseases that hinder the movement and freedom of souls, but how can she do that? And she does not realize she's sick yet! No one is aware that anger and envy, jealousy, hatred, etc., are diseases stuck in Hamid, the human being. Yes, in all his components: in his body, his mind, his soul. You, Hamidel, is overburdened with these diseases, and we can only cross your inner heaven instead of the second heaven.

I was afraid that Hamidel would not understand what I was going to say, but it's okay to try. I said:

"Whoever realized himself, Hamidel, has realized the universe. We found in the previous scene of the Eternal Theater that there is no difference between the second heaven and the inner heaven, there is eternal while here is perception. So, we will stay around your body, and together we will realize what it is, and we will see the whole universe in it, that the whole universe is reduced in man, in this body of your human being, Hamidel!"

Her ether hovered around his body; until he became blurry, the souls could see him sleeping or laying down, seeing him for what he really is from inside, and there we found the effect of the flash of Hamidel active in the heart, as the absolute can move the whole universe, we found in the brain a miniature state of those flashes that fill the universe, and it controls the system within natural law that does not deviate. They are flashes of assorted colors, dominated by red color if the body is sick and deprived of will, and flashes increase blue if they have good effective behavior. Hamid's body then became a cognitive or perceptive scene that resembled all the universe, in which you find the holy mountain of Turr, and on its sides the Tree of Durr and the Valley of Tuwa, where the theater of perception is held, through which we arrive to learn the secrets of the universal man in its comprehensiveness.

Hamidel jumped slowly, from her current location, she became able to attract the flashes of the universe and listen to all the sounds that were melting in the space of the lower heaven, she became able to restore and polarize them, and could retrieve every van in the sky of the world, restore time, sound, and light. She is now using the maximum capacity available to souls… she asked: Where will Pure Mind come from?

As soon as she spoke, immediately, Pure Mind slipped from the brain structure in Hamid's head, his flash came out with a bright light, and he settled into the orbit of the body thrown against us. I said,

"This is Pure Mind you were asking for."

"It's enough to telepathize." He said directly:

Hamidel spoke to him in the same way:

"Souls are influenced by feelings just like humans, so our estimates of things will change according to those feelings. But you, as an absolute value, are stripped of everything but your voice, so we want you to accompany us in this cognitive scene, so that we know which ways to follow."

Pure Mind kept silently where in his silence the perfection

of the answers. I telepathized with him about what happened in the first scene of perception, where after its end, Hamidel chose to return to the lower heaven; we're here on the Holy Mountain of Turr, waiting for the second scene of the perception. At this hour, we have chosen to change our seats, to change the angle from which we look at the same events. We sat on the left side of the perception theater platform, which is the opposite of where the actors, the humans, used to enter. Here we can see their faces as soon as they set their feet on the worldly stage that you now know in the theater of perception. Suddenly, Hamidel was asking me about the reason for that, I said:

"When we were wearing our bodies in the land of the world, we often judged the events from the location from which we see them, from the angel of view of our vision and mind, and here, above the holy mountain of Turr, the whole situation became different but contrary, the possibility is no longer impossible, but available and accessible; let's change what we're familiar with and what we're used to there."

And once I telepathized with Pure Mind to find out his opinion, he told us:

"Various readings are fertile material for understanding life, introducing you to the mysteries of the universe and the greatness of its creator."

"Am I really going to change my convictions if I can do that?"

"You will see that yourself, and you will know the spaciousness of the thought of perception and its usefulness in the high heavens, and you will also realize the narrowness of the worldly thought in its opposite; the gap is very much between the lower heaven and the afterlife; the more human beings rise, the more they could understand the meanings of difference as a matter of axioms. In this perceptual scene, we will see these actors of Soul of the King's novel is based on."

As soon as Hamidel read the characters of this perceptual scene above the preserved board, she was cheered and moved lightly. Her jelly limbs crumbled, and she rose from above her wavy holy seat, she began to hover around it in a circular motion, she telepathized me:

"You will be able to see your body hovering around it and watching it from all sides, and you will see its greatness when you notice it from outside, not inside! You could see the universe in the second heaven, and now you will see it in your body, here is the whole universe in your body, whenever you realize yourself and your body you have realized the whole universe, and we no longer need to go to the second heaven."

As we used to see our body dresses hanging, and as you are now moving away from your body; we belong to our bodies in fact, they are not part of us as much as we wear them only whenever we want, and we take them off and also clean them when we want, we throw our bodies and dispose them when they are unable to fulfill our desires, it is a temporary relationship based solely on interest, we have to wear the body dress to achieve actions in the world.

"Will I see Kamel's body too?"

"That was a major reason you were here. Did the theater make you busier? Did you forget your first message?"

"Don't we see there from here? Don't we see a worldly scene from this stage of this perception theater? And in terms of our council over the Holy Mountain of Turr?"

"Yes, but our feelings and emotions are constantly changing, the human beings in the world have been feeling materialism and terrorizing them, and here we are more concerned with morale, we are concerned with what beyond the material, do not the souls be nostalgic for their mud bodies? We were there seeing, and we are here cognizing."

Hamidel was shaken and repeating:

"We perceive and recognize? Is perception a blessing to the people of the world?"

I replied:

"The light cannot wish to fall into the mud and its filth, where the desires that hinder it from reaching the introductions of perfection, don't you find what the angels have become? they became luminous and forced to do nothing but goodness. If they wore mud, they would be soaked like human beings in the mud of pleasures… Let's start together and see the second perception scene now. Come on, come on."

The Second Perception Scene

Characters: Al Mualemi, The King, Shawzan, some Ministers and Officials.

Places: Royal Court.

Al Mualemi enters the Royal Court confidently, surrounded by the men of the Court, sees the king sitting with his artificial tyranny on the ruling chair, filled the whole chair with his body, almost prosperity speaks among his own. In his official council, five ministers sit on his right, who are listed near the king according to their positions and their importance to the decision-making center, and according to the level of responsibilities they have. On the opposite side, five others sit on his left, apparently private, advisers and those close to the Government's Cabinet of the Kingdom of Tablistan. Al Mualemi deposits something wrapped and leaves it in the guard's hand from inside the Cabinet, and then enters without anything but what he wears. In front of him is the director of the king's court, a wide-shouldered man who can be distinguished from his broad moustache, which covers a quarter of his face. Then, the king stands with his greatness welcoming the master, Al Mualemi; everyone stands for a tribute, loving or fearing the King.

"Mr. Al Mualemi, you are highly welcome to the Kingdom of Tablistan." The king addresses him.

"Welcome, your highness, I am so pleased with your kindness and nice to meet you."

"General people of Tablistan and I have been watching your

awareness program (My Success) on the local television every Thursday. In fact, we must first admit that we are going through a crisis, which you called the cultural crisis, and refused to call it a security or political crisis. You have described it a lot, you said it is a transient crisis and if we do not limit it and trim its nails, it will turn into a major security and possibly political crisis, I agree with you of course what you say. But we have to remember the beginning of the story, and remember how the government in good faith has always sent its young people to the universities of developed countries in terms of science, and we have never thought that our students will return with that knowledge, that culture, and carry the thought of those strange societies as well, it became clear to us, Master, that education does not increase the level of morality or happiness of man, and here lies the crisis with these young people, and hence it has crystallized and formed; our officials and ministers have worked to stop this destructive ideology and limit its extension and spread. As you know, Master, we have sent many of our young people to study in these distant countries, but, as I have said, our youths have returned with their certificates and sciences but also carry non-religious ideas, destructive ideas of religion and society as well. They wanted to poison them in a religious and conservative society, they have returned with left-wing ideas that are contrary to our traditions and customs. In doing so, they are trying to drag our kingdom with its youth to reject and refute all religions. You can also see the brotherhood of different religions here on the land of Tablistan, while we cooperate with all countries of the region to cultivate principles of freedom, the freedom of worship and cooperation between religions. Religion, master, as we all know, is a close relationship between the servant and his Lord, and what we concern here is the relationship of the citizen to his homeland, but the religion transformed into behavior that hostiles people's values and principles. The left has radicalized us with their ideas, and those who are enchanted by it have dared to compromise the security and safety of Tablistan, and this is our great misfortune and utmost."

Al Mualemi thinks well of the king's long sermon, recalls his ideas, and even retrieves them, and then points to the director of the Royal Court ceremony, to bring the box, he placed in front of the door of the court from the inside. By order of the Protocol Director, two servants bring the box and place it in the king's hands; Al Mualemi advances to where the box is, opens it slowly as the oysters open. The king and the audience were waiting to find out what was inside the box, so what would a cleric give to a king who put the entire world in his palace? Al Mualemi reveals from his box a ship with four different flags on its back. The ship did not surprise the king or the attendees because of its simplicity and modesty, no jewels nor diamonds from its owner! But the four flags aroused the king's curiosity:

"What are these four flags, master?"

Al Mualemi stood in the middle of the court and the eyes watched him and waited for what he would say. He speaks as he looks at the king's legs, and gradually lifts them up as if he were reading him from below to above, and as soon as their eyes meet, he speaks to him in a confident tone:

"This ship represents the Kingdom of Tablistan, and the banners represent the three heavenly religions that practice their rites freely on your land, and are, therefore, required to remain in one ship, in the event of hardship or ease."

The king turned around Al Mualemi: "But you put four, not three! Did I miscalculate?"

-"Absolutely not, because the fourth front flag represents

you, representing the King of Tablistan, who has excellent value in maintaining the brotherhood of those religions on his ship, even it is a very difficult task; he must be a wise commander of the ship; to proceed and sail with peace."

The master dazzled the king who opened his mouth so much, thinking. Then he said:

"How pure and smart you are, Master!"

"I hope you're always right." Al Mualemi answered him without hesitation, as if he were hiding his answer as gum under his tongue.

Everyone's silence between contented and hesitant, between confident and skeptical. It was a long silence while the audience was watching the king staring long at Al Mualemi. Hamidel took advantage of this period of anticipation and stillness; she came close asking:

"Why does the king stare at Al Mualemi as he's coming from another planet?"

"For the Gazer to be the Gazed himself, he wishes to penetrate and access him and know him."

"Did you feel that then?"

"The attendees and bodyguards of the Royal Court blinded me, hiding the injustices that were going on in my kingdom, and I now realize them not the way I knew them in the lower heavens. I was unfair to myself, so they were!"

The king woke up from the slumber, staring at Al Mualemi's own voice as he said:

"We hope that our message in this world will be purposeful and effective."

The glabrous Minister of Information asked the king to make his intervention, and the king authorized him by a gesture.

"Yes, master, we are following your awareness episodes, and

we are satisfied with your performance, but the trend of violence, as we all know, is escalating according to the investigations of the public security reports. Unfortunately, the dull and stupid ideas they always boast, have all turned into destructive behaviors, harmful to the individual citizen, society, and the nation. They undoubtedly worry the public security and civil peace; they have never stopped writing: the leader of Arak falls. This is considerable damage to our national security; the arm of the Arak leader extends to the countries of the entire region."

The Minister's words provoked Shawzan, the director of general intelligence who is sitting with five others on the king's left, he was trying to speak in a quiet voice in appreciation to the presence of the King, trying to be calm to avoid the King's anger if so. He said:

"I suggest, your highness, using excessive force to prevent leftists and those who follow them by writing slogans on walls and planning marches and possibly coups. This kind of human being, through my extensive experience in dealing with them, is undoubtedly destructive, and their activities will cease only with the use of excessive force and deterrence, the stick, your highness, is always to those who disobey."

The king takes his eyes to the reactions of all the audience; the approval is present on their faces, the smile is the title of satisfaction, while some hypocrisy hurts the soul before the eye. Then, he takes his eyes to where Al Mualemi is; reading in his face the desire to speak, Al Mualemi said, addressing Shawzan as he remembered his handshake, as if he were only talking to him:

"Excuse me, sir, these young people, without a doubt, have a psychological memory that drives them to this hostile behavior. They are, without doubt, suffer from many other and possibly compelling problems, and they have never been able to express them, so they are directing their energies to another path that is out of national consensus, they are planning marches, writing slogans, and repeating them like parrots. Mr. Shawzan, he who is strong can restore his soul. As a security man, you can use excessive force to defeat them as you say, but they or even others will come back, and you will not be able to wipe them from the whole earth. But if you understand what they want, and you can deal with their demands even if you disagree with them, you will uproot the problem, because you will know and diagnose their suffering accurately, and do not forget that the correct diagnosis of each disease leads you to half the treatment. Mr. Shawzan, you must forget your muscles and strength when talking about justice, freedom, and equality, about democracy in all its forms; you cannot demand democracy if you cannot live it inside you."

Without permission, and without regard for the presence, Shawzan intervened in a sharp voice, like a sword in his deafness, which angered the king himself. He wondered:

"And what is their problem specifically, Al Mualemi? Do they have a problem other than dragging Tablistan into ruin and internal and external conflicts with the Arak leader?"

In his session, Al Mualemi retreated, pulling his turban from his head to the middle of his forehead, taking the king's tacit approval, and taking out his voice in a deliberately heavy tone; he answered:

"They are a group of young people inevitably caught between two hells, between the fire of local religious extremism and its pressure over them to the point of suppression, and the values of the environment in which they studied during university. They are two contradictory environments that generate aggressive and impulsive behavior, yes, aggressive behavior in every sense of the word, which is enough to put a cloud over their eyes."

The Minister of Information suddenly interrupts him:

"This is where your role is, Master. The role of media as a fourth authority, we must spread love among all people, we must constantly raise awareness, spread all kinds of awareness, and stay away from misinformation and intimidation."

Shawzan did not like that whole talk; he still remembers those looks that provoked him when he first met with Al Mualemi in the Office of the Minister of Defense, and he said with a gloomy face: "But it remains a misguided party and will only meet love and charity with abuse and ingratitude, yes, they are envious of goodness."

Al Mualemi stands with permission as he hovers around the hull of the ship and touches it with all his body, then puts his palms on its four flags, he turns around and all eyes watching and waiting for him:

"What Mr. Shawzan is saying may indeed be true, but in our first steps, we must be wise, and meet their violence with love. Repression does not eliminate controversial ideas, while dialogue can undermine them. Despite all this, we must keep the law above all. Graffiti against the leader and against those who follow in his footsteps, and even the marches they organize are all an expression of internal feelings, and we should not punish anyone for their feelings and even their thoughts, but if that expression turns into hostile behavior, then we only use harmless force, because harmful force will also inherit hatred, anger, and counter-violence. Gentlemen, yesterday is not today, and the world is not like the hereafter. Brothers, we must realize the suffering of people before judging them. Don't you see that ninety eight percent of the world's population is poor, according to united nations statistics, but they are satisfied because they sacrifice their physicality for the immortality of paradise, and only two percent of the world's population is rich, rich but not self-satisfied, because they fear the hell and its torment, as the united nations statistics say, but they are satisfied, because they sacrifice their physicality for the immortality of paradise, and only two percent of the world's population is rich, rich but not in a state of self-satisfaction, because they simply fear hell and its torment, that promised fire, and they feel their own and public hatred for them."

The king raises his right hand and it is adorned with two shiny rings, showing his desire to silence everyone. Then, he repeats the same sentence as the previous:

"How pure and smart you are, Master!"

Al Mualemi answers him with the same speed and the same words:

"I hope you're always right."

Al Mualemi stands at a heavy pace slowly toward the king and puts his hand under his woolen cloak (Besht). Shawzan becomes suspicious, and his security sense pushes to move; he points to the director of the royal protocol to move quickly, and to intercept what Al Mualemi intends to do; he moves in his direction, and the security guards become ready, but the king or the ministers did not react negatively, they all smiled and laughed. Moreover, Al Mualemi came out a medium-sized white paper from under his cloak. It is the same book he previously dedicated to the Minister of Defense. He raises it in the face of the protocol director who slows down going back. Al Mualemi speaks:

"Your highness, this is my book which you have heard about from the Minister of Defense, it represents my experiences and philosophy in life, and you no doubt realize that the word is stronger than the sword and its sharpness, isn't life but a word?"

The king takes the book with a smile, and the Shawzan in turn retreats to his seat and the feeling of loss beats him and increases him with a frown, while Al Mualemi gets his cloak, and his eyes are inexhaustible from the King. The director of the Royal Court ceremony is more than two meters away without looking behind him.

"This is my book entitled: *'My Struggle,'* I left a copy of it with the Minister of Defense."

"So, this is *'My Struggle'* book that they're talking about."

"Yes, *'My Struggle'*, I put in it the most important ideological and moral pillars that help man to the goodness of his actions and intention, so that his behavior is promoted in accordance with what he believes, I derived its ideas from the Holy Quran and the Sunnah and adopted the political and military rules contained in the approach the rhetoric of Imam Ali. I also relied on the experiences of the pioneers of our great Islamic history, to find in this book that the backward and different images of intellectual deviations are acts adopted and practiced by the former and were for enlightenment thought. In short, in its first chapter, it represents the means of self-defense; Its second chapter contains the political and military rules of government, as described in the biography of Imam Ali, Muslims Khalifah, through the Book of Rhetoric."

The king places the book in the palm of his left hand, opens it with his right, slowly meditating, and reads the dedication to the audience: (Wisdom comes from those who want ŏ and those who come to wisdom have done a lot of good.) Then, he addressed Al Mualemi: The verdict is only wise, and you are the appropriate for that, Master. The king then stands smiling as he puts the book close to his chest and says:

"How pure and smart you are, Master!"

"I hope you're always right. Al Mualemi answered him without hesitation. The King: Make sure that I read this book with precision and focus, and then we will have a special session, in which we discuss the most important things in it."

The Minister of Defense asked politely to talk:

"I have read the biggest part of the book; I will be happy to be a part of the discussion to be held."

Al Alawi, the minister, also speaks, and he was in the row to the king's left:

"Will the king also allow me to attend? So that good will prevail and benefit swells."

The King:

"Our Council has never been filled with minds, and our heart is always and ever expanded to all those who want good for the soil of this country, and we open our chests to all those who work for the Kingdom of Tablistan."

Just before the hinged and dramatic scene ended, Hamidel came toward my side, stretching her limbs in the form of vibrations as she telepathized me:

"Why did Al Mualemi choose Kingdom of Tablistan specifically but not others?"

Al Mualemi, with his innate intelligence, never chooses. He goes to the sea, stays there for an awfully long time, meditates a lot, and reads between the waves and behind them, and he only catches fish ready to fish. Hamidel then went to the other side, where Pure Mind was in the cross, and she telepathized with him, and he replied:

"Good will, in the heart of any leader or king, is the best way to torture him, and it can be exploited to reduce the evil that comes from him."

The veil of the Perception Theater descends announcing the end of the second scene, and Hamidel returns to her dress, to her mud body.

(10)

Hamid went to the cemetery on Thursday afternoon as the people of the area used to, in a religious and social tradition. The people enter the cemetery to visit their dead, but Hamid entered the same place to examine the cotton grave and what happened to the imaginary grave of his father. He wanted to see how people adopt graves as an idea, and build them in their minds, and then sometimes they come to sanctify that idea, and embody it without a convincing reason. As soon as Hamid is certain that the bodies are clothes that man gets rid of and leave when they are no longer able to meet what is required of them, and after examining the cotton grave, Hamid took a solo tour of the tombs, looking for a suitable place that would not be suspicious if his father's body was officially buried. He felt that the place should be identified from now. There, the cemetery was filled with many who had just lost some of their relatives and acquaintances, and only a few who had lost their relatives a long time ago, as if they were saying with a unified collective voice: the severity of the loss would be reduced if it was gradual; then we reach the stage of oblivion without pain or agony.

You may read the sadness drawn on some faces because of the recent wound left by that loss, and you may read the joy and satisfaction on other faces that were caused by the prayer of those who left, satisfaction and an expression of the ability to keep the rope of communication with those who died.

As soon as his eyes fell on the fake cotton grave, people

gathered around him, and the Tablistan flag was raised next to two other flags, one black and the other red. On top of it, concrete rising about an inch from the ground, as well as a lot of flowers were scattered on it. Rosy water was poured. Some rings and green threads were attached to the grave limbs. All are waiting for the owners to recollect them and take their blessing.

The surprise was excessively big, when he found his mother sitting among the women, while Maya standing behind the women's row, leaning her waist aside, putting her hand on him as if leaning on him. She was watching the whole situation, as if she knew the truth even if Hamid nor his mother told her about what happened, because Hamid and his mother had promised not to reveal the secret of the body.

Hamid came much nearer, and then there was a silent conversation between him and his mother, which Maya received with muffled anger, so he initiated her with his new smile, while she was saying to herself:

"What is the secret of Hamid's smile, which does not disappear from his life whenever he sees me? Why didn't he ask me why I was here? Did the man find out something? Did anyone tell him about what's going on inside me? Nobody knows the secret but three: Allah Almighty, I, and that whom I do not want to mention say his name now!"

The constant truth to me was that both Hamid and Maya had their own secrets, which they are feared of reaching to the other, it is the secret that made anger and anticipation drawn on Maya's face, while the smile and contentment were etched on Hamid's face!

The mother advised the women to stay in their place and continue to recite the Qur'an, and then went to her son. She told him in a reassuring and deep voice:

"Ma, why did you come here, and you know that the body in this grave is cotton? And did Maya know anything from you?"

The mother explained, "Things must go on in a way that does not arouse suspicion, son, people must be sure that the one in the grave is undoubtedly your father. As for Maya, I think she hasn't known anything yet, I haven't spoken to her since she was satisfied with after coming back from her father's house. What strange is that she came here alone to read some Quranic verses even she was on a troubled relationship with you father, and foremost, she came first and alone as if she were watching people gathered around the grave without caring about who inside the grave. Why all that? I don't know, Hamid… I do not know!"

Hamid was unable to find a satisfactory answer to his mother's various and disturbing questions, he remembered earlier when we were there in the second heaven, when I told him: that's to let you know that mourners never cry but themselves; It makes no difference whether the body in the grave is flesh or clay, human beings comfort and cry themselves first, and then they make it possible to accept the effect of this loss, but at the same time they like to step up, sudden things are very harsh for all human beings.

The mother kept her eyes between Hamid and Maya, pulled him from his wrist, told him:

"As you can see, son, Maya is here behind the women, watching but not participating, she looks at us as you see, she looks at the grave and those around it, as if there is something she intends to do. We cannot tell her the whole matter; the feelings are very conflicting and contradictory; so, I think she came here to check on what happened or something else. God knows that, but tell me, Hamid, what brought you here, and you know the details of the whole story?"

Hamid shrugs off addressing me inside: "What does Maya want from me after I knew the end of her story with me, and how will things between us go? I know our destiny and our future now, and yet I have decided with determination to change everything and reject destiny, and our destinies are undoubtedly our actions, they are exactly what we want, not what heaven wants."

Hamid then went to his mother answering her:

"I came to know how my father's body could be buried in his grave tomorrow morning without raising any suspicions or questions, the week is over by tomorrow. Mother, tomorrow is the last day of the period set by Falah. We want to bury him peacefully; how will we be able to do that? The whole thing must be managed and planned well. But. Mom, I'm still wondering: What let Maya come today?"

The mother suggested, "It's not a complicated task, Hamid, what if we rumored among the women about a lady from the area who dropped her baby while she was three months pregnant, for example? No one will ever ask or care. The question now is: Did you know how your father was killed? And what's the secret of the seven stitches on his chest? What did they do to your father's body, Hamid? But. It seems that you have not completed the task, and it is impossible for you to achieve the desired results."

He told her: "I am only sure, Mother, of the wound and the seven stitches, but we need a forensic doctor to examine the body and open the stitches, which is impossible. Falah refuses that because that exposes him to deserved punishment, possibly dismissal and imprisonment as well. Anyway, we must thank God, and we must burry the body in the grave before they discover the whole task. As for your suggestion of burying the body, it makes sense, Mom, yes. It will be noiseless, especially when it's after dawn or early morning."

Hamid's mother left her son and returned to the women who were about to leave but saying:

"Give the martyr's son a place that nobody deserves but him."

The mother went to Maya behind the women, she can't stand upright. She greeted her and offered to go home together. Maya's eyes attached to her husband from afar; but he did not pay attention to her, she became angrier, and her face was red. The mother and Maya moved around between the graves as if they were on a tour or inspecting. The mother is looking for space to be able to take down her husband's body, without much curiosity and without Maya knowing anything about her intentions. She said to Maya, pointing her hand:

"This place is very convenient, we can choose one of the classes dedicated to the burial of children, and there in the last small graves, it would be the best place."

"What are you talking about, Aunt?"

"No, nothing in particular, I just liked to clear the line between children's graves and the rest of the graves of the dead, just a talking."

"That's it!"

Maya didn't know exactly what Hamid's mother was talking about, and she concluded:

"My aunt wants to get rid of my baby so that she can get me away from Hamid in revenge. Can she hurt me and hurt her son as well? But everything has become possible in the case of revenge."

The women moved from their places around the fake grave, and soon after they left the cemetery as a black group through the main gate, they turned back curiously as leaving, talking, and watching what was going on between Maya and Hamid's mother, who waved to them saying goodbye. Then she pointed to her son rushing to return home. He ignored them this time because he did not want to look at Maya's side. They went out but he headed toward the fake grave to complete the task.

He sat next to the grave, and soon some men of the region came behind him, they offered him warm condolences. They asked God to raise the soul of his father to the shrine of martyrs and believers, and they had a dialogue, which showed their mercy and contributed to the departure of Pilgrim Kamel.

One said:

"The deceased has remained in prison for less than one year, and I think that Shawzan punished your father unjustly as he usually does to others, punished him, and tortured him as he healed him to avenge. I think that Shawzan knows that your father did not commit any crime worthy of imprisonment, torture, or murder."

Another confirmed:

"They kept him in prison for almost a year already; and he must have left tortured, oppressed, even we didn't see the body ourselves when washed and buried. May God forgive you, Pilgrim Kamel, and bless your soul."

The first answered:

"Quranic Verses to his pure soul, may his Lord honor him well in the hereafter, and place him in a higher degree with the martyrs and believers. God bless your condolences, Hamid. We will erect a shrine around the tomb of your martyr father, and we have already begun to work on it, as his dignity and exploits began to be clear to all."

The second commented, referring to the headstone:

"I tied a green thread on the headstone, and I took it two days later, and tied it around the back of my son, the patient with bile a long time ago, and he is healing thanks to the dignity and blessings of the martyr."

Hamid raised his head toward his interlocutors as his tongue was held, and raised his eyebrows until the lines of his forehead appeared longitudinal, as if he had aged a lot during recent week, did not take much time before he was followed:

"It is the legacies and what they do, the recognition of them makes us always happy. But let us read *fatiha* now to the soul of the deceased and to the souls of all believers and believers."

He remembered his date and the need to meet with Falah tonight, and to see what happened about his father's body there, and began to realize that it would not be able to bury the body, he was expecting some bumps and difficulties, the worries became hardened and riddled him more, he used to talk with himself once alone: what things should I start with, and to which end? shall I track Maya's story here or there? What about the tombs, which one do I have first? And what crime did my father commit to be killed, as they say? Is his relationship with Al Mualemi enough to kill for her? And you, King, what's your story? you left your body, but kept your soul in my sight, close to me, wherever I go. What an unhappy life. Isn't the death of the body more comfortable than this world and its problems?

I said without Hamid hearing me, of course:

"No pleasure in life without affliction, Hamid."

He got a sudden tinnitus, and he started looking in all directions without realizing what caused it, pinching, and pulling the flint of his ears. He did not look for a long time before he decided to return immediately to the family home. And there, he was met by Maya who was waiting for him from outside the door, as she was putting her hand on the side of her waist as usual, forming the shape of a slanted triangle, she knows that the secret of woman's beauty comes from the angle from which we look at; he greeted her with a smile, and she became angrier with his current smile . He entered where his mother was waiting for him.

He greeted and kissed her head, then lay on the same seat in the middle of the house hall, his mother left for her room, while Maya stood waiting for him to start talking, but he didn't pay any attention. She said trying to provoke him:

"I'm going out."

"Goodbye." He answered her.

He remained silent and quiet, so she explained that as regretting and love, she thought of her deadly weapons, she hugged him as welcoming travelers after a long-time journey, just exactly as Al Mualemi hugged Kamel at the airport, she fell on his shoulders to confirm her love, and she didn't know that love is from the heart and adoring of the soul, therefore adoring is never influenced by place. He felt the heat of her soft flesh body; he became horny and couldn't do anything but to squeeze her from her slim waist, which the more he pressed it, the more it turned around. Then, he swooped down on the river between the breasts saying:

"If I knew the reasons for my love for you, I would have cancelled, myself, the possibility of it happening."

Then he wondered:

"Can't the scene of Maya's perception become an uncompleted destiny, I mean, it's pre-estimated and not what I want? Can't we on earth change the fate and destiny of our actions? Otherwise, what is the point of paradise, fire, reward, and punishment, if everything has already happened and is complete? Mind says: It was ruled, but logic says contrary to it: we can change every destiny with our actions, and I can keep it here, here in the world, just fate? We know the fate that could be changed; thus, I hope my God to replace it well. That's all to be held accountable for our actions, we humans. I want to change that heavenly destiny, yes, I will change it."

He took his wife to the stage of fight, and as soon as he finished from bed fight, he convinced himself that her love was sincere, he stuck again to the thread of hope: we will change it here in the lower heaven; In order for the scene to change, where the second heaven is, I will prove that man is the master of the situation, and he is the one who makes his destiny and his fate.

Nearly two hours later, after relaxing, Maya as he believes and wishes, Hamid said goodbye to his mother and wife and went to the morgue of the capital hospital, where his father's body was buried, and to Kingel, who keeps hovering in her orbits. After the usual steps there, he met the driver, Falah who was waiting for him, to rid himself from a self-made complicated trap. Falah greeted him after Hamid cautiously crossed all the steps and took all necessary precautions.

Falah welcomed him saying:

"We have no time but tonight to take your father's body to the cemetery, it would be better if you took it with your relatives, but if you want my help to maintain confidentiality; I won't be late at your service, but we must take the body tomorrow, take it to the cemetery as soon as possible, we don't want new complications that might take my job or my neck."

Hamid immediately replied:

"Don't worry, everything is in God's hands, the task will be done, if he permits, but now let me see the father's body alone, maybe something new has happened. Is it possible?"

There, where the promised refrigerator number five, which Hamid did not attack anymore as he approached it, he carefully examined his father's face; removed the shroud from the face of that blue body; found it shrinking steadily, reducing on himself every day. Then, he removed the shroud from the chest and checked it out; He found the seven stitches clearly stretching from above the heart to the navel. He pressed on both sides of the wound very slowly, but the strength of the bones of the rib cage prevents his hand from reaching the depth, does not allow him to examine the inside, place the thumb directly above the chest area, press and press… Hence now, the thumb finally sank somewhat into the space under the skin, he wondered:

"Did the heart shrink on itself as the whole body already shrank, or is the whole heart not in the body now?"

He snuck into the ground and squatted, and he leaned his back to the wall, turned his head back, thinking about this tale that does not want to end, he began to put the possibilities and ways to catch the truth, he closed his eyes as if he had been full of the worldly life, and may get a nap. I did not care about all of this. As soon as his closed his eyes, I came to him, burdened him with his eyelids, I came to his forelock exactly, and concentrated at the specified point on his forehead and between his eyes, the one that began to prevail and go inside from the frequent penetration, Hamid was resisting sleep, and I was focusing on separating his nervous system from the source of command from the brain. The attempt succeeded at the second time, and he turned his back, and his powers were lost with no resistance, so I settled to him, until Hamidel noticed my presence and said directly:

"I trusted your coming back and your presence without a doubt, but you are long overdue this time, I almost died without you, souls and good dreams that awaken the meanings of words and thoughts within us, I am like the dead without you… but anyhow. warm regards."

Whoever expected something, fell into it. My mission has not finished yet, soul. I had to come back but at the right time, and here you are sending me your warm regards, because heat means life and cold means the dead body. Let's go now, let's go, let's leave your body with half your ether and keep the other half in your body, let's see the universe by knowing your body. Then, let's go to complete the next scene from the theater of perception; Come on.

The Third Perception Scene

Characters: Pilgrim Kamel, Hamid's Mother, Hamid, Maya, Shawzan.

Places: The house of Pilgrim Kamel in the Kingdom of Tablistan.

The Eternal Veil was removed, and the image of Tablistan came empty from its noisiness after Al Mualemi had forced to leave her, and his closest friend, Pilgrim Kamel remained alone in the wind. He expected some events that would happen to his life, while the unseen hid a lot of issues, and would throw them on the back of Pilgrim Kamel and his family when time came.

After the police, intelligence and special forces surrounded the House of Pilgrim Kamel from all four sides, closed the entrances to the entire neighborhood, then entered the neighbors' houses from their doors and backs, destroyed what was difficult for them, they began to gradually break through from the far to the heart, where the traditional house of Pilgrim Kamel, a house built in the local style, which spent half of his life struggling to survive. They surrounded it and broke into it from his walls, one of them tried to open the courtyard door from inside, so that Mr. Shawzan, the director of general intelligence, entered with his selective and faithful men. The door remained locked, and the Shawzan asked to break from the inside. They did and then went to the inner door, and they also found it locked tightly. Shawzan pointed out to break it; They executed his orders with ease, as if they were used to breaking in.

The sound of the broken door was more frightening than expected because it broke the silence of the night and expelled his reassurance; so, all the people of the house were terrified.

Before the sound of dawn prayer spread in all corners of the neighborhood and streets, Shawzan's men filled the entire inner hall of the house, Pilgrim Kamel woke up and followed all the people of the house on the sound of breaking the door and the noisiness caused by Shawzan and his men, they went out successively. Hamid's mother was about to fall out of shock and horror, while Maya screamed loudly as if to appeal to a storm of inevitably a frenzy; She went out to the lounge in her semi-transparent pajamas and does not yet know what is happening; Hamid tried to cover his wife, manage it with his body and then to bring her back inside, but the Shawzan prevented him pointing his weapon at him, as he sees the pleasure of the scene, reads that in the eyes of all the security guards. Their eyes focused on what distinguishes her from the rest of the females to her slender waist, the above scattered and below sloped. Hamid begged Shawzan to let him bring his wife back to her room and promised to return her after covering up her body, and after she silenced her child, Kamel, who was crying, frightened by the sudden scare, she had to play the whole role of the mother as life goes on.

Shawzan agreed with him and allowed him reluctantly, he returned her to her room and was assured of staying by her son's side, he asked her to calm down and wear heavy clothes protecting from the arrows of the eyes of the rabid wolves as soon as they called her again. He went out to the lounge and left his wife and son in their room. Shawzan spoke after biting his tongue and tasting the sweetness of victory, revenge and even insult. He told Pilgrim Kamel, standing in the hands of two men who were tough police officers:

"As I promised you to hunt your master friend since I saw you in the office of the Minister of Defense, I also promised you that you would fall into my hands even after ages, now I am keeping my promise. I never break my promise. Remember that well, Shawzan never breaks his promise. As you know, your friend has revealed, we have received news from friends and from the regime of the Leader of Arak, we now realize why he was defending those left-wing slogans denouncing the leader, The leader of Arak falls, then this is what you wanted! Your friend left the Kingdom of Tablistan as soon as his plan was discovered and exposed, and if it were not for the morals of our redeemed king, he would have executed your friend or handed it over to Arak. But to know, man, Tablistan was not able to enter thorny calculations with Arak and its leader, nor with the Burqan or other countries of the region, now. Who else next to you?"

Pilgrim Kamel begged them to let Hamid's mother enter her room as Maya had earlier entered with her child. But Shawzan stomped them all out in a crude voice:

"Let everyone in the house go out to the outer courtyard, and no one stays here; we will search every corner of this house, you are the closest friend of Al Mualemi and the one who mutes his secrets, you must be working to achieve what he could not do, we will find all the evidence and that condemns you inevitably, there is no way to hide anything, and I will punish you as well."

"There is no power but by God." Pilgrim Kamel answered him, holding his son Hamid's wrist and leaning on him.

Shawzan laughed and sarcastically said: "This is what we know and learned long time ago, everyone repeats it, if the siege or illness intensifies with the criminal, he turns into God. You did not know your Lord except at this time. Why didn't you keep Tablistan safe as it's generous to you, you, agent? Why did you ally with our stalkers, traitor? Get all out yourself before we take you by force, hurry up."

Pilgrim Kamel took his wife by the arm and one of the security men put his gun on the back of his head. Hamid assured Maya and their son after she closed her door and locked it from inside with the key. They surrounded them all, and they put the weapon on standby in front and behind them. Shawzan asked three of his own to search the house one corner by another. The more he gets tired of the search and the more he gets lost, the more he breaks down the contents of the house and scatters its belongings, as if he were calming down himself.

After desperate searches and sabotage, Shawzan and his men found nothing; He went to Maya's room and knocked on her door, she opened her door and got out a part of her head, asking him:

"Yes, what do you want?"

Unexpectedly, he lowered his voice in front of her: "Excuse me, beautiful lady, we just want to search the room if it doesn't bother you."

"It's okay, but where can I go while Hamid is not there?" Maya asked.

"Hamid and his father and mother are outside, come outside and have a seat in the lounge, our men will search in your room, and they will not damage anything, I promise. We'll also ask you a few questions if possible." Shawzan answered.

Maya sat on the lounge sofa, and Shawzan sat proudly opposite to her, talked to her about Al Mualemi and his relationship with her uncle Pilgrim Kamel, explained to her that he was chased by the leader of Arak, expelled from Burqan and more recently from the government of his country Tablistan, then he added to her:

"You, as a good citizen, can protect your precious country from the danger of Al Mualemi and his associates, and you know that his closest associate is your uncle Kamel, this father of your husband who stands outside."

"How do we protect our country when the danger is gone? Al Mualemi left Tablistan as you say."

"Yes, beautiful lady, he left the homeland, but his followers and plans are still there, and there are those who work under his control. As an honorable citizen, you must stand by us to protect our country, and we will give you as much as you can to help you, we will do a lot of what you ask, and don't ask either."

Maya took her baby to sleep again,

"How can I help you? And what's the reward?" she asked.

"We will arrange for you some meetings in the Criminal Investigation Bureau, you will tell us about the meetings that took place here in this house between Al Mualemi and your uncle Kamel, we want all the minute details before the big. As for the reward, you have everything you want, and if you ask for your uncle's full heart, I will give you a gift in your hands, nothing more precious than your satisfaction."

Maya laughed as she bit her lower lip:

"My uncle's heart, my uncle's heart…"

He then handed her his own phone number and asked him to return to her room.

Shawzan and the rest of his men went out to the outer courtyard, allowing Hamid and his mother to return to the house. Shawzan addressed Pilgrim Kamel in anger with him, threating him:

"We have not found anything at your home, and this is another practical proof of your skill, the strength of your criminality and your smart and the skills that you have learned from your traitor friend, you have hidden the evidence that condemns you and your friend, because you expected us to be here, malicious, and this is another crime alone."

He then went on to talk to his men:

"Leave them all, we don't want them, just this Kamel, tie him by the hands and blindfold him. I will avenge you; I will avenge every word your friend has said in my right, I will avenge the obscenity of his tongue and his inciting the king and others to me. The scene of revenge will only be in your body, yes in this body."

They blindfolded him, and took Pilgrim Kamel in a black armored vehicle resembling a large beetle, took him directly to the National Guard Prison, two hours north of the capital of the Kingdom of Tablistan, a prison prepared specially for politicians and dissenters, and for leftists who once wrote slogans that provoke the neighboring countries, where Arak's leader was the first, the prison was also prepared to those accused of collaborating with foreign actors, all demons before people believed in their God just in this prison.

The great prison is surrounded by a 20-meter-high fence with electrified sharp thorns, monitored by precise security cameras, and at its six corners, watchtowers, a guard standing on top of each of them. Inside, the prison wings are painted black, each has eight opposing and compact cells and four other cells, with a narrow longitudinal red tunnel, which has been allocated to solitary confinement.

They held Pilgrim Kamel in solitary confinement awaiting the start of the investigation, kept him alone for three days, where he did not see the sunlight until his pupils widened, and his eyes were addicted to the stark color of the cell, he began to forget the light and colors. At the time of the two meals, they brought him water and lentils with white rice for lunch, brown bread with some tea in the evening. He stayed with the same-type food until he became familiar with it and feared change.

When the expected investigation came three days later, he was brought by two heavy guards who led him to the Special Investigation Office, they let him stand, handcuffed him from behind, then untied his head and ordered him to wait. Two hours have passed, and Pilgrim Kamel is waiting, and he doesn't know who is waiting or what to do.

Pilgrim Kamel was taken to Shawzan, they took him into the black room of the investigation, it is a cubic dark room except for two holes in the ceiling from which the light falls vertically. Pilgrim Kamel stood underneath them handcuffed from behind and his legs were tied tightly. In that cube, he could be seen but not seen. He heard a sound that looked like thunder in its intensity, a voice whose frequencies were distorted to become terrifying, but Kamel was able to distinguish it, he overcame the tools of disinformation to change the tone of that sound.

"That's you, it's you. Ahmed Al-Shawzan." Kamel said.

"It's nice that you know the voice of your enemy before your lover, and the most beautiful thing is that you know my real name yet, this is a good start to working and playing together."

Shawzan lit the two other holes to show the face of Pilgrim Kamel standing opposite him. Then, he came to his side carrying an electric whip working whenever he pressed it. The whip gave the sound of electric contact and sparks. Shawzan walked revolving around his victim, and without a word, stung him on his knees.

Kamel screamed affected of the intensity of electricity, and Shawzan turned around him as he gathered his throat and spit it green over him, then said:

"I remembered something important that Your Master, Al Mualemi said in one of his episodes: 'Man lives his life with samples of the torments of hell, because divine torment is the last sign of deterrence.' According to your friend's confessions, these are samples of the torments of hell that have been prepared for you and like you."

Then, he began to experiment with his whip in different areas; he may know the severity of his victim's tolerance, his weaknesses, and which areas are more sensitive and responsive to the electric current. Shawzan got the answer only two minutes later. He raised his fist screaming:

"Yes, the knees but from behind, excellent."

The opening session did not take place after discovering those weaknesses, ordered his executioners to stand Pilgrim Kamel on his legs for three full days, he was blindfolded, the guards rotated around their victim enjoying their job, and whenever he wanted to bend his knees or to sit down, he was struck with a truncheon on them from the front, and if he tried again, he was hit with the electric whip at the same time, but in front of the knees and behind them, he was tired and relieved of pain and his legs gave up, he was no longer able to stand. He fell asleep after a long and exhaustive day, until he nearly fell asleep in a stand-up position; tried to sleep, but they poured a bucket of chilly water on his head which mixed with his sweat; he woke up and fell into a sudden coma.

After the experimental program of various torture, Shawzan returned with his reddish eyes, ordered to untie Kamel's hands; The victim stood like the crucified Christ, and he sees Shawzan smoking his cigarette and puffing smoke in his face, he burnt his entire cigarette into different areas, and then started giggling loudly filled with the smell of barbecue.

"Your Master friend didn't get the honor of meeting me here, I wish I strongly could. but now, you must take his part before yours, to double the agony you have, I will punish everything that doubles in you: the legs, hands, lungs, kidneys, eyes and so on. I will uproot anything individual, because it will break the rule, it will torture you alone without feeling the torture of your traitor friend, and this is a great injustice, it is a great injustice to oppress anyone. I am so confident that you will admit and confess what you have done and what you have not done. You will admit what your friend did and what he didn't, you're going to tell me about every felony that happened or didn't happen, that's our fair law here, the law of binaries. But in the end, make sure you get all your part, and above all that a kiss, do you want it now?"

Pilgrim Kamel was about to speak or say even one word, but Shawzan warned violently: every word has punishment, beware to say what I do not desire and want, what your friend said in front of the king and Minister of Defense is enough, you know everything, his words were like bullets directed at my chest.

Kamel's legs were tied over his feet with iron chains, and he slowed down on his back, a large stick inserted from behind his knees, then folded the knees on the stick, tied the hands from the wrists and became over the legs, then lifted the stick and Kamel was hold of it; he swung in the cell space like a pendulum, groaned in pain and the tough stick. Shawzan stood holding the electric whip with his left and a bamboo truncheon on his right. The series of forced interrogations or confessions began:

"You will first tell me about your first meeting with Al Mualemi, when it happened, where and how it was."

"My first meeting with him was in Arak, specifically in the Husseini seminary there, and then we met in his council in the presence of his uncle Al-Faqih, and I do not remember specifically in any year, but it was more than twenty years ago." Kamel answered.

Shawzan put the power cord down the foot of Pilgrim Kamel, whose body rose and screamed terrified of the power supply, and said, laughing:

"This (tremor) disturbs your memory and will remind you in the smallest detail and with all the dates, you will not forget anything anymore. And where did you meet him, who else was with you?"

"After Arak, I met him in Burqan, then here in Tablistan."

"Where did your plan start for the coup attempt against the regime who hosted you?"

"There was no plan to overthrow anyone, the orders were given to Mr. Al Mualemi from the three ministers, and from the official authorities, so he appeared on the weekly television program known to everyone in Tablistan, he was appointed as a defense adviser, and then was granted citizenship in just one year by the King himself, his work in the light was clear, and with an official statement from the Kingdom."

"We know all that but want nothing but what you know. Do you get it, Kamel?"

The electric shock was put on where the kidneys are from behind, and as soon as Pilgrim Kamel was about to faint or die, the source of the pain was removed. Then came a bucket of chilly water filled with ice cubes:

"Who works with you in the Awareness Fund here?"

"All the people you know."

Then, Pilgrim Kamel fell into a coma, and ended one of the scenes of torture, so its episodes continue afterwards, and the series of torture and the removal of nails and confessions of

Kamel continue for less than a year, it was enough for him to lose his mind and to keep him weak memory which almost lost, to destroy his powers and follow various diseases, the first of which was high blood pressure, and diabetes.

As Pilgrim Kamel was about to die death, he was taken to be treated and recovered secretly in a private hospital. Then the whole scene is returned with iron hands.

Before the end of the ill-fated year, in a parallel event, the Royal Court summoned the kingdom's security officials, an official meeting was prepared on the royal order, at which the King spoke at a conference attended by senior officials and dignitaries in the Kingdom, it was covered by the international media.

He said, "The honorable presence, in my behalf name, The King of Tablistan, I would like to express my sincere thanks to you for what you have been doing to serve the beloved Kingdom of Tablistan and its generous people. I always recommend that you keep the human being in this land in your sights, and that every criminal should take his punishment, and that the dignity of the human being and his religion right and doctrine to be preserved, and that everyone receives equal rights. We also affirm our rejection of injustice in all its forms, reject individual transgressions, and punish them strongly, we are all responsible to Allah almighty, and everyone is accounted in no way, whoever wronged my name or abused the power available to him; I am innocent of him and his actions, and he must get his punishment in this world before the hereafter, peace be upon you and god's mercy and blessings."

I was, at that period, watching the king's inactive body, so I prepared myself to leave him for a final departure, I was waiting for the appropriate time and his final decision, souls never leave their bodies unless those bodies are bored or the mind declares its desire to stop the orders to survive, as soon as the right time approached, I found Azrael hovering in the space of the exhausted body. I do not deny the amount of awe that I have suffered as I prepare to enter the isthmus, the huge tunnel that will take me from worldly life to the second, while the body remains under the regolith. Therefore, I examined the matter with the king's mind, and together we came to a common conclusion: The king's body would not be able to perform the functions required to survive. So, the agreement came with the mind: I will leave the body to avoid the pain conveyed by the dilapidated organs of the mind. We agreed calmly.

At that time, the mind decided to recommend as he recalled his decisions, and to lament his status as the first official responsible for what happened to the King, acknowledging his mistakes and shortcomings. It's a kind of guilt, that trick which your inner ego sits on you; the sense of mind dissatisfied because the lusts of the body went against what he wanted. As an expression of this clash between mind and body, the heart reduces its supplement of blood, and man feels a tingling in the heart, thus, human beings are known to call it a prick of conscience; at that time, I was talking with the mind:

"The injustice of your entourage haunts you, and your throne has not guaranteed you eternal happiness."

From that moment on, I became more prepared to leave the king's body, waiting for the opportunity to slip from his body, to go from his distress, to cross the isthmus toward the heavens we are at now, and no one can know his end and feel his death but himself. I was able that time to read what is going on in the king's mind and his constant conflict with his body, the body that began to reject what he was dictated and suggested to him; therefore, I wanted the king to do a public meeting wishing that he will ease his scourge, every bad work going on the land of Tablistan, the king will be hit a lot, and I no longer like to stay in the whole world, I used to put obstacles between the king's mind and his body to separate, so the body himself helps me to leave.

I soon wished to meet Azrael, the majestic king whom Hamidel had previously seen, and she was appalled by him. No doubt, he appalled me too in our first meeting, and as soon as he accomplished his mission and took me from the legs of the king's body, his news was interrupted, and I didn't find him afterwards but here in the second sky. I left the lower heaven to the second, and my body continued to disintegrate under the regolith... But now, Hamidel, I am responsible for everything, it is a sustainable responsibility. I was feeling the grievances that were in Tablistan and I didn't know them accurately, but I became responsible here, and the responsibility is complicated, the pain of death was nothing but a simplified picture of the horror of the scene that I saw on my way to the second heaven. In those later hours, I saw the Kingdom of Tablistan from the high heavens, I saw all the scenes of injustice before the scenes of justice. Hence forward, I saw the torments of Pilgrim Kamel, who soon passed away from the world until I came to hover around his body, so I saw you in Hamid's body asking for knowledge. And here I am, Hamidel, following what happened to a whole body at the hands of the Shawzan and his statesmen. That man who used the powers misplaced; he abused me before himself.

Let us now come back together to follow the scene of the perception and see what has happened to the body of Pilgrim Kamel, and how the torment has claimed his body. Can I atone for the injustices that statesmen have done that will never end? Let's go, soul, let's follow the words and actions of the Shawzan.

The special security guard knocked on the door of Shawzan's Office, who authorized him to enter, he said:

"There's a lady out there asking to meet you, sir."

"Who is this lady?"

"I don't know, sir." The guard replied.

The Shawzan opened the surveillance screen that lies behind his desk and saw… He saw Maya standing in all her adornment and charm at the main door of the Criminal Investigation Bureau. He told the guard: Enter her in a hurry, I am waiting for her, enter her now and quickly.

Maya entered Shawzan's office, he greeted her from alongside his desk, shaking her hands warmly and saying,
"I've been expecting this visit for a long time. You've been late since your first visit, but you are always welcome, have a seat please."

Maya walked in front of him wearing her black cloak, and it appeared underneath her hooded body, while her hair appeared under the veil (Sheila) which was not fixed perfectly. Shawzan paused as Maya sat in front of him. He, as most men, collapsed under the magic of excessive femininity, Maya realized what the Shawzan wanted, knowing since begging that adultery is a slip for man but crime for woman. She gave him direct rejection with a sign from her palm; thus, he said:

"Welcome Maya, Shawzan is still on his promise, and I hope you keep your promise as well."

"How is he my husband's father now? Where is he?"

"Your uncle is between life and death because of his illnesses that surprised him while being in prison."

"I want to get rid of him once and for all."

"So, tell us first, let's listen from you to what was going on in your house between Al Mualemi and Pilgrim Kamel, and after we get all this information, I will give you what you wanted, I will give you the promised reward."

Maya began her series of revelations and confessions, while Shawzan kept listening and enjoying, smiling as he watched her body at the same time, as his wishes were fulfilled. He became at the top of the ecstasy as he enjoyed the spirit of victory, waiting to sip the toast of victory. As soon as Maya finished her audio recordings, he asked to return six days later, he now knows her much better, knew that conscience was not assassinated but gradually killed, then shook her hand as he reminded her:

"Shawzan is a word. If he promises, fulfills. You will come here on time, we will get rid of your uncle Kamel so that you take over Hamid, and you will take the big prize I promised you myself in the name of the King, you should remember that I will never break my promise, do remember that Maya… remember."

Maya left Shawzan who went out to the torture cell to finish his mission perfectly. Hamidel and I are watching what he will do, and how he will use the king's authority to achieve his goals and his chest swells. Shawzan came to Kamel who was exhausted, he was almost faint from the severity of fatigue and pain. He told him biting on his lower lip:

"Your end is so close; I'm going through all binary things from the legs to the ears."

Kamel groaned as he was moaning:

"Kill me and comfort me, this slow death is harsher than death itself."

Shawzan laughed at the top of his voice, which became like squealing on his lips, echoing: Murder is not a crime, Kamel, but the crime is our inability to kill those who deserve to be killed. Then, Shawzan stung his victim with the electric whip again asking him: What do you say? Pilgrim Kamel could not say a word, so Shawzan said rather than him:

"Very beautiful, silence is a sign of satisfaction… Good job."

While he was alone with Kamel, he laughed too loudly. Then, he started with Kamel's legs, so the rest of the body rose, went up to the knees, so the whole body collapsed, squeezed the testicles, so the eyes receded. He went on until he got to the heart. Hence Shawzan was angry of who created the heart, saying:

"This is never fair, this is an obscene injustice, the heart has no counterpart or similarity in the whole body; it must be uprooted from its place."

He took out his knife, tasted it with the front of his tongue, inserted it, kept it there, and pulled it out, tasted the blood and smelled it. He took his tongue out between his lips moving them to the far sides, he cheered up… then complete the mission. He put the heart in the grip of his right, raising his left fist, he looked at his fists parallel with a laugh: "This is justice, now the heart has a similar."

Shawzan put Kamel's heart in a black plastic bag and tied it tightly, washed his mouth and hands to remove all the red stains, and put the bag in his office refrigerator. He called his guard and ordered him to bring in the specialist who put in the seven stitches, cleaned the whole place, and hid the evidence from the investigational experts. Shawzan hid all the evidence, and he didn't know I was in second heaven watching him, and someone who has been watching the whole universe.

The curtain of that scene was cast, the scene which captures who sees or reads it. Then, he lifted the curtain on the other side, to see Maya greeting Hamid in her house, and saying goodbye while he smiled at her. She gave her baby, Kamel, to his grandmother. Maya left without being asked where based on the (honor agreement) between the spouses.

She arrived at Shawzan office on time, he didn't stand welcoming as the previous time. She sat in the same chair, and he stayed behind his office with a swollen chest, smiled at him and lured him to talk; he shamelessly asked to get her body, but she said, "Taboo."

He repeated it but she insisted on her refusal. He rose from his place saying: the forbidden relationship is also a kind of love, Maya, but religious people call it a sin, and we do not know why.

He went to the mini fridge to the left of his office, drank the toast victory, got the black bag, stood in front of Maya, who sat looking at him, and he said with a promising laugh:

"Always remember, Shawzan does never forget his promise even if immoral hated, this is what I promised you when I was at your house, on the night of your uncle's arrest, then confirmed my promise here, go ahead, take the prize, but do not open it until you are outside this building of investigations."

Hamidel has come out of her place, and the scene continues about Shawzan and what he's doing in his office. I asked her,

"What's wrong with you, Soul?"

She said:

"Let's just cast the veil of the perception theater a little bit, and let's just have enough now of what Shawzan has done, his role has ended, and his chapters are complete. We must follow Maya's path without being able to intercept her, because a woman who is not ashamed, can't get in her face."

They already followed Maya on her way home, she put the bag on the car seat next to her, pressed it and found it cold. She said angrily:

"You are a liar, mean and criminal, Shawzan does not lie!"

"It's just a piece of cold candy. She opened the black bag suddenly. She was stunned while Hamidel was watching."

The next noon came, and she waited to precede everyone to Pilgrim Kamel's grave, and she went ahead of everyone. She dug up by her hand on the side of the grave and buried the greatest secret ten inches or more. Then she retreated and stood. Women came to visit their dead, Hamid's mother came with them and read few verses from the Holy Quran. Hamid's mother was afraid that the tomb would be exhumed or that some dirt would be removed from him because of a deep fear. Maya feared that matter twice and more, she would be so happy if a shrine were built on the tomb that all secrets would evaporate and go to their creator, hence forward. It is available for those who are concerned of the perception theater, to follow its chapters. Maya left a few minutes later with Hamid's mother, marching along the line between the children's graves and the rest, waiting for the promised hour.

While waiting for that promised and anticipated hour and what would come to that matter, and from the holy mountain of Turr, the veil was lifted to the third scene of perception.

(11)

It became very difficult, and in the world life that Hamid still clings to like all human beings, he can see with his own eyes those cruel scenes that Shawzan and his collaborators inflicted on his father, torture based on healing, revenge and the uncontrolled use of power handed over to him and his associates, as we saw in the previous scene of perception; the trust given to him was based on the closest and most loyal authority to it. While freedom from the body has given Hamid a great spiritual energy, his presence in the lower heaven has made him carry many of the diseases that burden and prevent him from flying to the second heaven as he always wishes; that's why his eternal visits were replaced by other preceptive.

Despite all this, it has become more difficult to visit him. So, what is the way to your soul, Hamid? And how to telepathize with Hamidel? Hamid has become a grudge against the people, led by Maya and Shawzan, which stands as a barrier to the movement of lights from which we, the souls, were created.

It was not possible for me to visit him again, despite Hamidel's habit and anticipation of him, those visits were easy at beginning, because his spiritual readiness was innate, based on love and a desire to know the truth, that love is the secret of the survival and happiness of souls. As love has been set aside and became timid, it is difficult for me to express to his soul through his forelock, through that point between his eyelids and at the bottom of his forehead, Hamid did not realize that the greatness of the whole universe involved his two sides, he didn't know that his soul is the creator and the creature, the sender, and the receiver; therefore, the mission is difficult and may impossible. But… It was possible to find another way, and an alternative way to perform the task that lifts me from the second heaven to those highest, I searched for a soul that is healed in the earth and has no human diseases, pure and still hovers between a human being's sides who is closer in his purity to the world of souls. I searched for that soul that bears those special characteristics, which are still suffocated in a body of a human… Until I found it inside a man known between his family and his acquaintances Ibrahim Garien.

In order to carry out that alternative mission, which will help Hamid to reach the truth. I tried to telepathy with Garien's soul that was satisfied and confident and satisfied, she was at the height of serenity, never desecrated by the qualities of humankind; his soul (Ebrael) overtook his mind, and the body is under control by his soul. As he differed from human beings, they called him in vain the madman or Garien, because he has a pair of jinn as they think, and they didn't know that he was superior to them, even though he exceeded the laws that human beings had set for them! I came one morning to Ebrael while her body was awake, distracted, soul sized.

"Can you help Hamid see what happened to his father while he was still in the lower heavens?"

Ebrael showed no resentment other than a usual and predictable question.

"Why did you choose in particular?"

"You know, Ebrael, that the human body falls between two forces that try to move it as they desire, namely, the power of soul and the power of body, and often the mind obeys the power of desires, so that the body performs its desires while the soul becomes only a witness to the act."

Ebrael was listening to me, as if I'm adding nothing new to her knowledge, as it is only a spiritual postulate, then I found acceptance to do the good that she used to do not long ago, she said:

"You know that I supported the body of Ibrahim Al-Garien to disrupt the work of his mind, so people called him crazy since childhood, and so also all his movements and actions became in accordance with my orders, while I left to his mind some things that concern the body only such as eating, drinking, sleeping, urine output and others."

I was happy with this brief telepathy with Ebrael, I found her acceptance and self-evident, which helped me to speak increasingly.

"So, it's all possible!" I spoke.

"Say what's behind you, I'm receiving your words as rain atoms."

"You must take Garien to the way of Hamid on his way to Friday prayers, and you must engage him in a dialogue through which Garien can attract him. Hence forward, your mission is going to be possible."

"What mission are you telepathizing about?"

"To tell him and through the tongue of Garien what happened to his father while he was in prison. Whether Pilgrim Kamel was killed or died naturally."

Soon after, the promised Friday came, which preceded the burial body day. Hamid went out toward the awareness mosque built by Al Mualemi in the capital, he saw Garien sat as usual on the step of the mosque, wearing a white dress and a red scarf (*Ghitra*) on the head, and above his head put (headband) as if he wanted to assure the predominance of his mind in front of the aspirations of his soul. Hamid shook hands with Garien with the same reassuring and does not know what that man hides, and then welcomed him warmly:

"Peace be upon you."

"Peace be upon you too." He said it as he barely opened his mouth to get the letters clear from his mouth.

Hamid asked Garien, shaking his hands:
"You knew me?"

Ebrael's answer was shocking while coming on the tongue of Garien, and she wants to get directly into the subject that oversees and to accomplish it:

"What I know is that your father is dead, you are not important to be known!"

Hamid was shocked by the Garien's answer, and Ebrael addressed him with another, more perplexing request:

"I now want this watch in your hand."

"Do you know how to read the time from the watch? Why do you need it?"

"What do you need, and your father is dead?"

Hamid left Garien stunned after he promised to bring him the watch later, Hamid was filled with the request of Garien, what does the death of Pilgrim Kamel have to do with the watch that Ibrahim wants?

As for Ebrael, the mission began successfully and linked Hamid to her to get to him again, so that she begins to inform Hamid and a hint of what happened to his father in the central prison during being interrogated by Shawzan and his officials.

The Imam of Friday began his weekly sermon, and when he talked about the political affairs in the Kingdom of Tablistan, he became cautious in addressing the bitter conflict between the leftist's movement and the government, and therefore deliberately went on to talk about the sedition that started there from the Republic of Arak: Ideological differences and their impact on the awareness work between the Alawite seminary and the Husseini seminary.

Here Hamid put both his palms on his head asking himself: I have seen everything this Imam is talking about beforehand, I am sure of that, but how did I see all this and where? Then the Imam talked about the most effective way to confront the oppressor, and should Imam Hussein be invoked as a model in his revolution against the oppressor, or to humiliate the unjust ruler for the good of the nation and to save blood of the people as his brother Imam Hassan did? Hamid began to reveal to himself: the unjust ruler must be confronted, even with a word or poem, even if this results in stalking, the overthrow of nationality and exile from the country! Then he asked himself: Who told you all, Hamid, where did you get these images and views?

After Friday's sermon, Hamid quickly shook hands with some worshippers and went out to his house. But Garien kept waiting for him repeating:

"The watch, the watch, your father died, and you don't need it anymore."

Hamid pulled Garien from his wrist saying:

"I'll give you the watch if you tell me about the watch's relationship with my father's death, deal?"

Garien was waiting silently while Hamid was reading the details in his face, seeing the movements of his lips as if there were some hums. When Hamid's eyes met the eyes of Garien and fell into her beam, he found her pupil changing in assorted colors, until it became a transparent gel that almost saw what was behind. Garien's soul asked her body to close her eyes and turn away so that she would not be discovered while she was standing behind them. Hamid left Garien in front of the Awareness Mosque and said: I will meet you tomorrow here before noon prayers. Qarien replied: Don't forget the watch.

Luckily, Hamid arrived at his house, and his mother greeted

him while Maya was out. The mother said:

"Your wife went out two hours before the prayer, she maybe now at her family's house, I did not ask her considering the agreement between you."

Hamid felt that better, and his mother left for her room with the Holy Quran in her hand. Hamid lay in his usual chair on the side of the hall. He seemed happy as he stared at space across the same point, realizing that silently contemplating is the right way to wakefulness, and that misery is once your mind stopped meditating. He began to breathe deeply and regularly (Bot/To, Boot/Too). He forgot the world gradually, so did the world. He spat to the world, so she welcomed him. When his breath was set, he closed his eyes; he became clear and high.

He began to look deep down for Pure Mind until he found him waiting for him there in his depths. He started by talking:

"The stripping of the world and its luxuries allows your soul to search for images of perfection and total qualities, that's why you have found me now, Hamid."

"Garien has linked the watch I wear to my father's death. And I never understood that troubled relationship!"

"You will understand it well, Hamid, if you dismantle what he said and then re-install it, and if you think that words don't describe things as much as our feelings do."

"Our feelings?"

His exhalation and inhalation have risen, the space between them grew and expanded steadily. In this space, Pure Mind has found the opportunity to set things in their appropriate places: "You are fully aware of what human beings are saying when they classify people as sane and crazy. A reasonable person who observes custom and general laws in public, but penetrates them in secret, and the madman or crazy does not recognize those laws in his secret nor public. But may I ask you?"

Hamidel was amazed by this question itself: "I asked you to

answer my bewildered questions with her, but it's okay if you ask too,"

"You know envy, jealousy, hatred, etc., and you know that they are human diseases, but have you ever asked yourself who gets them, the wise or the mad?"

"Wise, of course." Hamid answered without any slight reaper of what would be.

"Your minded people are sick, your mads are healthy. Your wise people are bodies, your madmen are souls."

In the still sitting room, the mother put her right on Hamid's shoulder, inviting him to lunch, but she listens to him whispering, repeating: your madmen are souls, your madmen are souls, your madmen are souls.

It did not frighten her, she used to various stages of Hamid and strange since the departure of his father, woke him up and said:

"You will not stop these things and wonders if your father's body is not buried, we did not get to know what happened to your father until now, and we did not relax his body in his grave."

They had lunch together silently as if nothing had happened, they left, each to his room. When Maya came, she found her husband sitting on the edge of his bed, she sat on the other side, and her child left her to his father who kissed him and held him to his chest.

Hamid waited the next day until the end of the morning, and soon left for the mosque, saying,

"Can Qarien keep his promise?"

Then he quickly turned around: "Who was the madman in fact, is it me or him? We are sick with our minds, and you are healthy with your souls, we must warn some legacies, some of them are mad."

Hamid sat on the same step as Garien does every day, dressing like him, and as soon as someone crosses, he greets him wrongly. Nobody realized the truth but some. A few minutes later, Garien came to him automatically and he knew where his legs would take him except through habit.

Hamid took off the watch he was wearing and gave it to Garien.

"Take it, that's what you asked for, but tell me what my father's death has to do with this watch?"

Garien took the watch for joy and didn't seem to know anything to hide. He took the watch and before he left, threw the same fluctuating and jelly-eyed look into Hamid's eyes, and then said to him,

"Stay here, be me and you'll know everything on your own."

Hamid turned his back on the wall behind the step, recalling the words of Garien:

"Be me and you will know everything, be me."

"How can I be him? And who is this Garien? He's crazy and mad. He has no mind, who is he?" Hamid wondered.

"It is a soul that lives in inner peace, a soul that moves a body without a mind subject to its desires…" I answered Him.

Hamid ran after Garien, so he might come back. He came closed to him saying:

"We haven't finished our conversation yet."

"I'll see you. I will find you before you do, but once necessary."

And he's gone.

(12)

By the end of the seven dramatic days which followed the departure of Pilgrim Kamel, and being his body in the refrigerator of the morgue of the capital hospital based on an unwritten agreement between mother and her son Hamid, with Falah the driver of the morgue, Hamid has no other choice but to ask Falah to take the body of his father to the cemetery before things get complicated, and the man falls in the forbidden, as soon as the duty supervisor on the morgue inspects it tomorrow morning. For all these, Falah called Hamid:

"Hello, Hamid, I'm waiting for you on the same date."

"It's Okay." Hamid replied.

"Your father's body must be exhumed, before things get complicated and we fall into the forbidden, I think you understand me, and I need no more to explain."

"Never mind, Good. Wait for me at 10:00."

Hamid came on time, followed the same previous steps, and Falah brought him to the morgue in his usual secret manner. From there, Falah was sure that his guest would do what he wanted, and he would take his father's body to where it should be. That was his final impression. As soon as the two entered the land of the dead, the land phone at the receptionist's desk rang, Falah asked Hamid to leave and said:

"I hope it isn't the supervisor, and he is not on his way to the morgue, listen… If this happens and he suddenly enters here, you must hide inside, If the supervisor sees you here, Hamid, we will have a disaster."

"Where can I hide?"

"Open one of the refrigerators and throw yourself inside, that may help." Falah quickly replied.

Falah's intuition was right, and while talking to the supervisor in charge, he pointed to Hamid by rotating his lips, and with the movement of his right hand like he was throwing out flies! Hamid understood who was lurking behind the call; Hamid entered refrigerator number six, near his father's body in refrigerator number five, lay down with his head deep, and then pulled the door of the refrigerator from the inside with his toes; it was almost closed completely, but he kept a small amount of the door open, to see through it the life of the world.

As time passed, Hamid felt the wintry weather inside, holding his hands to his chest, pulling his knees to his stomach, perhaps warming each other. But… His teeth started to catch you and applied to each other from the cold.

He said:

"In the name of Allah, they will say, Our Lord, you made us lifeless twice and gave us life twice, and we have confessed our sins. So, is there to an exit anyway?"

"Finally, Hamid, here you are dragging yourself to death on…"

He warned that he would not move so as not to draw attention, and soon his heart had diminished, he closed his eyes and his sense of life faded; hence forward, what a wonderful moment! I came to him:

"You are welcome, Hamidel, our meeting is renewed as usual until the goal is complete."

"Kingel, where have you been? I have been waiting for you."

"Next to you, I'm always watching you. Lest a bit of you

leaves your body and see the whole universe by examining the movement in your body, to stay in the heaven of your body that resembles the second heaven and follow another scene from the theater of perception that you know, an advanced scene in order of the previous perception scene."

"Let us leave with some ether, may I get rid of this heavy body soon."

"You were just clinging to the life of the world, and now you are clinging to the afterlife, it was only one hour in between, as if you had seen death for what it is; whoever hoped to die, he didn't fear him."

Hamidel accepted the irony with satisfaction and willingness, she realized that stability is not possibility. We left from our moment to the heaven of Hamid's body. And there, we did the whole usual steps quickly. We removed the veil of the Theater of Perception, which looked like the Eternal Theater as we settled together to the Holy Mountain of Turr. We began to follow another perceptive scene, an advanced scene which is full of details in the history of the Kingdom of Tablistan, combining Al Mualemi and its redeemed King.

The Fourth Perception Scene

Characters: Al Mualemi, The King, Ministers, Shawzan.
Location: Al Mualemi's office at the Ministry of Defense, King's Court.
There is only Mr. Al Mualemi sitting in the middle of his office, his name stands out gilded over the lavish brown office: Mr. Mahdi Al Mualemi/ Ministry of Defense's Advisor, Kingdom of Tablistan. The Master leaves his seat with a bumper velvet back, puts his black turban on the his desk, hangs his worn cloak over the hanger that holds nothing, like an autumn tree, and then begins to talk to himself, laments and blames it, adores her: Since you left Republic of Arak and God almighty takes care of you, he stand by you and correct your mistakes wherever you go, as if the whole thing is prepared in advance, you have no dog in the race, your life may have tough situations, but I know that it is for your goodness and guidance, it paves your future and your coming affairs. You gave a poem there at the ruling party's celebration in Arak on their Republican day, and you, unlike all the attendees, gave a poem of no praise as the others used to, your goal wasn't to fight the regime there but uniqueness and prominence, the best way to achieve those goals was to expose the leader and get out on him, it is The Ego that is between your side, master, your desire to be always a pioneer in the vanguard of people, knowing that the power of the masses wherever they are is the only force capable of change, to defeat the prevailing and inherited. You had to be the leader of those masses, ride its

back, and control the conditions, to use them in your future favor.

The master then lay on the black couch opposite his office, put his back on the end and his legs on the other end, and he continued to remember the events, admitting to himself:

"You wanted to move the masses that, once they meet, choose a leader. You know that the public is a herd that does not spare its leader and his guide. You, as a leader, were basically bound by a specific idea, the idea of pure opposition, and became obsessed with it over time. Nothing, even prison, could displace that idea from your mind but death. You knew that leaders are not men of thought but men of practice and engagement, oppression and excessive cruelty is only increasing their insistence."

Moreover, Mahdi, you left your homeland, fleeing, not afraid, as you claim, to the state of Burqan, to be haunted by the hands of the leader of Arak and his intelligence, as if it were an octopus with no borders; so, you will be commonly known. You would expect your uncle to be killed accordingly in the Cedar Republic, and from your crisis, you run back into the hearts of people before their homes in Burqan, to the country of light and peace, as if it were a rest stop for a breathtaking warrior.

But now, you have already been involved in the situations and behaviors of the Kingdom of Tablistan. How will you survive and where to go? You are now here in Tablistan, and you have been asked to raise the banner of reform, fight the poisonous left-wing ideology, and spread the teachings of the religion; its request has been officially requested by the King himself.

Al Mualemi moves in the corners of his office in a circular image, he continues to talk to himself as if he were arguing with her, blaming, and telling her:

"Your luck is hidden in one corner of your life, beware that your life is circular, master."

Here, Hamidel personally attests the loss of Al Mualemi and the state of contradiction he is experiencing; so, she comes near asking me and Kingel, whose signs of disease are invading his body there:

"What does all this theatrical scene have to do with the death of my father, who is looking for satisfactory answers to his death?"

I Interrupt her:

"Did you forget that the king himself is one of the main actors in those scenes? And those kings are the first to be questioned on the promised day, didn't you see me there as a body? Didn't you realize what I was aiming at in the world? When I watch myself from here, I know that the King's crown and its power are nothing but a mosquito wing."

Hamidel shuts up and nods her head in approval. And we go back to follow the scene of the perception, so Al Mualemi sits in the bumper seat. He continues to address himself:

"From the state of Burqan, you land on to the Kingdom of Tablistan, master, the events take you here, to the land of Tablistan, between a master, a merchant, and several ministers, then in front of the king himself. By time, you suddenly find yourself carrying its nationality, and you are appointed a defense adviser based on the opinions and ideas that have been accepted by the King and his advisers, which is all to complete your plan and your religious role, as you would like to be seen by others."

Suddenly, without introductions, the door is knocked on, and the director of the Royal Court enters and invites him to meet the promised and anticipated Date. He stands beside him while his escorts stay near the door, inside and outside. Al Mualemi then finds himself inside the Royal Court again, seeing that the number of ministers has been greatly reduced, with only the ministers of defense and information remaining silently, nothing moves but their eyelashes and breathes. No officials remain but Shawzan, the director of public security who seems to sulky as when he usually meets Al Mualemi. This time, the king stands in honor of the comer, he takes three steps toward Al Mualemi, while the director of the Royal Court retreats and remains silent and rages badly on his face.

"God bless you, your highness."

"Good evening, brother."

"Your brother?"

"I have seen your book."

'The Struggle', I have read it in letter by letter, I have been very impressed by your attempts to develop a new modern concept of political and military concepts, those derived from the book Approach of Rhetoric as you mentioned, but I did not understand what you said specifically about the issue of leadership, how can leadership be more self-satisfied than a service to peoples and the masses?"

Al Mualemi expected this question because it is the cornerstone of many of the historical events of humankind. He said: - Your highness, let me give you a historical example, you must have read and heard about Napoleon Bonaparte, the man who once said in the French State Council:

"I could not finish the Vande War until I pretended to be a true Catholic, and I could neither be settled in Egypt, until I pretended to be a pious Muslim, and when I pretended to be an extremist papal, I could get the trust of the priests in Italy. So, if I had been able to rule the Jews, I would have given them the Temple of the Prophet Solomon."

Your majesty, Napoleon was thinking only of himself, but he

couldn't get his strength only by adopting the voice of the masses and became obsessed with the voice of the people even on his deathbed!

Whenever Al Mualemi talks about something, or cites an incident, the more the king and the rest of the audience are attached to him. As for Shawzan, the sense of security remained at the ready, he does not trust or believe the others, sleeps only like a wolf, closes one eye, and keeps the other to protect him!

The king praised Al Mualemi very much and referred to him in pride, and explained that based on security reports, the level of violence has decreased and the number of people writing left-wing slogans on the walls has decreased, as confirmed by reports since Al Mualemi began presenting his weekly program called *'My success.'*

Al Mualemi lowered his eyes as he was listening, then spoke in a more modest form saying:

"I did nothing to people but let them feel my love and my scare for them, I let them feel that those feelings represent the officials of the whole government."

Shawzan did not like the speech and humility of Al Mualemi; he replied:

"Hey, you, what love are you talking about? Before you, I was doing the same thing with them, and I think that the intensity and even power have helped us to deter the so-called leftists, we are almost deterring them by force from writing slogans and marches... There is now nobody who writes slogans on the wall's slogans hostile to the Arak leader calling for him to fall."

"Their beliefs and ideas represent a big rock that presses on their chests, and to remove that rock, as you are an experienced security man, you must enter their chests and push it away, but do not remove it from the outside. If you were inside them, the energy of goodness will help you, but if you removed the rock from outside them, you would add a greater load on them. Mr. Shawzan, listen to me well: complete love makes you religious, even if you are not a Muslim, Christian or Jew. Because love makes you pure and clean, you may realize one day that love is also the maker of civilizations."

The King, suddenly, rebuked Shawzan and warned him if he does not stop contradicting the Master, or respect the crown as well:

"Stop it and be polite, unrespect leads to obscenity, beware or I will throw you in prison, where the jailer is equal to the prisoner."

Then, the king smiled half a smile, and added it with an artificial giggle, so the audience laughed sarcastically. The king went toward Mr. Al Mualemi, reassuring him:

"In recognition of your clear efforts in the television awareness program (My Success), and in gratitude for your sincere rhetorical style, considering the great effort you made in writing your book to benefit every citizen in our presence, and in all subsequent civilizations, and your urge pushing people to get around the ruler, for all of this, we find that you are a worthy example to be emulated; For all what we mentioned, we decide, as I am the King of Tablistan, we decide to grant you the nationality. So, you become a citizen we a proud of, who instills the good values of the citizens and works to serve the country through his leading media position. The position that is undoubtedly influential and enlightened pioneer."

"I am at the service of religion wherever." Al Mualemi replied.

"How pure and smart you are, Master!"

Al Mualemi does not hesitate to answer him in the same

tone: "I hope you're always right."

The king then explains that they are in the process of building a military army based on contemporary pillars, and since he found his stray in the book (The Struggle), this bodes well for that project, and here the king asks Al Mualemi confidently:

"I hope that you, Master, will feel comfortable working as a special adviser for defense in our Kingdom, and I hope that you will provide us with all your suggestions that are in the interest of national unity."

"It is a great responsibility, your highness. I hope to be good as you expect me to be, so I serve the Tablistan and its people, as a lift to the religion of Allah almighty, to preserve the Kingdom of Tablistan from every unjust hand. But excuse me your highness, I do reject this position."

"Why? Are you mean to give us?" The king asked and ordered the Head of protocol at the Royal Court to bring what was previously agreed upon. He brought him what he asked for and put it in front of him. The king did not give any chance to Al Mualemi in terms of rejection. The king stood up and so did all the attendees, including Mr. Al Mualemi himself, he asked him to get close, so he did. Al Mualemi stood in front of him looking at the Medal of the Kingdom while it was still in the velvet box. He said:

"I work in the Kingdom as a cleric with a heavenly message, but I am not a politician."

"And who is the politician then?" The King interrupted him.

He said without looking at the two ministers present:

"Only a politician deserves to be honored here, and I don't want to be a politician; a politician is nothing but a smart criminal."

The two ministers were shocked by what they heard and

confronted the king with a smile of satisfaction that reduced the effect of the word. The King lifted the Medal of the Kingdom imitated Mr. Al Mualemi, then gave him a wrapped gift that nobody doubted that it's value, worthy the prominent event of His Majesty the King... The passport of Kingdom of Tablistan, besides an amount of money may tempt Al Mualemi to install the foundations of his citizenship project.

I telepathized with Hamidel, I read her desire to fold this scene after she knew the Al Mualemi's upward line in Kingdom of Tablistan. I knew that she wanted to see the next scene of Maya, but I told her:

"The driver Falah is coming to you, and you must get back to your body immediately."

With this emergency intervention, the fourth scene of perception is over. And then we go back to what is happening in the events of the lower heaven.

Falah found his friend, Hamid, is semi-frozen in the refrigerator number six, pulled him out and lifted to him and then put him with all his weight on the ground, and then brought a heavy blanket from the near reception, put it over Hamid's body, and began to measure his heartbeat through his wrist, and when he sensed the remnants of pulses, he pressed Hamid's chest to speed up those impulses... minutes later, Hamid began to regain consciousness but remained sunken eyes, while his tongue was almost frozen. Falah poured warm water into his mouth, which helped him wake up. He said:

"And where will Al Mualemi go?"

"The name of the morgue supervisor is Ali, not Al Mualemi!" Falah denounced his question.

"And where will my father stay after Al Mualemi leaves?"

His life is now in danger. Shawzan will chase them both. He will punish him. Let's hurry up to him so we save his life.

Falah ignored Hamid's senilities while he was semi-awake, but he captured Hamid's urgent desire to exhume his father's body.

Falah jumped and he pulled Hamid to him: "Your father is there, let's take him back, remove him!"

Falah opened the dead's refrigerator and went to bring the bed of bodies' transporting, but Hamid pulled his father's body, dragged him to him, put him on his shoulder, and walked him to the gate where he met Falah who shouted at him:

"What are you doing, crazy? You're going to get us into a disaster."

He was asked to put the body on the bed, but Hamid refused insisting on carrying his father's body, keeping him away from the hands of the Shawzan. Falah pulled the body from the legs while Hamid from the chest and then the hands; the body slipped out of their hands and fell to the ground. Hamid shouted at Falah:

"You killed my father."

Falah left the body on the ground and grabbed Hamid and dragged him inside and... He slapped him with force that knocked him to the ground. Hamid screamed jerky, so Falah left him and returned to the body, put it on the bed of the dead, tested the outer passage... no one, thank God so much. He pulled the bed into the car, pushed the body inside, closed her door and returned to Hamid's side. He started patting his cheeks as he read verses from the Holy Qur'an, brought him water, washed his face. So, Hamid opened his eyes, and Falah gave him warm water. Hence, Hamid began to regain his worldly senses, but he still feels a terrible headache pressing his head. Falah helped him to stand up, and took him toward the car of the dead, let him in the chair next to him. Hamid slowly regained his breath, his balance, and his consciousness. He recognized Falah next to him, asked him:

"Where to?"

"Cemetery to bury your father's body."

"And where is she now?"

"Behind you, you can see it. Let's read Qur'anic verses to his soul."

Falah drove fast to the cemetery which he knows very well, while Hamid knows the small pre-prepared tomb, which his mother suggested its place. They went with the body to the land that people think is monstrous, and the souls count it as a land of immortality.

On the way to the cemetery, where the end of the world's life is, the human body is hidden in its own tomb, left alone with the wind above, and worms mess with its contents. The driver, Falah, and Hamid drove the car of the dead silently, under the weight of the holiness of death and his majesty.

On the way to achieving the common goal, they met at a security checkpoint, where security officers scattered around it like black locusts; Falah panicked for fear of being exposed, asking about the papers of the deceased, and about the cemetery to which the body would be taken, he told his escort:

"That's what I was afraid of, Hamid. Surprises never occurred to the mind."

He continued sarcastically:

"This is the predicament I put myself in, and it is the same one that will put me in jail hopefully."

Hamid saw fear on the face of the driver Falah for the first time since they met at the entrance to the morgue, since his face was cleared, and saw the black zippers on his forehead.

Hamid rectified, and asked Falah to do the siren, which in

turn could use its influence and give them the way. At the checkpoint, security officers received the letter; they gave away recognizing the impact of disease and death. Falah felt relieved as they made their way to the cemetery in the south-west of the area.

As soon as they crossed safely, Falah shut off the ambulance siren, went to the street he still remembers its details, he parked the ambulance at the same place where he first carried the body, stopped it only two meters from the back entrance of the dead washroom. It was one of the rare times that he carries dead and do not see mourners in the cemetery waiting for their deaths. The two men pulled the body out of the vehicle, put it on the dead-wheel-drive bed, put it into the dead shower place with no effort, and then stood looking at each other.

"What shall we do now?" Falah asked.

"I don't know and honestly, I can't wash my father."

"I think dead washing is like *Janabah* washing, all are similar, but we must change the intention. We just take the water and put the eucalyptus on the shelf there, right behind you."

The two young men agreed to mix water with eucalyptus in the bucket, and Falah would play the role of a washman while Hamid helped him. Hamid turned his head back when Falah was about to open the morgue cloth from Pilgrim Kamel's chest. As soon as he removed it, Hamid was astonished, took a deep breath, and Falah said:

"O, God, we are to God and to Him we shall return."

"What happened and what do you see? I can't look with you."

"You should see with your eyes, Hamid, this situation is not normal."

Hamid forced himself to come to his father's body while it was lying in the shower, remembering the chest image as he last saw it, the seven stitches and the blue body. Then he looked at his father's chest, found the wound site had fallen inside, the roof of the chest and the skin fell inside. Hamid screamed in horror:

"The father's heart was ripped out, and it may have been stolen and sold as well. Oh, my God."

"I'm sorry, but we belong to God, and we return to Him. We were in one disaster, and now two. It is said that the body of the deceased is the remains of man, and his heart is the conscience of man; oh Hamid, this who steals a heart, is like he stole the conscience of humanity."

"That's what we have been promised. And that's exactly what I saw. You are honest, Falah. Therefore, the Pure Mind must find a heart to rest, the heart where stillness and peace are."

"What are you hallucinating? what pure are you talking about? you're back to your madness, Hamid. I saw the wound a week ago with your mother, the chest was intact, but now, the roof of the chest has fallen inside." Falah was explaining.

Hamid said: "Oh my God, you will never understand me as Garien does."

Then, Hamid began looking for me in all the corners of the washing room with his eyes. He said addressing me: "You're here, you must be here."

He is aware of my existence, but he cannot see me, he must meditate carefully, forget the place, stop moving, and be stripped of everything. In the past, he used to come out of the narrowness of the world and its material imprisonment, ascent into the space of the second heaven where he touches the truth and learns the facts. When it is difficult for him to do so, he must meditate now, he must cross from the outside to the inside, from the narrowness of the world to the spaciousness of the soul. He must realize that ascent is either to the vastness of the whole universe, or to the self where the heart is concentrated, as if the center of the whole universe were in the heart of man himself.

He muttered himself: "He who knows himself, he knew the

universe."

Falah interrupted him to ask: "Did a fit of madness come to you again?"

"Who the hell you are talking to, Pure mind, Garien or your ruins? No one here but God, you, and me. You have truly gone mad, Hamid."

Hamid asked Falah to get out of the dead washing room, and stay in the car of the dead, as he did at the first time. Falah deplored this request. At Hamid's urging, Falah left for the car and sat behind its seat. Hamid stood in front of his father's body, focused his attention on the place of the wound that he saw before and still knows him well. He began to look at the places of the stitches accurately as he recalled the moment when Shawzan came into their house at dawn, how he broke the door, and broke the house from the inside. At that time, his father stood in the middle of the hall, and Hamid's mother came next to him, and then Maya and her baby came out, she stood next to him. He remembered how Shawzan and his men looked at her. At that moment, Shawzan asked everyone to go out, to the outside courtyard to search the whole house and check it out; so, Pilgrim Kamel went out first and then his wife, and finally Hamid came out at gunpoint. While Maya had already gone inside with her baby, but she went out to the house yard about ten minutes later, she went out while a lot of the security men were outside, but Shawzan and five other men remained inside. Hamid gazed in the places of stitches; he found the roof of the chest falling inside, so he forgotten the world around him. He then lost the ability to use his five senses, and now able to see me when performing to him, I was in front of him above the wound.

Thus, he saw me and started addressing me:

"This body, Father, is a miniature model of the universe that I used to see at the top, and he who wants to discover the universe, must know human beings. As for that who tormented and killed you, then kidnaped your heart, he knows that your heart seeks the love of God, while heaven and earth do not; congratulations on your body's death, Dad, because you got the second life, you were reborn."

And because Hamid then sees what beyond death, I can breathe words in him as thought, that he can pick them up slowly. I said to him:

"As we removed the eternal veil for the first time, while we were in the second heaven, you always must remove the veil of vision here in the lower heaven, you will see the truth, and you will see the theater of perception. Hamid, you have been given the grace of knowing the annihilation of your father's body, and since you realized the annihilation, you were not afraid of death and its nearby. You are now fully aware of the timeline, and you know that every number for the end is zero, and no matter how long man remains before the resurrection, the whole time is nothing but an hour."

(13)

Hamid and the driver Falah finished burying the body at seven a.m. Then, Hamid returned to his humanity and to his worldly heaven.

His heart was filled with rage and hatred for the king and his ruling regime, I really wished he would keep his human ego recessive and low inside him, and to be dominated by his spiritual egos, which he mastered there in the theaters active and controlling, but now he has returned to his humanity, and to his predecessor as he was. He was angry at Shawzan particularly, because he used his deadly security arm in the wrong way, he used his power violently to control the people of Tablistan. Therefore, how can I address Hamidel and contact her? She has been contaminated by multiple mental illnesses; I'm feared she may fight me too! Anger is a spiritual disease that is like envy, jealousy, hatred, etc. All of them have now made him do not distinguish between the act of Shawzan and the king's desire, between the king himself and his soul who now lends a helping hand to him. When the soul is infected with one of these diseases, it becomes heavy, loaded with more energy that cannot be held. Thus, no one, even me, can lift Hamid's soul to the second heaven of her body or any new heaven, she becomes too heavy for its diseases. Here I must think of another way, such as that of Garien, I must change the way I communicate with his soul, the soul that was transparent when it flew to the second heaven as well as to the heaven of his body, but it becomes heavy gray when filled off with worldly diseases. I became required to talk to her in the lower heavens, to break into his inner heaven together. But can I? Will the task become difficult or impossible? There is no harm in the results whatsoever, but I must try to do my job and my duty to those who have been oppressed in the King of Tablistan; I may get another ascent to Highness.

I came to Hamidel on that night when he buried his father's body in his tomb. I came to her as was Hamid asleep, addressing her in constant vigilance and ready:

"It will be difficult for you, Hamidel, to accompany me to second heaven to complete and preview what happened to Hamid's father, you will never see the Eternal Theater anymore, and it will be difficult for you to fly in the heaven of Hamid's body. But you can help Hamid to master other ways, inspire him that transcendent wisdom. He must think and meditate on the things around him, in the wonders of God's making, he must look at himself, himself only but not others, and when he knows himself, he will know the whole universe. Then, he will achieve the same effect that his soul has achieved while ascent beside me to the high heavens or the heavens of his body. A human who realizes himself individually, realizes the universe and if he can forget the weight of his body while meditating on those creatures; and if he can see what's behind those materials around him. Only then, He's going to find his way into one of them, the universe is in you, man, and you don't realize. That time only, he could talk to the absolute values without the need to leave or ascent. He will be dominated by perfection, and he will be able to interact with the Pure Mind and live conscience and others, and he will know that the world is lighter than a mosquito wing!"

Hamidel, a prisoner in the body of her owner, rose, and as

she found my presence near the body, which was steeped in deep slumber, and she found the image of ether in the body as well, Hamid turned into his right-hand so that he might address me... She said:

"Will I be able to defeat human diseases from Hamid, and become a full light like angels? Am I going to see Pure Mind whom you insist on his presence? will I address him if I perfectly know the work of meditation?"

"Soul of Hamid, the grandson of Adam, human being must first realize that man is better and higher than angels; that's why God glorified her to him and let her prostrate to Adam that first human being. Besides that, Hamidel, angels must also put their hands in the fire once to feel the meaning of pain as human, but they cannot. As for your Hamid, he is the man, who carried good and evil in his chest, and by his choice, he is the master of creation. Ah, Hamid, you may master meditation, so that your soul will rise to you and materialism will be removed from you. Man, thus, sees the creatures with his eyes and feels them with his five senses, but he only realizes them in his spirit, and when he has mastered that, he will see the greatness of the universe and its Creator behind those creatures, including the (ego) between your flanks."

Hamid's body breathed deeply and his eyelids closed to his eyes, as if he realized that there was no need for the eye when talking about apparition. It is like that, if you look at a tree with your eyes, you'll find it with a trunk, roots, leaves, but if you meditate the same tree, and you master the work of meditation, you will find a fully well-established life, breathing, nourishment, sense and even worship. Then, the inanimate will become a living creature, and then you will find me manifest in one, and you will find Pure Mind and patience in the others. You will find the greatness of your Lord in all his creatures. You will see me, Hamid, in you, as your soul saw me for the first time in heaven, you may now consider the goal!

The weight of the speech has become heavy on Hamid's ears, he moved his head to the right and left, as if my conversation with him became a mischievous tinnitus that he would like to get away from. Then, he started gasping and repeating what I said: A tree, Creature, Life, Meditation, King, Shawzan, then, his pronunciation accelerated, recalled the initials tied together: TC, LM, KSH…

His mother came scared, mourned her bad luck: my husband, Kamel died, and my son got crazy, my Lord, your mercy.

Maya followed her as she was watching the results of her plans, even Shawzan had left her, and she did not receive his promised reward but gave her what he can't be given! His mother came to wake him up with some water and Qur'anic verses, then she said:

"This is what we got from Tablistan and its King, the death of the father and the madness of the son, O, my God."

She continued to read verses from the Holy Quran.

As for Maya, she went to her horror and started listening to her husband's delirium and saying: "I don't wish you could be delirious with what's going on around us, Hamid, madness is disclosure, I seek God from you, you're crazy, but you're better than the sane ones."

Hamid woke up from what he was in, and felt as usual a big headache, his center of balance has differed again, his body is between his family and his relatives, but his soul is still in dialogue with me and waiting for the next of the events of Tablistan, he took a drink of water from his mother as he sweats, while Maya repeating:

"I seek refuge with God from the accursed devil."

Then, she read two verses in a voice that hides what's inside. Hamid began to separate his apparition from his reality and regain himself; so, he calmed and settled down himself, he told them:

"I'm fine, don't worry… I want water, then to sleep a little." It seems to be the result of fatigue during this week, please… He drank water and said: I want to sleep a little.

They left the room while Hamid was trying to recall the details of the dialogue that took place between us, and then he wondered about the first steps of meditation, perhaps reaching through it to know the self, and how to know and practice and even master it? He went to his small library, so he may find some books that help him learn the easiest ways of meditation. He searched and searched but nothing. He then sat on the floor facing his books and his father's books, which were arrayed on the shelves of the house library, sorting with his eyes the books he had read from those he had postponed reading, and then recalling the ideas and topics contained in them. After that, he came to the books he was keeping on the waiting list, focusing on every title, and meditating on the book, perhaps knowing what the title was hiding and what was behind the cover, until he took longer at the same shelf, and moving from one to another unconsciously.

He looked at a white book, written its address on the side: *'The Struggle.'* He pulled the book, slipped back stunned, widened his stare, and at that moment wanted to hear himself, but he had to silence all the sounds of the senses inside him first.

He kept looking at the title and found the name of his author: Mr. Mahdi Al Mualemi. He closed his eyes, breathed deeply as he repeated (Bot/To, Boot/Too) and saw the biography of the author which had already been written in his depth. He found him there in Arak, Burqan and Tablistan. He followed his life from that moment until he was expelled from Tablistan, as if his life were in a permanent movement resembled a bicycle if it stopped fell… Then he saw his father in one of the pages, suffering in the hands of the Shawzan.

Now when Hamid had forgotten himself before the universe, he reached his peak; so, I whispered him:

"Hamid, meditation is to cross from the outside to the inside, from the narrowness of the world to the spaciousness of the soul, and without the need to move from the narrowness of the world to the spaciousness of the seven heavens. Self-knowledge, Hamid, is the knowledge of the universe.

And then telepathy became possible to him, I came to him asking his soul to surround her as she remained in the space of self-lurking in his heart, in Hamid's body. I asked her to follow together the next scene of Perception… She accepted.

The Fifth Perception Scene

Characters: Al Mualemi, Kamel, The King, Shawzan.

Place: Tablistan: Al Mualemi's Apartment, King's Palace, Airport.

We are at an advanced scene ahead of what we have seen, showing Mr. Al Mualemi lying in one of his cramped rooms, the house allocated by the General Endowment Department to host him in the capital of Tablistan, and next to him, his friend Pilgrim Kamel, both on a cotton bed, lies on the ground. Suddenly, without any introductions, the phone rings in the hall of the house, and Al Mualemi answers the phone without hesitation:

"Peace be upon you, God's mercy, and blessings."

Al Mualemi did not receive a response to his greeting, no one answered him on the other side. But as soon as Al Mualemi answered the call, the wooden door of the house was forcibly broken, so Shawzan and the security men broke into the whole place, armed with all their equipment, as if they were in a raging war.

From here, the two men met face to face, while Kamel stood by and reads them, perhaps finding the hidden animosity between them. Al Mualemi did not give Shawzan long to say hello and repeated his previous phone greeting: Peace upon you. But Shawzan insisted on not answering him. So, Pilgrim Kamel, in his turn, repeated the same greeting, but no answer, Kamel says denouncing:

"Peace upon you, God's mercy, and blessings."

Shawzan doesn't care about them, and he refers to his men with an understandable head gesture, and the men gather around the Al Mualemi and Kamel, they put the handcuffs on their hands from behind, the two friends showed no resistance. Then, security officers begin to search the whole small house, from its hall to rooms and bathrooms. Chairs and tables are turned, books and notebooks are thrown away, objects are scattered, mattresses and pillows are cut through. But nothing they were looking for was found.

Shawzan speaks to them in a sharp voice: you have been exposed, the Ministry of Foreign Affairs has received a call from the intelligence of the leader of Arak to judge you, and as you know he is the fiercest and most brutal leader of the East, he called us to tell us about a scheme led by you, Al Mualemi in Our kingdom of Tablistan, and led by other followers from Arak. We are asking you now and with a clear royal decision, we ask you to leave Tablistan within three days. You must hand over the passport to the officials at the airport, there is no time for the leader of Arak to wait for investigations and the work of intelligence. But you must thank your Lord so much, His Majesty wants to meet you face to face, it is a farewell meeting. You will come with us now, and we will take your friend to his home until his turn.

But the King, what does the king want from this meeting after I have already been accused without any investigation, and the leader of Arak has become the truest of anyone else?

Listen to me with all the focus, don't make it a long story. In recognition of the place that you had with His Majesty, we will limit the problem to expelling you from Tablistan only, and release your friend, Kamel. Otherwise, all security measures would have been taken in complete secrecy; and it would have been different, and maybe it's all over before it starts.

Al Mualemi replied: "In appreciation of the King as well, can you explain the circumstances and details?"

"You will listen to everything there, in the presence of the King, in the same place where he handed you the honor of nationality and awarded you the first Medal of Honor of the Kingdom."

A part of the veil of perception is lifted, and another part is removed, Shawzan is allowed to enter to the king's court, dragging behind him Al Mualemi handcuffed and behind Kamel behind him. The king sheds his eyes on the Al Mualemi and says:

"How malicious and evil minded you are, Master!"

"I hope you are always right." Al Mualemi answers.

Everyone is silent, amazed by the severity of the situation and its strangeness… Hamidel takes advantage of the tragic situation, asking me as I watch my body and what its five senses have done, and I see that great scene… Hamidel asks me:

"How does Al Mualemi say that to you, excuse me, say that to The King? How can he say: You are right in both cases, when he was satisfied with him, and when he became angry at him?"

I answer her: "Because when you judge someone, you judge your inner self, depending on the ego that controls us, we make judgments. Al Mualemi is not pure or malicious in himself, but he fluctuates according to the psychological state of the king."

Hamidel wonders: "What is my father's situation? I mean Pilgrim Kamel. What is his situation and Al Mualemi is about to leave Tablistan?"

"It was presented in the final chapters of The Perception Theater, and we will probably know more details of what happened between Kamel and Shawzan." I answered.

"Isn't it Shawzan who killed him?" Hamidel sobbed.

"Maybe." I answered.

Then, we remove the veil of perception on another part of the play, and here begins the scene in the waiting room at the International Coast Airport, after the Al Mualemi left Tablistan, he arrived alone at the arrivals gate at the airport to drag his small bag, and as usual, he does not smile, cry nor appear to be affected.

He must check with the transit officer before continuing the expected return trip to Burqan as planned. He has received information from Al Wajih that the threats of the Arak leader no longer exist there, so he can return to Burqan, and stay there without the need for media appearances.

Al Mualemi finished all the official procedures and got a ticket on the international lines of Burqan. But nearly three hours later, Al Mualemi went to the waiting room, put his leather bag next to him, and lay on the chair breathing tight and deep.

The passengers began to occupy the waiting room and fill it gradually, and then one of the travelers arrived wearing the traditional costume of the residents of the region, was carrying a rosary of yellow amber reminded Al Mualemi of Al Wajih's rosary when he first met him in Burqan. The man sat in the row opposite to Al Mualemi, and put his scarf on his eyes as if he wanted to take a nap to sleep in.

Al Mualemi received a sudden telephone call that confused him a little and began to walk around the waiting room. Al Mualemi's dialogue turned into Persian, perhaps it will be difficult for any listener to understand him. It seemed, on the other side, that the caller did not master Arabic and may not speak it, which also means that Al Mualemi has various linguistic abilities enabling him to speak more than one language. He said:

"Peace upon you and god's mercy."

"…"

"I'm very fine."

"..."

"Go to Burqan, take a fake passport, and then go back to Tablistan? Is that possible?"

"..."

"Okay, okay. Goodbye."

The masked, sleepy traveler lifted his mask from his face, looked at Al Mualemi trying to ascertain his identity, and as soon as Al Mualemi noticed him, the man quickly put his mask again, acting as sleepy. A few minutes later, the man left, and when he gave his back to Al Mualemi, he removed his scarf, leaving the passenger lounge area, looking at every direction. An hour later, three security officers came to Al-Muallem's area:

"Can we see your passport and ticket, please?"

Al Mualemi took out what they asked for, gave them. They told him:

"Could you please come with us?"

The officer walked in front of Al Mualemi with two security officers behind him. The eyes of the passengers chasing them, and curiosity fell the departures hall.

Al Mualemi was entered to the detective office who was on duty, he was sitting on his seat, and in front of his desk, this masked man with the gold rosary sat. Al Mualemi knew that the planned plan had been revealed, but he wondered: How did that happen as I spoke in Persian? This man in Arabic must be fluent in Persian as well, it's a slip that might cost you your life, Master.

The officer asked Al Mualemi to sit down after he gave him the passport and his ticket.

Why do you want to leave for Burqan, and they have already asked you to leave, did you forget?

Each situation can remain but impossible.

The officer pointed to the masked man sitting in front of them:

"Do you know this man sitting in front of you, this man who listened to your call?"

The man removed his mask; Al Mualemi was shocked and recalled a Qur'anic verse:{ we have certainly created man in the best stature; then we returned him to the lowest of the low[3]. You are Dherar, the head of general intelligence in Burqan, who offered me help, and he dropped me off before he disappeared at Tablistan Airport. You played your role perfectly; you saved me there to hunt me down here. That's the intelligence, well done.

The officer and Dherar giggled as they looked at Al Mualemi. In a sarcastic way, Dherar said a sentence that Al Mualemi was repeating in the Council of Wajih in Burqan: to realize that you are a liar; you are half honest.

Al Mualemi pulled the mobile device out of his handbag and said with a smile that might prevent them from seeing the destruction of the interior that had happened to him: this mobile is undoubtedly the idol of the era. Dherar stood as he walked into the interrogation room saying: You were in Burqan, Master, and I know your prestige very well. I also know that our national security was compromised, and we had to do what the leadership asks for beside what we want. Then, you came to the kingdom of Tablistan where they asked you to leave after a long time, and here you want to go back to Burqan so that you change your passport and then come back here to Tablistan. That is impossible Master, which is impossible, we can't allow you to get to the prince (Amir) there. What a hellish plan, but it's become disgraced.

The officer then spoke from his chair: We have received

---

[3]. The fig surah:4,5

orders from the Burqan, from Tablistan, and both governments want to deport you to Persia, where you can do whatever you like. And if both governments were aware about to those who hosted you in the two brotherly counties, and if both governments were not accountable to the personalities that hosted you in the two brotherly countries, It would have been hard for you to leave alive. We will withdraw the passport that you have now, give you a pass document to Persia, and after you are on its land, we will have cleared our legal and humanitarian responsibility. Now, go with the security officers until the time of departure, it is the punishment of Allah almighty for your actions, even if they look good.

Al Mualemi nodded as he looked into the eye of his interlocutor and said:

"God's punishment is really his own mercy."

Here, the fifth scene of perception theater closes announcing the end.

(14)

Hamid finds everything that his body lacks in his wife Maya, he happily wanders every time they are alone, he senses her love in the depths, he never imagines leaving him, and the farther he is away from her, the more adored he comes back. Sex is an urgent need such as water and food, fills him and then he is thirsty and hungry, always yearning for it as the infant to his mother's chest, he didn't educate himself to get as much as needed. Therefore, Hamid believes that the bed is the truest meaning of Maya's love and loyalty to him. He may (remember) their future together in that eternal scene, which speaks of her abandonment to him, and her sudden denial of the love between them, but he does not care about that, because life, for him, is fate and destiny, and fate may be repealed by our will. For all that, Hamid now realizes that he can change what he has been destined for in a better way. Even though his destiny is originally black, he is also able to erase his blackness by his will and make it a bright white space.

I am the Soul of the King of Tablistan, and as the mission that I chose to help you, Hamid, I found obstacles in your way preventing you from realizing that idea, that inevitable end. How can I stand against your youth like an impregnable dam? I am confident that a person is not accompanied by blind trust except in his youth or the height of his stupidity! So, how can I help you when you can't help yourself? You found Maya in her most participatory forms, which gave her family responsibility a clear holiness. The family responsibility that she performs is another face of sacred ligament, and this is what convinces you and satisfies your egos between your two sides. Maya has never spared any sacrifice for her family, so you struggled, Hamid, to maintain that ligament.

Your convictions have been firmly established in Maya, and your desire to have children has increased, then you have always expressed your love for her in private or general. Then you came once asking me as you were collecting your strength and increasing your convictions:

"Does not family responsibility mean that you can meet its requirements and answer its questions?"

I said: "The lust of soul, Hamid, tends to God, and the lust of the body tends to man, and the unseen will not prevent you from what you want and claim to do, man will only be hit to the kind of his work."

He said motivated: "But Maya is immaculate! Don't you see how she does her homework perfectly?"

I said: "The mind always loses in front of passion, and your passion moves out of your sexual lust, listen to what Pure Mind says."

"And where is Pure Mind and who has been gone from us long time ago? We don't find him in second heaven, nor in the heaven of the body."

"Oh, Hamid, Pure Mind is part of the universe, and since you have been able to return to yourself and within you to find the whole universe, the mind is also within you. No need to leave for anywhere while everything is firmly in you."

As soon as Hamid got rid of the dirtiness of the world and meditated on what's within it, the voice of Pure Mind came to him over the ether, the mind answered him in the language of telepathy and without having to listen to him. He replied:

"You must know, Hamid, that sexual relations are the pinnacle of autism with the other, because it gives you joy, strength, energy, and confidence… but don't rely on it because it doesn't last. I am now inviting Hamidel, who is between your two sides, to follow another perceptive scene on a journey with me in the cosmic ego of Hamid, in his inner heaven."

The Sixth Perception Scene

Characters: Hamid, Maya, her sister.

Places: The home of the two families in Kingdom of Tablistan.

After several jumps on the timeline left or right, front, or behind as human beings realize. Hamid returned one evening missing his wife Maya. While driving, he wanted to replace her name with another that would make her happy and joyful, to let her feel her pride and love in his heart. He decided to call her a soul mate. He bought her a gold necklace, put it in his pocket, entered his house and shouted happily to his beloved:

"Soul mate, soul mate, where are you?"

She came from her kitchen drying her sweat and stood in front of him silently wondering about the secret of the sudden label, hiding her smile, and waiting for what was behind this new label. I was able to read what was in her mind, she was saying in her silence:

"After these bitter sweetly years, Hamid can't call me that absurdly, unless he's hiding something, a terrible betrayal, or a great secret! Men don't change their attitudes in vain without a slip or mistake they made. They are like this. This is the sort of men; they are the crooked side from which women were created."

"Hi Hamid, what do you have today?"

Hamid asked Maya, smiling, to close her eyes for a moment. She did, he took out the box and wore her that gold necklace, and he was keen to challenge and defeat the unseen. She opened her eyes, went to the mirror, her eyebrows bounced up with astonishment and half happiness. She whispered to herself:

"This is further proof of the magnitude of what your hands have done, Hamid, atonement as much as sin. I will follow you, son of who betrayed his homeland, until the end of the story."

She thanked him, teared her eyes as usual whenever she wants, and realized that the shock of the joyous news is no less than the sad news, and the eyes tear for both.

"Oh, Hamid, a new name, and a new gift. Soul mate and gold necklace. So that's it!"

"This name is to prove that I see you as my mirror, I find a lot of you even before I ask, you look a lot like me, and this is a source of pride and happiness that never ends."

She said to herself:

"I'm going to catch you in the act of your crime."

I also whispered to him at this moment: You must warn, the similarity is a danger equal to the difference in its magnitude and value, and its claiming will fall you into it, and if the alleged similarity occurs, it will make it easier for your twin to discover your mistakes and flaws, and then he will give you, and this is an alarm bell and an upcoming obsession.

Hamid suddenly shouted to get me away from him:

"I don't want to hear from you now!"

Maya was stunned by what Hamid said, she wiped her face whispering:

"Was I thinking aloud and Hamid heard me? Is he able to read what's inside me?"

"Just laughing with you, you're like a satanic devil, you even smell the words, by the way, I want to put a tattoo on my shoulder, a tattoo that I like, I'll draw it tonight, and I have made an appointment." Maya said.

Hamid's mood turned up down, and the anger spread among him as a snake writhing, infiltrated him and spread his poisons lowly, starting from the feet until his chest and moved his trace to the head:

"We are back to the same topic, I rejected it in advance, Maya. It is over, you do not have to repeat the same request every day."

"True, you refused, but this is my body, and that's my right, it's not your business."

"Don't go to draw the Tattoo. It is over. If you go, don't come back, I don't want any disagreement in front of our baby, Kamel."

Maya left in the evening insisting on breaking her husband's control, realizing in her own decision that he loves her, but it is love of sex and domination, and she stubbornly refuses this kind of love.

In the evening, Hamid returned as usual, but Maya didn't. She stayed with her sister in her father's house to break what she calls a love of control, she stayed there waiting for Hamid to come or even call her back, to preserve her pride, and even change the equation of their relationship.

A disagreement that the most optimistic did not expect, but I did my part toward Hamid to the fullest. I warned him repeatedly, and so did Pure Mind. Despite all this, Hamid chose to speak to her at her father's house, he didn't want to lose his family even though he lost his dignity. Her sister greeted him with their father, who arranged for them to meet in his presence. He promised to remain silent as long as their dialogue was within reason, Maya entered the Council. After the brief greeting, she said:

"If you love me, you must prove it?"

"How?"

"Change your behavior as we agreed earlier."

"I promised you many times that we would change our behavior together and overlook some things, but once I change what you ask, you also change some of your behaviors but temporarily; It wasn't a radical change or a change of conviction, it was just to prolong our relationship, and to keep my love for you, you expected the whole of our love to be bigger, but we always bump into each other together, I think you feel less attractive these days, and I can see it so strong and influential inside me."

"Have you finished developing your theories?" She said sullenly.

I whispered to him that there is no point in her begging, that she feels unattractive, that her happiness is declining, and that her self-confidence is diminishing, so she wants to set off in forbidden areas, to express her self-confidence, she is in short, Hamid: You will not be able to love the other if you do not love yourself first, your success is not what your partner does but in your reaction.

"What shall I do now, do I have to keep the situation as it is?" he asked me out loudly.

"It is up to you both," Maya's father said.

"It's over," Maya said.

"Hamid, you should have asked yourself from the beginning: Who am I and what do I want from Maya?" I spoke.

"How can I ask if I have not tried yet?" he said.

"Haven't you been through a while since the beginning anger, and a negative feeling toward Maya?" I spoke.

"Yes," he answered.

"That was enough to make the decision and activate it," I said.

"I'm not wise enough to know that" Hamid said.

Interventions and solutions were useless. So, the relationship disintegrated gradually, an unexpected misunderstanding, and the attempts of restoration became a bigger mistake, because the role of the soul mate has finished his mission. The task of stripping you in front of yourself and in front of others has begun, it became a way of exonerating the self. The interpretations have become more, there are those who say like her father: it must be a slip of a bed, and another sees it as the repercussions of betrayal... while I say nothing but the heart of prisoner Pilgrim Kamel, with its removal, the conscience has snatched.

Hamid was not able to scatter his family with both hands, he was very stubborn and stuck to a fine thread of hope, bringing the whole family together and getting her together. It was not necessarily to ask him about his final decision, simply because he was addicted to Maya and his family responsibility, your addiction to your lover or couple makes it difficult to part.

I had no choice but to explain to him that love results from touching the depth of the heart of the beloved, to reach his core, and if the relationship fails after that, you must replace your loved one with the love of the universe. If you reach the depth of the world, you will realize it, you will love and adore it and heal from your first love, that is what I trust. The human act in its reality is based on two: love or awe. Maya loved to be a mother, so she married you, Hamid, and Maya was scared to be old, so she destroyed her family. Then, she'll love what she destroyed and so on. Man is forced to repeat the experience because he follows his feelings, seeing the unseen will never dissuade him from his decision, man is hostage to his momentary feelings.

Silence fell on the place; the star has fallen. He may consult Pure Mind who addressed us, and in turn realized our dialogue and said:

"The mind is not a solution to problems, the mind knows all the problems and classifies them only, but he is, as words, do not give man happiness, the feelings of doing right and wrong are the ones that give man his happiness. Therefore, you grieve and rejoice, Hamid, but I, the Pure Mind, stand helpless, aimless and without life."

This tragedy has destroyed Hamid, so that his mind is let down with Pure Mind, and he stopped working, he became captive to his heart, which could not accept the truth: you are similar, and the similarity is like difference are both destructive, you must share the differences with her, and maintain your privacy in similarities, that's it simply. They both wanted to control each other through their false love, but Maya did not understand the secret of Hamid's enduring happiness, because she did not realize our existence in his life, Me, and Pure Mind. It was only after, Maya realized that everything had two different poles, and if they were similar, they would destroy each other.

After worldly days, Hamid always asks me the same question about what happened: Why do we destroy what we have been building?

"Maya destroys what she has built because of the great love she has given, she destroys it out of greater fear, parallel to its direction and intensity. Your relationship with Maya is based on something that can be invested between them, and when she gets what she wants, the necessity of the relationship is gone, then the discomfort is formed, and hatred takes shape. You, Hamid, felt that you were nothing without Maya, while you were an important thing, but your patience ran out of waiting because of the sexual energy driving you. After the age of forty, a person begins his relationship waiting for the worst, because your partner does not believe in or agree with your new goals. The more Maya loved you, the more she loved herself. So, I told you since the beginning, it is man who decides all his life, no one forces you. You should not call what you are a calamity, because you grow and learn from these experiences, and you can invest them in what benefits you personally; The wise man is the one whose reacts are more than acts, remember that you are a soul with higher needs than her body. Do act that way."

(15)

My body was lying in one of the rooms of the Royal Pavilion, and some of its organs began to declare their rebellion, silently declaring their refusal to carry out what the king's mind demands, with no power to carry out the orders, because they were out of power one by one. I thought that I would then be able, as I am the King's Soul, to take the lead, to remove the role of his mind and his physical desires. I thought I would finally be able to carry out the right act, to force the king to do good in his last stages of worldly life. In his whole life, the lusts of the king's body have defeated his mind when they wrestle. And now, I hope the conflict will be only bilateral, between me and the king's mind. But, at a sudden, the unforeseen happened.

After sunset, two of the king's sons entered their father's room, they came stealthily and without the knowledge of their older brother, the Crown Prince, the two sat around the King's bed. The elder put his palm on the king's forehead to feel his temperature, and soon said to his brother:

"I think the King's temperature is low, and this is a sign of death."

The younger brother sensed his father's death and said:

"Therefore, we should not sit idly by as we follow the king's transition to the Crown Prince appointed by his father himself, for nothing but he was born before us."

"Yes, the Crown Prince must only be to the parents of Tablistan. Kingship mustn't go out to a man whose mother is not originally from Tablistan, although they were all migrants.

Although all of this is contrary to the king's own wishes."

The elder took out of his pocket a piece of paper bearing a Royal Decree, he held it, reading loudly what it says:

In the name of God, the most Merciful, the most Compassionate. Every soul will taste death, and you will only be given your full compensation on the Day of Resurrection. So, he who is drawn away from the Fire and admitted to Paradise has attained his desire. And what is the life of this world except the enjoyment of delusion. [4]

I am the King of the Kingdom of Tablistan, relieving the Crown Prince of all his official positions in the Kingdom, and appointing my second son in the mandate of the Covenant in the general interest of the Kingdom of Tablistan. God attest to what I say.

With all my regards to the Royal Family, and to the people of the loyal Kingdom of Tablistan.

May 22.

The elder took his father's thumb and buried it with blue liquid, then put his mark on the second commandment.

The younger brother stood stunned: what if the first will appeared, with the signature and the Royal seal as well?

"Don't worry, our mother, the Queen gave me the pin number of the royal treasury that is over there. We will also seal the will, and then we will lock the royal treasury until the king leaves."

"I asked you, what if the first commandment comes up?"

"Don't worry, the current Crown Prince has only the first commandment, but we have the second, the Queen, and Shawzan as well are on our side."

"Shawzan?"

"I promised him the portfolio of the Ministry of Interior on

---

[4]. Al-Imran Surah: 185

condition that we get rid of this Crown Prince, in the same way that he tried it with Kamel, Al Mualemi's friend."

"What about the public opinion of the Tablistan's people?"

"Everyone knows the dangers of the leftists to the kingdom, and we only must spread the relationship between the Crown Prince and the left movement, and the risks it represents to the kingdom, conspiring against the kingdom and extending the ties of convergence with the left, all of which are sufficient to remove the Crown Prince, and get rid of him through Shawzan."

"What a shrewd person you are!"

"I am my mother's son, brother."

The brothers left the Royal Pavilion after receiving a call informing them about the arrival of the medical staff, and the chief medical officer of the Royal Palace, accompanied by three others, was admitted to the Pavilion, which became a mini hospital. He came to know the latest news of my healthy body. My body was lying on the white bed, and a lot of pipes penetrated the palm and arm; until many black spots floated on it, shiny black spots resembled those giant spots that I saw with Hamidel in Burqan desert, both of which were oily black colors that reflected what beneath their crust, earthy or fleshy!

The Crown Prince entered with the medical team, the doctor found the heat of my body in constant decline, and the mind was finally unable to give his orders to my body. I was pleased with this event. Finally, I will be able to be liberated from the oppression of this body, which is easily obeyed for lust. When he claims to have risen, he allows the mind to act and control the body as it pleases. I wanted to tell the Crown Prince and the medical team what the brothers had done. But how do I get to them? I can't contact them all, their souls must ask to meet me, and then I can only meet them in one of the heavens, in the second heaven, or the heaven of the body or its inner heaven as well! I come to them by apparition or perception. Otherwise, they get rid of all traces of the five senses, stop working on them, and then they'll also realize me by meditating to contact them. All these matters are impossible in their current situation. I kept a part of me in the King's body and scattered the rest of my ether with the light in space. I was watching them all as I did with my exhausted body. The doctor told his team:

"We belong to God and to Him we shall return."

"What is the matter, doctor?" The Crown Prince asked.

"The heart will stop pulsing forever within two hours, and until then, the abilities of the mind to give signals to the rest of the body will be reduced… my sincere condolences."

At these moments, I began to see the weight of ether among the light atoms scattered in the Royal Chamber, expanding the space, and the atoms began to lose the flash from their outer orbits. Then, I felt the presence of someone who was crowding me, who wanted to take me away from that electronic flash, until he brought me together between his dangling limbs. He took me to him strongly. And I'm still looking for this invisible object, I sensed him but haven't seen him yet. I said addressing his ether:

"Who are you?"

"I'm Azrael."

"And what do you want?"

"Get rid of that body and take you to the second heaven."

"Why did you slow down?"

"Because of your body's desire to live, but having been unable to live, I will do fulfill your desire now."

"So, you are Azrael, there is no difference between you and The Mind, both of you do what the human body wants, but you do not give souls any attention, as if we are marginalized and have no real roles in this life. Ah, from all this existence, when can I see death helpless in bed?"

"Your Lord created the whole universe just for man. He created souls for him as well. Everything was created for man, what is great. Even death was created for human to understand the meaning of life."

Azrael came close to me, and all his limbs drooped, and here I saw him in his first original image and form. He was the absolute light, but he recited as the likeness of his victim's actions. Azrael became gray as he squeezed me, his color became a black-and-white color, he caught me and brought me back to the king's body; the body was re-filled as if it had been restored to life, and then he began to take me to him from the bottom of the king's legs, turning my body leg into each other, and they were tangled like two sticks.

When he took me all out of my body, the air bubbles came out of the body, and soon he was stowed with the last bubble of the King's mouth. The voices in the Royal room were raised and the Crown Prince fell onto his father's body... while, at this moment, I felt the joy and freedom of the world of eternity. And while Azrael still held me for his grooves, I asked him: "Where to?"

"To where you were before you chose the King's body, a fetus in his mother's womb."

"It is ages, I have forgotten."

"We will go to the Holy Mount of Tuwa, there, to the endless world."

He grabbed me by my forehead as we were crossing the isthmus, as if we were in a dust tornado, moving from the first heaven to the second... suddenly, there was another soul dragging me from my tails to the lower heaven. Azrael stopped wondering, we telepathized with that soul catching my tails,

"Who are you?" Azrael asked her.

"I am Kamel's soul, asking her for my rights."

The Conclusion

My mother visited me in a dream, asked me to write the *Soul of the King* novel, she promised to visit me again after I finished writing. More than three years later, I could say that I waited for you, mother, for a long time.

I used to ablute every night before going to bed, read *Al Fatiha*, and I may pray on Friday night to be close to God; hope something happens, hope you Mom will come back to tell me how to write the end, but you never came again! I understood your message, knowing long after that *Soul of the King* novel has not been completed yet; it will never be complete until the end of life on the earth.

When I closed the file of *Soul of the King*, I agreed with the publisher to print it, even it is not yet complete, my mother came at the same time of the first apparition on Wednesday, 29 November, but she abandoned me this time, and did not mention all the details left in the novel. I stood bewildered looking at my mother's face, as she was still in her youth, full of beauty, smiling and reassuring, not as she left this world in her late sixties. She only left me one sentence:

"Son, the novelist who authors his novel in three years, just like you did, is the one who thinks and wonders, while the politician, who tends to be smart up, ignites a war in three days, because he doesn't...! The smart one, my son, is the one who tries to change the world, and the wise one is trying to change himself."

Then she left.